THE VANQUISHER OF WATER

Also By Logan Young

Coming Soon
The Power of Princirum, Book 2

Coming Soon
The Power of Princirum, Book 3

The Power of Princirm, Book 1

The Vanquisher of Water

Logan Young

THE VANQUISHER OF WATER by Logan Young
Copyright © 2020 by Logan Young

First Edition, September 2020

Edited by Suzanne Johnson
Cover Design by Levierre

ISBN 978-1-7347879-0-0 (Paperback)
ISBN 978-1-7347879-1-7 (Ebook)

Published by Sanctuary Press
www.imloganyoung.com

10 9 8 7 6 5 4 3 2 1

To My Family—

* * *

For never doubting

the workings of

my crazy mind

* * *

CONTENTS

THE VANQUISHER OF WATER

W H A T ' S   H A P P E N I N G ?

KYM SAT ON THE SAND BENEATH THE INKY-BLACK SKY, THE GENTLE rush of water filling the air. The river may have been beautiful once, with clear water and vast banks. That is, before the Rulers built the wall to keep the death demons out. Now, the river flowed into the city through thick, iron grates, surrounded by those smooth, tall walls. Trash peppered the surface, collecting around the grate near Kym's house. There, it became part of an ever-growing mess, unable to escape to the world beyond.

She sighed, watching the garbage slowly build around the grate. This forgotten stretch of riverbank had been Kym's place ever since her friends abandoned her nine years before. The trash, which hadn't been as bad back then, always gave her something to do when she'd sneak out for some air. And tonight was no exception.

Kym dove into the river, and the cool water stung her warm skin. She maneuvered easily around the familiar rocks and sand beds, reaching the grate in seconds. She held onto the rough bars, hoping to see the river disappear as it kissed the distant horizon. Was the world really so different out there beyond the wall? She wouldn't know, thanks to the thick layer of trash in front of her face.

She shoved her hand into the muck, grabbing a handful of what used to be plastic bags. They ripped away from the bars, staying mostly intact but covering Kym's hands in a layer of slime. Her skin tingling slightly, she continued to pull, removing handfuls of the slimy black gunk. Finally, when she couldn't hold any more, Kym kicked herself to shore. She dumped her armfuls of garbage onto the sandy ground, shoved her wet hair from her face, and dove back in for more.

She concentrated on the biggest piece she could find, determined to free as much as she could from the grate. If she could clear enough of it away, maybe she'd get a glimpse of the outside. It took some time, but she finally pulled a large piece of plastic from the bars and dragged it, along with several smaller plastic chunks, bottles, and cans, back to shore. Kym sighed, smiling at her work as she threw this collection in with the rest.

A shiver ran down her spine that had nothing to do with her wet skin. She turned around, her damp hair whipping her in the face, sure someone was watching her. But no one was there. This stretch of riverbank was hardly ever patrolled since there hadn't been a death demon attack here in years. Her spine still tingling, Kym dove back into the river.

She glided under the surface, feeling the current pull her toward the grate. She knew she had to leave soon, even though she'd rather be here than stuck in school. She surfaced, eager to look out at the world beyond the wall. Suddenly, extremely hot water surged past her, forcing her away from the grate. She tried to swim out of it, but the powerful current swept her beneath the surface.

She struggled, swallowing several mouthfuls of water as she tried to claw her way back to air. But the hot current pushed her still deeper under the water. Lights popped behind Kym's eyes, and it was like every muscle in her body was being squeezed by a million tiny hands. Her throat opened and closed rapidly as her watery vision began to darken. The water holding her began to glow bright blue, emitting a faint, high-pitched hiss. Every part of her body relaxed as the ringing filled her ears. The glow faded like the embers of a fire, as did the temperature. Now free from the water's grasp, she rose back to the surface.

Kym gasped, her heart pounding in her throat. Another shudder ran through her body, and she thrashed around, and sank like a rock.

Spluttering, her body shaking, she splashed back to shore. She crawled onto the bank, slipping on the small rocks lining the sand. Had anyone seen her? She looked around, but the riverbank was still deserted. She shoved the garbage into the largest bag her shaking hands could pull from the pile, threw the bag over her shoulder, and sprinted away from the river.

Kym ran through the narrow streets. The thundering of her heart filled her ears, and the morning air caught like ice in her raw throat. She needed to get home. She could figure this out if she just made it there. How could this happen? Her parents said she was safe. She'd never shown any of the signs. They'd promised nothing would happen to her, especially after what happened to her aunt and uncle. But something had happened, and now, her world could implode around her.

"Home," Kym ordered herself, an ache growing in her side. "Just get home."

She made it home faster than she thought possible. The mere sight of the small house was enough to slow her breathing, but only slightly. She was safe. And anyway, getting sucked down the river by glowing water didn't prove anything. No one saw her. She shouldn't get herself worked up over a freak accident. Her hands still shaking, Kym dumped the bag of waterlogged trash in the bin and unlatched the old gate.

She slipped through her bedroom window as quietly as she could. She tiptoed across the floor, praying it wouldn't make a sound. The last time Kym's parents caught her coming in this early, they had grounded her for a month. After a short struggle with her wet clothes, she tossed them into the hamper by the door before pulling on a ratty old shirt and shorts. She crawled gratefully into bed. The touch of her old, worn sheets made her worries fade away. Instantly, her eyes began to droop. Maybe she'd get a couple of hours' sleep before she needed to go to school. She'd probably just overreacted about the wave in the river.

"Let's get a move on," a voice called through Kym's door, sending her heart racing. "We're leaving for Temple in thirty."

"Thanks, Mom," she breathed, trying to keep the panic from her voice.

How could she forget about Temple? They went at least once a week. Kym fell back on her pillow, her heart once again returning to a normal pace. For a split second, she'd thought her mom knew she'd been out all night. But she didn't. She'd managed to get in without either of her parents noticing.

In the heat and steam of the small bathroom, Kym could smell the river on her skin. She washed her body three times, hoping to mask most of the smell. She dried herself off and ran a brush through her hair a few times before going back to her room. The small room, with only a bed, old dresser, and small table, was tidier than when she had left it. A pale-orange dress sat ready on her bed. Mom really didn't understand Kym's desire for privacy.

"Did you even try with your hair?" her mom sighed when Kym walked into the living room. "No one ever sees how blue your eyes are when you cover them like that."

Her dad shepherded them out the door. They joined the already-formed crowd in the street; no one acknowledged them. They worked their way to the city center, where massive, shining buildings replaced the small houses of Kym's neighborhood. The Temple, constructed of white stone, sat in the heart of the city, although Kym wouldn't have called it white. The tall walls and pillars must have looked magnificent when it was new, but the passing centuries and lack of care had taken their toll. Cracks spread through the greying pillars and grooves, worn by countless worshipers, led the way up the steep steps.

Temple was never the highlight of Kym's week. It wasn't that she didn't believe in the gods, but bowing to giant statues always seemed a little pointless. What difference did it make, really, in the long run? No matter how hard she tried, she couldn't see the gods in her everyday life, not even with her father's constant reminders that the gods always had a plan for her and for Princirum. So, was it part of the gods' plan for her aunt and uncle to be killed?

The Temple's main chamber was a massive, round room filled with benches that faced the large altar at the center. Six smaller altars were set into niches around the curved outer walls, while shafts of light filtered in from the many skylights in the domed ceiling. Kym followed the crowd to the center altar, where she thanked the Great Mother, Pheil, for the life she had created before moving on. She gave thanks for the earth, light, fire, air, and darkness the other gods provided, but her mind was blank. She'd gone through this so many times that she probably could have done it blindfolded.

Kym moved more and more slowly as she walked from altar to altar. As the high priest began to address the now-seated crowd, Kym finally ambled up to the final altar. The statue of a young woman with a kind face stared down at Kym from the center of a shallow pool. Reta; goddess of water and purification. Kym stared into the face of the goddess, and for some reason, she couldn't bring herself to move her feet.

There was something off about the statue's eyes. It was like they were looking at, and even through, her. A jolt surged through Kym, but it wasn't discomfort or even fear. It was the same sense of calm she'd felt once the water started to glow in the river. Kym stepped forward and, without thinking, placed her hand in the altar's pool. It was hot; almost the same temperature as the wave.

"A plan, hm?" Kym sighed, stepping back from the altar, starting to lift her hand from the pool. "What a joke."

A bright, blue, glowing spiral appeared on the back of her hand the moment she moved it. It looped around several times until it reached her wrist. From there, it wrapped around her arm until it reached her elbow, where it stopped. The spiral's glow was just like the water in the river.

Kym couldn't breathe. This couldn't happen again, especially not inside the Temple. What if someone had seen her? She jerked her hand out of the water so quickly someone might have thought it hurt her. She stared at her trembling hand and watched the spiral begin to fade. A moment later, it was like it was never there.

But what just happened wouldn't fade from Kym's mind. She couldn't convince herself nothing was going on. Something was happening to her, and it was only a matter of time before someone found out. But how could she keep it quiet? The priests, teachers, and city patrol were always looking for people showing the signs of magic, and Kym had shown two in the past few hours.

She sat quietly between her parents, trying to keep her face as normal as possible. Just like at the river, Kym was sure someone was watching her. Every cough and scrape of a bench sent fear coursing through her body. She needed to get back home. There, she'd be alone. There, she could figure this out.

Kym stood the moment the high priest finished speaking, but leaving Temple was a struggle. Even though it was one of the city's largest buildings, the only exit was the main entrance. The tightly packed crowd moved so slowly that it took nearly ten minutes before Kym could get outside, and even then she couldn't leave. Her parents, chatting quietly with the few people who'd still speak to them, didn't realize Kym was already waiting for them at the bottom of the Temple steps.

Most days, Kym would have already been in school by this time. But since this was a Temple day, school didn't start until half-past eight. She walked back home in silence, always staying a couple of paces behind her parents. Once inside, Kym shut herself in her room; she needed to be alone, and hopefully come up with some sort of plan. But her parents had different ideas. After only a few minutes of peace, her mom called her out to help with breakfast. They made scrambled eggs, crispy bacon, fried potatoes, and glasses of orange juice. Honestly, Kym just stirred things while her mom did the rest.

"Anything good in there?" Kym's mom asked her dad. He'd opened his news projector, filling the room with a soft, orange light.

"Not really," he murmured, his eyes darting quickly over the floating headlines. "Wait. There is something. A spokesperson for the Rulers released a statement saying the Rulers are refusing the mayors' request to expand the four cities. According to them, 'allowing the cities to develop past their originally intended sizes would upset the delicate balance of power we strive to maintain within Princirum.' "

There were four massive cities in Princirum, but Kym had never been outside of the City of Contellus. Every time she mentioned visiting the other cities, her parents told her not to worry about it. According to them, every city was the same, so there was no real point in leaving. But even if they were all the same, the thought of being beyond the walls of her city made Kym's imagination soar.

"The Rulers know what's best," her mother said, sitting down at the table. "They're the children of the gods. Who would know better than them?"

"I don't know. I just wish they'd leave the palaces and visit the cities more often. I can't even remember the last time they came and actually looked around."

"I'm sure they're very busy," said Kym's mom. "They've ruled Princirum for centuries, and I doubt they'll ever change their ways."

Kym's dad gave a huff in reply as he dished some bacon onto her mom's plate. Kym only saw the Rulers a couple of times a year. They'd come to her school to inspect the students, and they'd only speak when greeting them. She could never bring herself to look at the Rulers as they moved through the students, not after everything her family had gone through. Instead, she'd stare at a point above their heads until they moved on to the next student. Would that be the case now, with her showing signs of magic left and right?

"So, sweetheart," Kym's mother said gently, pulling her mind back to the table. "Did you enjoy Temple today?"

"It was fine," she murmured. "Same as it is every week."

"Really?" Kym's dad asked slowly. "You took your time at Reta's altar. Is everything all right?"

Kym opened her mouth, but she couldn't think of anything to say. She couldn't tell her parents what happened at Reta's altar. If she did, she'd have to tell them about the river, and then they'd know exactly what was happening. She couldn't do that to them, not after everything they'd already been through. They'd lost so much to magic, and now it could take Kym away from them. She'd never wanted to be part of that world, even after learning about all the incredible things people had done with magic. But showing magical signs meant her life could change forever if anyone found out. So Kym decided to lie.

"Everything's fine," she said, hoping her fake smile would convince them to drop the subject. "I just had a lot on my mind."

"All right," said her mother, a faint smile on her lips. "Oh, how was the river last night?"

At the word *river*, fear shot through Kym like an electric shock. Her mind froze, and she dropped her forkful of scrambled eggs onto her plate with a clatter. How could she know Kym had been out? She hadn't made a sound when she sneaked back in. And if her mom knew that, what else did she know? The glowing wave? The spiral on Kym's arm? She had felt like someone was watching her, after all.

"Or was it this morning. From the looks of things, you got in pretty late."

"How…how did…?"

"I took the garbage out before we left. I saw the junk you brought back. You also left your wet clothes in the hamper."

"Sorry," Kym apologized, staring at her lap. "I just wanted some me time. I shouldn't have gone."

"Don't worry about it, Kym," her dad said, turning off his news projector. "You're not in trouble."

"Really?" she asked, momentarily forgetting her fears.

"Really," her mother answered. "We talked it over, and you're too old for us to ground anymore. You're sixteen-years-old now, and you have the right to make your own choices without fear of us disapproving. Besides, you're just cleaning up garbage, and we can't tell you to stop doing something like that."

"But, what about the curfew?" she asked, remembering one of her more unpleasant times at the river. The city patrol caught her out at night and escorted her back home.

"Its never really enforced," said Kym's dad. "The city patrol has far more important things to do with their time. You're a smart girl, and nothing ever happens to you when you go out there."

Kym stood up so quickly she banged her knee on the bottom of the table. Her chair toppled backward, and the shaking table caused her full glass of orange juice to tip over. A bright orange stain spread through the old, faded tablecloth, but Kym hardly noticed. She couldn't do this. She needed to get out of there.

"What's wrong?"

"Nothing." Kym needed to think of something semi-believable to say. "I'm just supposed to meet someone to work on a project before school."

"Well, I'll drive you on my way to work," Kym's mom said, already starting to stand.

"No. It's fine," Kym said. She dropped her dirty plate in the sink and grabbed her backpack from beside the door. "I can walk."

Kym was out the front door before her parents could stop her. She walked as calmly as she could down the rickety front steps and onto the uneven walkway. She couldn't keep what happened a secret for very long. No matter how hard she tried, sooner or later it was going to get out. Someone was going to find out. And if her parents hadn't thought anything was wrong, they certainly did now.

Kym needed to be someplace where people wouldn't notice her, a place where she could be invisible. So she turned left and started walking to school. No one there would notice her acting odd, since that would require people knowing how she usually acted. She'd had no real friends since she was seven, and she had the Rulers, the gods, and the priests to thank for that little bit of bad luck.

Years before, Kym's aunt, Lydia, and her uncle, Herald, stopped going to Temple. They spoke publicly against the Rulers and the gods, and the priests arrested them for it. They refused to take back what they said, so the priest executed them before the Rulers could find out. And because of their relation to Lydia and Herald, Kym, at only seven years old, and her parents were shunned by everyone they knew. No one would go near her family after that, wanting to distance themselves from traitors to the gods.

Kym tried to make friends for the first few years, but even kids didn't want to be near what her aunt and uncle had done. So, she gave up on having friends. Everyone would forget Kym as fast as they could. Even her teachers, some of whom had taught her for years, still called out her name like they'd never seen her before. School was the place where she felt her most invisible, which was precisely what she was looking for. She needed time alone to figure out what to do now that she was one of the Favored.

The Favored of Princirum were those who, like the Rulers, could control one of the seven elements. When the Rulers found a Favored, they'd take them from their homes to live at the Rulers' palaces. As far as Kym knew, they never came back. They may get on her nerves at times, but Kym's parents were all she had, and leaving them was the last thing she wanted, especially for magic.

What if she refused to go when the Rulers found her? Just stayed at home and ignored them when they came to collect her? What if she insisted they made a mistake? Even as she thought it, Kym knew it wouldn't work. The Rulers never let a Favored out of their grasp, and there was nothing she could do to stop them. If they ever found her, they'd take her.

But that wouldn't happen right away. The Rulers only came to her school two, maybe three times a year, and their last visit had been less than two months before. Kym felt herself relaxing as the thought set in. She had time to prepare, even if she wished she didn't have to. She could tell her parents when she was ready. Her life wasn't going to end right away.

But when she got to school, she stopped dead in her tracks. Parked alongside all of the teachers' cars were six magnificent horse-drawn carriages. Every fiber of her body ordered her to scream, to run away and hide where no one could find her. But she couldn't. The time she'd thought she had vanished. The small ray of hope she'd built for herself slipped hopelessly through her fingers. It was over. Her time was up. The Rulers were at Kym's school.

CHAPTER TWO

FINDING THE FAVORED

"ALL CLASSES ARE POSTPONED. DEPOSIT YOUR BELONGINGS IN YOUR lockers and gather in the gymnasium."

The school's main hallway was packed with students. Most talked excitedly, filling the already-cramped hall with noise as they discussed the Rulers' sudden arrival. No one paid Kym the slightest bit of attention as they pushed past her, but she barely noticed. She shoved her things into her locker, following the instructions blaring over the loudspeakers.

The Rulers' arrival at Kym's school couldn't be a coincidence. They'd just been there a few months ago, and they weren't supposed to return for another month. Someone must have seen Kym. Why else would they show up now? She had felt like someone was watching her at the river and in the Temple. Anyone could have turned her in. But how did the Rulers get there so quickly? Her stomach twisted into the world's largest knot at the thought.

Kym walked into the gym, the largest room in the school, on trembling legs. An enormous stage sat opposite the door, where seven shabby, throne-like chairs faced the gathering students. She wandered through the students in a daze, not even noticing when she walked between two people having a conversation. Kym situated herself among a group of high-heeled girls in the middle of the gym, hoping to disappear in the crowd. The school bell chimed at exactly eight-thirty. The gym doors closed, and the students instantly fell silent. It was so quiet Kym was sure everyone could hear her heart pounding.

Kym heard them before she saw them. Their heavy footfalls and swish of their long, elaborate clothes, was unmistakable. The Rulers mounted the stage, the crowd bowing to each one before the next stepped forward. With each bow, Kym's legs shook more and more violently. The Rulers were tall, taller than anyone Kym had ever seen. Their elegant gowns, embroidered vests, and flowing white shirts made it look like they'd traveled from a different time.

"We welcome the Rulers of Princirum," the headmaster said in a tremulous voice, bowing low to the Rulers once again. "And we thank them for gracing our school with their presence."

At this point, the Ruler of Life was supposed to address the students, but she'd never come to Kym's school. So one of the other Rulers, a tall woman with long, brown hair wearing a pale-yellow dress, stepped forward. Kym bowed, along with everyone else, to Lady Evanna, the Ruler of Light.

"Thousands of years ago, long after the gods created Princirum and left us, their children, to guide it, I discovered the first Favored on the side of a road. She made the light from a candle's flame vanish before my eyes. I brought this child before the Ruler of Life and demanded we kill the urchin for stealing the magic that should have belonged solely to myself and the bringer of light, Thilg.

"Lady Zara, The Ruler of Life, refused me. She called upon the gods, who graced us with their presence. They decreed that possession of magic was not a crime, but a gift. The gods charged us with locating and training Princirum's magically Favored. So we stand before you, humble servants of the gods, searching for those who hold the gift of the element inside them."

Every person in Princirum heard the story of the first Favored before they could walk. When she was little, Kym had never understood why Evanna always told a bedtime story when the Rulers came to her school. But as she got a little older, Kym realized Evanna's version was very different from the one her mom used to tell her. In her mom's telling, the first Favored was going to be banished for having magic, and Evanna happily trained her in the end. This was very different from Evanna's version, where she wanted the Favored killed for having something Evanna thought was hers. Yet another reason why Kym never wanted magic.

The Rulers descended into the crowd, moving silently from student to student. Kym's palms filled with sweat and her stomach lurched every time a Ruler stepped in front of her. She stared up at their crowns, hoping they'd pass her by. They were the same color as the wearer's clothes and had seven tall points. But Kym needn't have worried. None of the Rulers observed her for more than a few seconds before moving on. Kym held her breath, hoping to be dismissed with the students who didn't pass the first round. She didn't even know how many rounds there were. The Rulers had always rejected her during the first.

Teachers dismissed over half of the students, but Kym was not among them. She watched them leave the gym, wishing she could join them. Instead, she joined the other students the Rulers chose to keep. Each Ruler made his or her way through the smaller crowd, grabbing each student by the hand or shoulder before moving on. Kym's body shook more violently as the Rulers drew closer. She wiped her sweaty palms on her orange dress, but it didn't do much.

As each of the Rulers stepped in front of Kym, she couldn't keep the fear from her face. James, the Ruler of Fire, grabbed her upper arm so tightly she felt her heartbeat beneath his fingers. But still, the Rulers didn't say a word. Their faces were so blank, Kym couldn't tell whether she had interested them or not. What were they even looking for? Could they tell if someone had magic just by looking at and touching them? Kym prayed they couldn't see the magic inside her.

When they finally finished, the Rulers gathered at the foot of the stage. They spoke in hushed whispers, ringed by the teachers who'd stayed in the gym.

After a couple of minutes, which felt like hours, teachers began walking through the students, dismissing those the Rulers chose to release.

Kym stood with her fingers crossed. All she needed was one teacher to tell her to go, and then she'd be free. But one by one, every teacher passed her by. Most avoided eye contact, but a few looked Kym right in the eye, and there was something there she'd never seen before. Regret. A minute later, Kym stood in the nearly empty gym with four other students. The Rulers, now seated on their throne-like chairs, all stared down at them.

"Congratulations," said Lord Kai, the Ruler of Earth. He stood and walked to the edge of the stage. "To determine whether magic truly exists within you, you will each be tested by the Ruler who chose you. We shall begin with the child I selected. Boy, hold out your hands."

Teachers rushed past Kym and to the opposite end of the line. The boy looked barely old enough to be in her school, and after not moving for several seconds, a teacher pushed him forward. Kai held out his hands, and the boy did the same. There was a flash of green light, and Kym squeezed her eyes tight shut, but it was gone as quickly as it had come. She opened her eyes and saw a chunk of earth floating in Kai's outstretched hands.

Kai pushed his hands forward, and the piece of earth drifted down toward the boy. Kym's eyes darted between the earth and the boy. She'd never seen magic before, and couldn't tell what Kai wanted the boy to do. Was he supposed to catch it? Stop it? Do something with it? Either way, the boy looked like he thought the earth was going to slam into his face. But it didn't. The moment the earth reached his hands, it dissolved into nothing.

Two teachers silently escorted the boy from the gym while Evanna took Kai's place. She'd selected two girls a few years younger than Kym, but neither of them caught Evanna's ball of light, and teachers sent them out as well. These three dismissals ignited a spark of hope inside Kym. They'd all failed, so maybe she'd fail too. The wave at the river, the spiral on her hand, and being chosen by the Rulers could all just be one big mistake.

Nila, the Ruler of Water, glided to the front of the stage, her elegant blue dress rippling around her. Something jabbed Kym sharply in the back, and she stumbled forward several steps before regaining her balance. She stared at Nila, her hands already raised in front of her. Kym braced herself, her hands shaking more violently than ever, and mirrored Nila's actions. There was a flash of blue light, and an orb of water floated in Lady Nila's hands.

Nila pushed the orb toward Kym, who just stood there, unsure what she was supposed to do. She closed her eyes, praying the orb would vanish when it reached her. Several seconds passed, and Kym didn't feel anything. Optimistic, Kym opened her eyes a fraction, but her hands were not empty. Spirals glowed on both her outstretched hands, and the orb of water floated above her palms. Kym looked up in Nila's impassive face, and all the feeling seemed to drain from her body. Nila waved her hand lazily, and the ball of water faded away.

"Behold, a new Favored of Water," Nila declared to the room at large. "What is her name?"

"Kymbralyn Collins," someone answered.

Two teachers half led, half dragged Kym up the steps and onto the stage. Everything—the noises, the colors, even the air around her—seemed to be slipping away. Her mind couldn't process the last minute. If it had, that would mean everything that happened was real. But she couldn't let that be true. Kym was so out of it she barely registered the last student catch the silvery ball of air Lord Stailin sent him.

Something tapped Kym's back. Turning almost in slow motion, she saw it was one of the teachers. Grabbing her by the arm, he led a dazed Kym off the stage and into to the gym teacher's office. She'd never been in there before. It was small, occupied mostly by a large desk with several chairs pressed against the walls. The teacher silently deposited Kym in one of the chairs before hurrying from the room. He returned a minute later with the boy who passed Stailin's test. Kym just stared blindly at the floor, not even looking at him.

Several long minutes later, the headmaster walked into the silent office. A short man with a round belly and a gleaming bald spot on the top of his head, he took the empty seat behind the teacher's desk. Slowly, Kym looked up from the floor and was surprised by his expression. His typically stony face was softer, and there was something in his eyes Kym had never seen before. He started to speak, and his words had a rehearsed quality to them, like he'd said them many times before.

"Congratulations to you both, on receiving this highest honor. As Favored, you're entering a world that is very different from the one you leave behind. The palaces of the Rulers are ancient places, teeming with magic and touched by the gods. The Rulers who discovered you will arrive at your homes at seven o'clock this evening.

"As of this moment," the headmaster continued, his eyes darting between Kym and the boy, "you are no longer students at this school. I'll be contacting your parent or guardian to inform them of your departure, but the reason is better coming from you. Go home, collect your things, and see your families."

Kym didn't breathe the whole time the headmaster spoke. She wasn't sure what she expected to happen, but it wasn't this. Telling her parents in her own way was a thing of the past. They were taking her that evening. She needed to leave and get home before her parents did. She needed time to figure out how to tell them she was leaving. But before she did that, she needed to make herself get out of her chair.

Kym stepped out of the office and found the gym buzzing with activity. Groups of students stretched and chatted while janitors slowly broke down the stage, but Kym never felt more alone. She could feel every pair of eyes lock on her as she walked by. Why did they have to stare? Why couldn't they ignore her like they used to? Her desire for solitude grew with every step she took.

Kym half walked, half ran down the now-deserted halls to her locker. Her fingers trembled as she punched in her combination on the worn touchpad. After several failed attempts, she finally yanked the door open. It flew back, banging against the locker next to it, but the metallic ringing barely registered in her ears. Kym scooped her things into her arms and threw them haphazardly into her backpack. She slung her bag over her should and walked right out of the school, not even bothering to shut her locker.

Kym wasn't sure how she got back home. One moment she was walking down the school steps, then she was standing in her empty living room. Her backpack lay on the floor, its contents spilled around her feet. Kym stepped right over the mess and began to wander aimlessly through her house. Somehow, she wound up lying on her parents' bed, staring up at the faded blue ceiling. Then she was in the pantry, running her hands mindlessly across the old shelves. Finally, after stalking through the bathroom and hall closest, Kym arrived at her room. And it was there, in the safety of her tiny space, that the tears began to fall.

She fell on her bed, and the thoughts started to roll over her, one by one. Everything was over. Magic was tearing her family apart once again, but this time, it was all her fault. She didn't want to go. She didn't want to learn magic and live in a palace for the rest of her life. But that didn't matter. No one cared about what she wanted. Nila would arrive to take Kym away that evening, and there was nothing she could do to stop it.

Her parents must have heard from the headmaster by now and were probably on their way home. They must be going crazy since the headmaster didn't give a reason why he sent her home. She didn't want them to find her like this; her face all blotchy, covered in tears, and unable to string two words together. Losing her was going to be just as hard for them as it was for her. So, for her parents' sake, she needed to be strong.

Kym attempted to pull herself together. In the small bathroom, she splashed some cold water on her face, hoping to cool some of the red from her skin. Her hands shook so badly most of the water didn't reach her face, instead falling onto her dress and floor. Kym tried her best to clean up the mess, using the thin towel that hung from a hook on the wall.

"Kym!" It was her dad, and she could hear the panic in his voice. "Where are you?"

Kym walked out of the bathroom, and her legs trembled so badly she thought she might collapse. Her dad sat silently on one side of the small couch, leaving space for her mom. Kym just stood in the middle of the room like a statue, her dad staring at her through narrow eyes, his brows pushed tightly together. Kym wondered why he looked so angry. He didn't think she'd gotten into trouble, did he? Why did he think she'd been sent home in the middle of the day?

"What's going on?" His voice was softer than before, but his face was still stern. "Your headmaster said you'd been excused from school and that your mother and I need to come home right away. What happened?"

"Where's Mom?" Kym's voice was no more than a whisper.

"She'll be here in a few minutes," Kym's dad answered, the concern evident in his voice. "She couldn't leave work right away. Did something happen at school? You know you can tell me."

"I'd rather wait until Mom's here," she mumbled to her shoes.

"Kym, it can't be that bad."

Kym didn't respond, and her dad didn't press the issue. Neither of them spoke until Kym's mom arrived five minutes later. Kym stayed where she was, rooted to the spot, while her mother sat next to her dad.

"What's going on?" she demanded. "Your headmaster said I needed to come home at once. What's the matter? Are you hurt?"

"No, I'm not hurt." Kym couldn't stop her voice from trembling.

Kym shifted uncomfortably from side to side, staring at her shoes. She needed to tell them. There was no point keeping it from them any longer. But once she told them, she'd never be able to unsay what she knew she needed to say.

"It's all right," Kym's dad said slowly. He had a strange look on his face, like he knew exactly what Kym was struggling to say. "You can tell us anything."

"So," she began, determined to say it all. "I told you nothing happened at the river this morning, but that was a lie. Something did happen while I was in the water."

"Oh, Pheil." Kym's mom's hands shot upward, covering her mouth.

"And after Temple, you asked me why I spent so much time at Reta's altar. I said it was nothing, but that was also a lie."

Kym's dad wrapped his arms around her mom's shaking shoulders, resting his chin on top of her light-brown curls. Kym's insides felt like one large knot, and she wanted to take all her words back. But she couldn't, not now that she'd started. She had to tell them the rest.

"This morning, at the river, the water pulled me under. It glowed and made me feel strange; it stopped me from panicking. Then at Temple, I put my hand in the water of Reta's altar, and a blue spiral appeared on my skin, but it vanished when I took my hand out."

Kym looked deliberately at a spot a good six inches above her parents' heads. Saying all this was hard enough without looking them in the eye. But she could still hear their gasps and sighs, which were horrible enough on their own. A slight thump told Kym her mom's hands had slid from her face, and Kym's dad made a sound like someone hit him in the stomach with a bat.

"What the Thed were you thinking, Kym?" her mom asked, her voice a mix of sorrow and frustration. "Why didn't you tell us?"

"Two years ago, after I hadn't shown any signs of magic, you said I was safe," she said, finally looking at her mom. "I didn't know how to tell you I wasn't."

"Why did your headmaster send you home?" Kym's dad asked in disbelief. "What happened at school?"

"When I got to school, the carriages were outside," Kym sniffed, blinking rapidly. She was determined not to cry. "The Rulers looked for new Favored, and I passed Nila's test. The headmaster sent me home to explain and so I could get ready."

"Get ready?" Kym's dad asked while her mom cried out, collapsing onto his shoulder. "Get ready for what?"

"Nila will be here at seven," she croaked, unable to stop the tears from running down her cheeks. "I have to leave tonight."

Kym fell silent, having said everything she needed to say. Wanting to give her parents some space, Kym went into her room to pack. After only a couple of minutes, her parents came in and started to help. She wanted to apologize and tell them this wasn't what she wanted, but the words caught in her throat. So they packed in silence, gathering everything they could think of, until the clock read five till seven.

Out on the front porch, Kym stood between her parents, her bags held tightly in their arms, when the giant blue carriage arrived. Nila climbed out, her dress shimmering in the setting sun, and glided up the front walk. With her massive crown, dark hair, and towering frame, Nila looked like something from another world.

"You must be Mr. and Mrs. Collins," Nila said briskly, her narrow face impassive. "I am here for Kymbralyn."

"I can't believe she is leaving us." It was the first time Kym's mom had spoken in hours. "I don't know what we'll do without her."

"To be chosen as a Favored is a great honor. You should be proud. Learning the art of magic at my palace is a rare opportunity."

"How long will that take?" Kym's dad asked, his voice full of strain. "When can she come back home?"

"It is different for everyone. Some have been at Wadita for nearly ten years and still have much more to learn. But there are those who mastered the art of water in only six years."

"Can we visit her?" asked Kym's mom.

"I am sorry, but that is impossible," Nila said, though it sounded like she was as far away from sorry as anyone could get. "Only those with a magical aura can enter any of the palaces. Before we started training the Favored, anyone could come. But now, the gods decreed only those with magic can be allowed entry."

"Why is that?"

"So we can teach the Favored without interference, of course."

Tears rolled silently down Kym's mom's face, while her dad's body shook on her other side. Slowly, Kym wrapped her arms around her mother, who placed her shaking ones over Kym's shoulders. Her dad's hands passed over Kym's head, wrapping around her mother, gently pressing Kym between them.

Kym was the only one not crying. She'd worried and cried so

much, she must have used up all the emotion she had. All she wanted was to be with her parents, to feel the love passing between them in the hug they shared. She embraced them for as long as she could, knowing that in mere moments, she would have to let them go.

"Kymbralyn, it is time," Nila said, indifferent to the moment Kym and her parents were sharing.

"Just because I won't be here doesn't mean I don't love you," said Kym, finally pulling herself away from her parents. "You're the most important people in my life. But I'm one of the Favored now, and I can't change that. I need to learn what that means, and how to use what the gods gave me. Please don't worry about me."

"Well said, Kymbralyn," Nila said briskly. "I will give you a moment for one final good-bye."

Nila walked back to the carriage, and Kym looked into her parents' eyes.

"We love you, sweetheart. We'll miss you," her dad whispered, giving her one final squeeze.

"I thought the gods had forgotten us long ago," her mom sniffed. "But now, they've given you a second chance, my love. Make it count." She kissed Kym gently on the cheek. "And make us proud."

Kym walked slowly toward the carriage, her parents right behind her with her bags. She looked up at Nila, who was more than a foot taller than her, and all Kym could think about was how small she was. Climbing into the carriage, Kym took her place across from the Ruler. Her parents began lifting Kym's bags into the carriage when the door closed with a snap.

"She will not need any of that," Nila said through the carriage window. "Not where she is going."

With no warning, the carriage lurched forward. Unable to speak, Kym watched through the ornate back window as her parents grew smaller and smaller, her bags still held in their outstretched arms.

CHAPTER THREE

A FRESH START

KYM STARED OUT OF THE CARRIAGE WINDOW LONG AFTER HER parents vanished from her sight. With no emotion left to use, all she could feel was emptiness. Every time she closed her eyes, she saw her parents standing there, tears running down their faces, their arms held out to her. And even though her body shook with grief, not a single tear escaped her eyes. Tears were for those who had something to lose, and with no parents, or belongings, or home, she had nothing left.

As the carriage rolled through the city, past the wall, and into the sprawling countryside beyond, Kym realized she had no idea where she was going. Whenever her teachers taught about the palaces, they'd show elaborate maps that looked way too artistic to be real. She knew Princirum had seven realms, one for each of the Rulers, and the four cities were somewhere between the realms. She was pretty sure Nila's realm was called Undarunci.

Kym concentrated, trying to recall anything she'd learned about Nila's palace. She knew the Palace of Life was in the middle of Princirum, but other than that, she had no idea where the other palaces were. Maybe Nila's palace was near the ocean? It made sense, Kym thought, for the Palace of Water to actually be near the water. She'd never been to the sea, but she'd seen plenty of pictures. All that pure blue water, stretching right up to the very edge of the world. Her parents would have loved that.

The smile fell from Kym's lips as quickly as it appeared. Her parents would never see it; they were stuck in the city, unable to see the ocean even if they wanted to. The brave face Kym put on for her parents melted away. There wasn't any reason to pretend. She didn't need to be strong anymore.

Nila leaned across the carriage and grabbed Kym's hand. She may have intended to show some sympathy or compassion, but Kym never felt it. Her grip on Kym was way too tight, and her long, ornate nails dug into the side of her hand. Kym tore her gaze from the window and tried to turn her look of pain into one of gratitude.

"I know leaving everything you know and care about is difficult. I am sure you must feel like your whole world has ended. But it has not. On the contrary, this is a gift. Today, your life begins anew. Do something in this life that you failed to do in your first. Not many are blessed with such an opportunity. Do not waste it."

Nila released Kym's hand, restoring the feeling to her already-numb fingers. She sat back in her seat, Nila's words filtering slowly through her mind. Was there anything she'd do differently with this new start? There was. Thanks to the priests, no one ever associated with Kym. As far as she could remember, there hadn't been any Water Favored chosen from her school since she'd started there four years before. No one would know to stay away from her. She could have friends.

Kym smiled to herself. Maybe her new life wasn't going to be as bad as she thought. It was a chance for a fresh start, and she owed it to her parents to make the most of it. She turned back to the window and watched the sky fade from soft pink to dark indigo, her eyelids growing heavier as the carriage rolled on. She fought the urge as long as she could, but finally, Kym gave in and fell asleep.

Someone gave Kym's shoulder a shake, jolting her from her slumber. She jumped, sliding off her plush carriage seat and catching herself just before she hit the floor. She looked around for who woke her, but the carriage was so full of bright light it was hard to see anything. Nila's vast silhouette filled the open carriage door, blocking some of the intense light shining just outside. Nila exited the carriage and turned to face Kym, still propped awkwardly between her seat and the floor.

"Kymbralyn, welcome to Wadita, the Palace of Water."

Kym didn't know what she expected, but what she saw far outstretched her expectation. The palace sat on the beach next to the sea, with piles of golden sand gathered around its base. It was constructed from what Kym could only call blue marble, but that description was far from accurate. The walls twinkled in the morning sun, and as she turned her head this way and that, they seemed to wave like the sea. Multiple small towers rose from the highest roof, surrounding one massive tower, which Kym thought must be in the center. It was the most magnificent thing she'd ever seen.

Kym's mouth fell open, and she heard Nila let out a little laugh. "Every time I arrive with a new Favored, you always act so shocked."

"It's just so beautiful," was all Kym could quietly answer.

"I am glad you approve, seeing as it is your home."

Kym climbed out of the carriage, which rolled off the second her feet hit the hard, graveled drive. Bright blue banners hung on either side of the massive front doors, each embroidered with a giant wave. A little man with wisps of gray mixed in with his dark hair bounced down the sweeping front stairs toward Kym and Nila. When he spoke, his voice was high and fast, reminding Kym of a squirrel.

"Welcome home, my Lady and young Miss," he squeaked, bowing low to both of them. Kym shifted uncomfortably at the gesture.

"Come, Kymbralyn," Nila ordered, ignoring the man, walking straight past him and up the stairs.

Smiling down at the little man, Kym hurried up the steps after Nila, trying her best to keep up with Nila's lengthy strides. The massive doors swung open of their own accord as they approached, and Kym's excitement grew as she followed Nila into the palace. They were standing in an enormous round room. Tall, thin windows lined the front half of the wall, while several identical doors covered the opposite. Kym turned slowly on the spot, trying her best to take in every detail.

"Before you can see the palace," Nila said, "you must be redressed."

"Redressed?" asked Kym. She was still wearing her best orange dress. "What's wrong with what I'm wearing?"

"Those common clothes are not acceptable here. You are part of a higher class of people, Kymbralyn, and you must dress as such. Do not worry. These lady's maids will ensure you look presentable."

Nila clapped her hands, and the sound echoed around the vast hall. A door on the very end of the hall swung open, and two women walked in. They looked a little older than Kym's mom and had their long, brown hair twisted in buns on the backs of their heads. They wore simple blue dresses and beamed excitedly as they joined Nila and Kym in the middle of the hall.

"Redress Miss Kymbralyn and have her ready for a tour in one hour," Nila ordered.

"Of course, Lady Nila," the lady's maids chimed back in unison, bowing low to her.

While Nila strode through one of the many doors, the lady's maids each grabbed one of Kym's arms and half led, half dragged her back through the door they'd come out of. Their constant smiling sent an odd tremor down Kym's spine, and she wriggled uncomfortably, trying to make them let go. Instead, they tightened their grip on her arms. The room they entered was about twice the size of Kym's old living room. Magnificent gowns lined the walls while a raised platform surrounded by mirrors sat in the center. The lady's maids placed Kym on this platform, and then they slowly started to circle her.

"She should be in a full-length gown with sleeves cut off at the elbow," one of them finally said.

"Marvelous idea, Veronica. And wouldn't it look fantastic if the cuffs tapered to the floor?"

"Genius, Isabel! That would really complement her long hair." They both spoke in very high, tremulous voices, like the man who welcomed Kym on the front steps. It was almost like they were singing.

"Am I wearing one of those?" Kym asked, looking around at all of the other dresses in the room.

"Oh no, Miss Kymbralyn," gasped Veronica, shock visible in every line on her face.

"It's just Kym," she said quickly.

"Those have already been used, Miss Kym," Isabel smiled. "We can't dress you in clothes someone else has already worn."

"First things first. You must get out of those old rags."

Kym started taking off her dress, but the lady's maids wouldn't allow it. She tried to help, but they smacked her hands away every time she tried, saying that wasn't her job anymore. They pulled what had been Kym's best dress from her and tossed it carelessly to the floor. Realizing there was no way to fend them off, Kym finally gave in.

Veronica and Isabel draped fabric over Kym, picked colors, tailored the sleeves, and sewed it all together, all while they chatted away endlessly. She didn't listen, instead looking at the beautiful clothes around her. She couldn't believe they were going to this much trouble just so she could get a tour. On very rare occasions, Favored would visit the city for important events. The last one Kym could remember was seven years ago, and the Favored arrived dressed like she was going to a ball. Kym always assumed she'd dressed like that for special occasions. She never imagined they dressed like that all the time. She wasn't even fully dressed yet and she was already uncomfortable.

"So, what do you do here at the palace?"

"We take care of you, of course," Veronica said with a dazzling smile.

"Take care of me?"

"We'll dress you in the mornings and bathe you and prepare you for training and get you ready for dinner in the evenings," said Isabel.

"And of course, we'll clean up after you," added Veronica cheerfully.

"So, you're my servants?" Kym asked tentatively, not wanting to offend them. "Why would you want to serve someone day and night? That sounds horrible."

Both Isabel and Veronica gasped, exchanging identical looks of shock.

"Oh no! Serving one of the Favored is the greatest honor in the world," said Isabel.

"There is nothing more fulfilling anyone could do with their lives," Veronica added. "Serving those touched by the gods. What more could anyone want from life?"

Kym wanted to shake both Veronica and Isabel by their shoulders. Why did they think serving someone was the best thing they could do with their lives? Unable to stand still for another second, she stepped forward, and her bare feet caught on the hem of her dress. She righted herself, and for the first time, properly looked at herself in the wall of mirrors. The thought of shaking some sense into her lady's maids faded from her mind.

She'd never seen anything so beautiful. Kym wore a shimmering blue gown, with sleeves that stopped just past her elbows and cuffs that trailed to the floor, just like her maids said. The fabric was light as air and felt smooth as water against her skin. Silently, Isabel stepped forward and slipped Kym's feet into a pair of high heels. Kym couldn't help but smile.

The door to the dressing room swung open, and Nila glided in. Immediately, both of Kym's lady's maids greeted Nila with "my lady" as they sank into deep bows. Nila ignored them. Instead, she raked over Kym with her narrow eyes.

"Much better," she said with a reassuring nod. "Much more normal looking. You are ready to see your new home."

Nila led Kym back into the entrance hall, leaving her lady's maids in the dressing room. Nila took Kym to the door on the opposite side of the hall, where a steep flight of stairs led to the bedchambers. Kym wanted to ask how many Favored were at Wadita; it looked like it could easily hold over a thousand people. But before she could ask, Nila shut the door and moved to a slightly larger door in the middle.

The dining hall was filled with large round tables and had a giant fire-place set into one of the walls. Before she could see any more, Nila shut the door and moved to the next room.

"The palace is thousands of years old, and built from solidified water," Nila droned, sounding almost bored.

"Solidified water? Like ice?"

"No," Nila laughed coldly. "It is nothing like ice. The great Reta herself solidified the water used to construct this palace when the gods roamed Princirum. Every drop is infused with her magic, and only the might of the gods could ever bring down Wadita's walls."

They walked on, exploring even more rooms. Everywhere they went, Kym saw more servants, all dressed in simple blue clothes, running all over the place. No matter what they were doing, the servants greeted Nila as "my Lady" and Kym as "Miss," and bowed low as they passed. And as she saw all these people running around, something occurred to Kym; none of them were Favored.

"Um, Nila, Lady Nila. Can I ask you something?"

"If you must."

"You told my parents only people with magic could come here. But the servants don't have magic, do they? How are they here?"

"Clever girl." Nila stared down her nose at Kym. "What I told your parents was a lie. They could step through our doors anytime they pleased. But why would you want them here? They would get in the way of your training. This is better."

"If you say so," Kym said slowly, not really sure if she agreed.

Kym couldn't believe it. She'd spent the entire ride to Wadita convincing herself to accept the world she never wanted to be a part of, and Nila had just admitted she lied to Kym's face. How could she live with these people? She wanted to go home, to just run out the doors and leave this crazy place behind. But she couldn't. Aside from knowing she was by the sea, Kym had absolutely no idea where in Princirum she was.

Nila showed Kym several massive, empty chambers used for large gatherings she hosted as a Ruler. If she needed a new outfit for a simple tour, how was she supposed to dress for a party? At the very least, it wouldn't be comfortable. Nila led Kym through several narrow hallways before they finally walked out into the garden.

Kym's growing feelings of resentment faded slightly as bright light hit her eyes and the smell of saltwater filled her nose. A waist-high wall separated the mass of green grass and plants from the sandy beach. The heels of her shoes sank into the soft, green earth, and she stumbled with every step. When she finally reached the wall, Kym just stood there, mesmerized by the view of the sea.

Nila cleared her throat, forcing Kym to tear her eyes from the glittering water. Nila retreated back into the palace, and Kym hurried after her, trying her best not to fall. She finally caught up to Nila in the entrance hall. Veronica and Isabel stood waiting for them, bowing once again as Nila approached. Was bowing all they knew how to do?

"Your lady's maids will show you to your bedchamber. Dinner starts at six o'clock. Do not be late."

On that note, Nila left Kym, flanked by her smiling lady's maids, alone in the middle of the entrance hall. There was so much about this place she didn't understand. Of course, she didn't want to be late for dinner, but was it such a big deal if she was? With hours to spare before dinner started, Kym followed her lady's maids through the door to the bedchamber stairs.

"Where is everyone?" Aside from servants, Kym hadn't seen any Favored since she arrived.

"Who, dear?" Veronica asked, not even looking back at Kym.

"The other Favored. I haven't seen any since I got here."

"Oh, they're training, Miss," said Isabel. "You'll meet all of them at dinner."

They exited on a landing, walked down a long hall, then turned up a spiral staircase. They climbed for several more minutes, and Kym had absolutely no idea where they were. Finally, the maids stopped in front of a door identical to many others they'd passed and opened it. The bedchamber was massive. An enormous bed draped in blue hangings sat against one wall while a set of glass double doors stood opposite the main one.

Kym walked over to the double doors, pulled them open, and stepped out onto the balcony. She stared down at the sea, and several minutes passed before she walked back into the room. She started opening a door opposite the bed when Isabel quickly stepped forward, and Kym could hear the panic in her voice.

"Don't go in there, Miss. None of your clothes are prepared yet. We should have the closet filled by the end of the week."

Trying to ignore Isabel's comment about preparing Kym's clothes, she opened the door next to the closet and saw the bathroom. The bathtub was the size of a child's swimming pool, and the counters were covered in more bottles than Kym could count. Shaking her head, her mouth slightly open, Kym walked back into the main room. There was at least fifteen feet of space between the bed and the opposite wall. Several chairs and couches were set up next to her bed, like a little sitting room. Kym's whole house could have easily fit in this one room.

"It's so big," was all Kym could bring herself to say. "I don't really need this much space."

"Don't be silly. You're one of the Favored, Miss," Veronica said. "You've earned a life of luxury while you learn to use your god-given gifts."

"You'll need this space to practice what you learn in training, Miss," added Isabel, gesturing to several large urns next to the balcony doors.

Puzzled, Kym walked over to the urns and peered inside. Other than being full of water, Kym couldn't see anything special about them. If they were there to help her practice magic, shouldn't they be more magical? Kym really didn't understand this place. Why did being a Favored mean she got all of this? It wasn't fair. Surely there was someone in Princirum who needed this stuff, especially since she didn't want any of it. The room, the clothes, the maids; it was all too much.

"It's just water," she said, still confused.

"You'll need it to practice, Miss," Isabel sighed. "Learning magic takes a lot of hard work and practice."

"Right. I hadn't thought about that."

Ever since Nila had chosen her as a Favored, all Kym could think about was that her world had ended. She'd never thought about actually learning magic. But Isabel was right; Kym was there to learn magic, and she had no idea how that worked. She wasn't even sure if anyone outside of the palaces knew how to teach magic. She looked at her smiling maids, standing on either side of the front door. If she was going to ask, these two were as good as anyone.

"So…how exactly do Favored learn magic?"

"We don't know. You are the first Favored Isabel and I have cared for. This is our first time at the palaces too."

"But before you arrived this morning, the head housekeeper gave us a brief overview of what we should expect. She said our Favored, you, could be exhausted during the first few days of your training, and we should provide you with a little extra care."

Kym figured Veronica and Isabel wouldn't know much. But what the housekeeper said about Kym being tired didn't make any more sense. Since she was new to magic, wouldn't she start by learning the basics? They couldn't be that hard. The housekeeper must want to prepare Veronica and Isabel for the worst, just in case it happened.

Kym spent the next several hours in her bedchamber, bored out of her mind. There was absolutely nothing to do in there besides lounging on the chairs and sofas. There wasn't even a television. After nearly falling asleep three times, Kym knew she needed to move. She slowly walked through the entire room, taking in every detail she could, except for the closet. Kym's maids stood on either side of the door, not wanting to subject her to the horrors of its bare shelves. By five o'clock, having exhausted every possible option, Kym decided to go back down to the entrance hall.

Veronica and Isabel started to lead the way out of the door before Kym stopped them. She wanted to try and find her way down on her own. She didn't like having to rely on them for everything. Since this palace was now her home, she should start learning how to get around it by herself. So her maids stepped back and let Kym lead the way, staying a couple of paces behind her.

After four rounds down the spiral stairs and two turns down random halls, Kym was utterly lost. She tried to keep going, refusing to ask her maids for help. She knew she could do it if she found her way back to the staircase. But, after wandering aimlessly for half an hour, she finally had to concede. Her lady's maids took over, and in less than ten minutes, Kym was down in the entrance hall.

The dining hall was set for dinner. Glossy blue tablecloths covered the round tables, while each place had four different-sized plates and more silverware than Kym thought she would use in a week. A fire crackled merrily in the large fireplace, and light from the setting sun shone through the vast windows on the back wall, offering a spectacular view of the sea. Since dinner didn't start for over an hour, Kym was the only person in the room. She picked a random table, and as she sat, she noticed Veronica and Isabel standing just behind her stiff chair.

"You don't need to stand there all night," Kym said tentatively. "I think I can manage on my own."

"Don't be silly," said Veronica in her singsong voice.

"We're here to serve you, Miss," chimed Isabel.

This was ridiculous. Not only were Veronica and Isabel going to dress Kym every day, but they were going to serve her at mealtimes too? Kym could handle them dressing her, since it was in the privacy of her room, but serving her where everyone else could see? What's next, watching Kym sleep? Bathing her? With a pang, she remembered her maids saying one of those was already part of their duties, and it wasn't watching Kym sleep.

As seven o'clock drew nearer, the rest of the Favored entered the dining hall. They sat down at the other tables, talking excitedly, surrounded by their servants. As the room filled, Kym realized how few Favored there actually were. Even though Wadita was massive, she counted no more than fifty well-dressed Favored sitting at the tables, and none looked older than twenty-five. This couldn't be all the Favored there were. There had to be more. These Favored must be the ones still training, just like Kym.

Somewhere off in the distance, a clock chimed seven. Everyone stood as Nila, accompanied by her entourage of servants, glided over to one of the tables that still had an open seat. Once at her chair, she waved her slender hands, and everyone sat, though Nila remained standing. Her arms spread wide, Nila looked to the ceiling and began asking the gods to bless the meal they were about to eat.

Even her father, one of the most devout worshipers Kym knew, never asked the gods to bless their meals. She sighed, realizing this was probably just the beginning of her religious re-education. And how could it not be? Her magic came from the gods. It was a package deal.

"And Great Reta," Nila added. "Mother of the oceans and water, bringer of water's purifying touch; we thank you for sending us our newest Favored, Kymbralyn Collins."

Silence fell over the hall, and Kym felt every eye lock on her. Why did Nila have to put her on the spot like this? Unsure what to do, Kym raised her hand, waving awkwardly, and couldn't stop the nervous laugh from passing her lips. Her face felt like it was on fire, and she wanted nothing more than to dive under the table.

Finally, after what seemed like a lifetime, Nila invited everyone to begin eating. The servants walked to long tables along the sides of the hall that Kym hadn't noticed before. They returned moments later with plates piled with food. Veronica and Isabel gave Kym mounds of steaming red crab, rows of brightly colored fish, bowls of massive shrimp, piles of potatoes, thick cuts of steak, vegetables dripping in butter, and much, much more.

Kym could still feel people watching her, so she tried to control herself. It was a hard task since she'd never seen so much food in her life. She piled as much of it on her plate as she could, but that barely made a dent in the mounds Veronica and Isabel brought.

Kym ate her food in silence while the rest of the hall filled with the sounds of happy conversation. Only one other girl, whose long, dark hair matched her eyes, sat with Kym. She'd been one of the last people to enter the hall and only sat with Kym after finding no other options. Kym hadn't helped matters, waving and laughing like she didn't know how to behave. But this was Kym's fresh start, and she wasn't going to let the entire evening be a waste.

"Hi," she squeaked. "I'm Kym."

"I heard," the girl said flatly, quickly glancing at Kym before returning to her food. "Kenna."

"So," Kym said, trying and failing to sound a little more confident, "have you been here for a while?"

Kenna looked Kym up and down, as though she was debating whether or not she should even answer. Apparently deciding that she needed to say something, Kenna replied, "Over four years now."

"Oh. Do you ever miss home after being away for so long?"

"At first." Kenna shrugged. "But after a while, you get over it. The magic we learn here is well worth the price of leaving home."

"To our three new Favored who arrived this past week," Nila's voice rang through the hall, causing all conversation to die instantly, "your first lesson begins at sunrise tomorrow. As for everyone else, your training schedules remain unchanged. I will meet our three new Favored in the entrance hall and take you to the training rooms myself. Be sure to rest well. You are going to need it."

CHAPTER FOUR

LET'S
BEGIN

KYM SAT BOLT UPRIGHT. SHE LOOKED WILDLY AROUND, HER ENTIRE body shaking, trying to catch her breath. In the darkness, her new bedchamber looked so strange, with the plush chairs appearing twisted and warped by the night. Shafts of silvery light spread across the dark ground from the balcony door, left ajar by her maids. A light breeze drifted through the room, working its way into even the farthest corners.

Kym pressed her back against the ornate headboard and pulled the thick covers over herself. She needed to get back to sleep, but every time she shut her eyes, dread over her first day of training invaded her mind. So she stared at the ceiling, unable to turn her brain off. What would Nila do if Kym's magic didn't come? She wouldn't throw her out, since her test already proved Kym had magic in her. Would she put Kym in a lower group? But how could there be a group lower than the one she was already in?

Kym got out of bed, realizing sleep wasn't going to happen. She started walking toward the balcony, but her feet got caught in the hem of the thin, silky nightdress her lady's maids insisted she wear. She slipped and crashed forward onto her hands and knees. Why was it so important for Kym to dress nicely even when she slept? Annoyed, Kym pushed herself up, hiked her dress up over her knees and walked the rest of the way to the balcony.

The ocean lapped gently onto the sandy beach, and the bright moon glowed silver against the velvety black sky. Since sitting out on the balcony seemed better than lying in the dark, she settled onto one of the lounge chairs. She closed her eyes, and the rush of the waves filled her mind. The cool night air seemed to calm her slowly from the inside. It was so peaceful, she almost forgot about her impending training. Unfortunately, when she finally felt relaxed, her bedchamber door burst open.

"Miss Kym, it is time to get ready for your first day of training."

"Veronica, she's not in her bed."

"Miss Kym, where are you?"

"Miss Kym?"

"I'm out on the balcony," she groaned, bracing herself for their arrival.

Veronica and Isabel each grabbed one of Kym's arms, heaved her out of her chair, and pulled her into the now-candlelit bedchamber. They filled the large tub with slightly steaming water, and subjected Kym to numerous scrubbings and soaks. They used so many different kinds of smelly soaps and oils that Kym's head started to ache. When they rinsed her down for the last time, Kym looked around for a towel, praying they'd let her dry herself off.

But it was not meant to be. Veronica and Isabel patted down Kym's entire body while she tried not to look too embarrassed. When she was dry, Veronica wrapped Kym in a light robe while Isabel brushed Kym's hair, tying it in a ponytail. Veronica left the bathroom and returned moments later with a simple blue shirt, tight pants, and flat running shoes. After the elaborate dress from yesterday, this outfit seemed almost foreign.

"No gown today?" Kym asked, her eyebrows raised.

"Oh no," said Veronica seriously. "You can't wear a gown while you're training."

"We don't want you ruining something that nice," Isabel added, helping Kym slide into the stiff, obviously new, shoes.

"Well, you look fantastic," Veronica sighed, sounding like an artist forced to work with limited materials.

"Thanks," Kym said. For the first time since arriving at Wadita, she finally felt like herself. "Thank you both."

"We'll have something more suitable for you to wear when you return for dinner."

If Kym thought getting to the entrance hall was challenging with her maids' help, it was even worse in the dark. The torches were unlit, and Kym found herself making even more wrong turns than she had the day before. But finally, Kym burst into the entrance hall just as light started to creep in through the tall, thin windows. Two other people dressed in similarly normal clothes already stood in the center of the hall.

"Hi," she panted. "I'm Kym."

The two other Favored, a boy and girl, simply stared at Kym before turning back to stare at the floor in the middle of the hall. They'd been watching it when she arrived and clearly thought it was more interesting than Kym. Upset, she opened her mouth to speak, but stopped abruptly. The floor before them shook and split open, revealing a vast staircase descending below Wadita. Kym couldn't even see where it ended.

"Follow me," said Nila, standing several steps below them on the newly revealed stairs.

Kym walked behind the other two as they all followed Nila down the dark stairs. Torches, set in brackets along the walls, illuminated the dark passage as they walked deeper and deeper belowground. After a couple of minutes walking, the straight staircase began to spiral, which branched off to doorways that appeared every so often. Nila led Kym and the others through the very first door, and Kym couldn't stop her mouth from falling open.

They were standing inside a giant sphere filled halfway with water. The room was enormous, at least fifty feet tall and just as wide and made entirely of solidified water. Giant basins filled with fire hung from the domed ceiling, and torches were set every couple of feet along the curved wall, filling the room with bright blue light. A ring of solidified water stuck out a couple of feet from the wall, sitting about an inch above the waterline. A little island sat in the center of the water, just big enough for one person to stand on. Kym and the others followed Nila along the ringed path until they were on the opposite side of the room.

"As you know," Nila began, "the gods banished Thed, the God of Death, from Princirum, condemning him to an eternity in Nothingness, where he rules over the death he cherishes. However, they could not cut his presence from Princirum entirely. His power seeps back to our land, creating the death demons that terrorize Princirum. Here, you will train to use the gifts the gods gave you to defend Princirum and keep the power of Thed at bay."

Kym could remember six different death demon attacks in the City of Contellus. Whenever one appeared, alarms sounded, the citizens stayed indoors, and the city patrol went to defend the walls. Each attack always ended with several demolished city blocks. However, Kym couldn't remember a single attack where a Favored came to help. If it was the Favoreds' job to fight them, why hadn't they shown up?

"Magic," Nila continued, calling Kym back to her surroundings, "is becoming one with one's self. You were chosen because of your connection to the element of water and the goddess Reta. However, magic requires tremendous skill and even more power. In this room, you will learn the basics of water magic. You will start with water walking."

Nila turned on her heel and walked straight onto the water. Kym instinctively stepped forward, her hand outstretched, but she needn't have bothered. Instead of falling into the water, as Kym feared, Nila stood on top of it like it was stone or wood. And even though Nila's gown covered the water around her feet, Kym could still see the water glowing bright blue beneath her. As Nila walked across the water, her feet made no disturbance on the glassy surface.

"Summon your courage. Do not let your fear take hold of you. If you do, it will pull you under. Trust in your power and take a step."

Kym stood there, hoping one of the others would step forward. Until ten seconds ago, Kym thought walking on water was impossible. But Nila made it look so easy. What if she couldn't do it? What would happen if she stepped onto the water and fell through? Beside Kym, neither of the other Favored stepped out onto the water. The girl, no older than thirteen and at least a foot shorter than Kym, kept glancing and snickering with the boy next to her, who must be around her age. They must be even more nervous than Kym was.

After nearly a minute passed, Kym knew she couldn't put it off any longer. She took a deep breath, focused as hard as she could on not failing, and took a step toward Nila. It felt like her insides turned to cement the moment her feet touched the water. Her knees shook violently, and sweat poured down her face, but she didn't fall in. Kym stayed where she was, not daring to move even an inch.

Slowly, the corners of Kym's vision began to blur. Beneath her feet, she felt the water start to bend in on itself. It snapped, and Kym sank like a rock. Coughing and spluttering, Kym dragged herself back over to the ringed edge. She tried to climb out, but it was like the magic sucked all the strength from her body. Hopefully, she looked up to the others. They each grabbed one of her arms and hauled her from the water. Even through her blurry vision, Kym saw the girl roll her eyes.

"Kymbralyn lasted nineteen seconds," Nila announced, her flat voice ringing through the vast room. "Matt, step forward."

Kym, her clothes soaked through, stayed where Matt and the girl left her while Matt took his turn. Kym was able to stand when the girl took Matt's place, though her legs felt like they were about to fall off. Both Matt and Chloe, the other Favored, lasted much longer than Kym did. Nila even told them to stop after they each stood for over a minute without falling in. Once Chloe was back on solid ground, Nila turned back to Kym.

"Again."

They practiced for hours. Each time Kym took her turn, she tried to stand on the water longer than her previous attempt before falling through the surface. And even though her body shook with exhaustion, she managed to improve every single time. She thought this was a good start, even though Matt and Chloe didn't step off the water during Kym's last three attempts. Kym was just about to step back onto the water when Nila, who hadn't spoken in over an hour, told all three of them to step back onto the ledge.

"That was a good start," said Nila, her eyes lingering on Matt and Chloe. "Now that you can stand, you will learn to walk. Take five steps onto the water, and then return to solid land. Kymbralyn, you will go first."

Walking on water was about fifty times harder than standing on it. Her first couple of steps were the best, with the water remaining smooth as glass. She'd get a surge of energy every time she lifted her foot from the surface, which vanished the moment she put it back down. Tiny droplets bounced around her feet as the glowing water rippled, and even though her legs shook worse than ever, she never fell in. Matt and Chloe did better; the water remaining as still as stone every time they stepped. Kym was too exhausted to even feel upset.

"Your training ran longer than I expected today. You will have dinner here this evening." Nila gestured to the island behind her, where a table Kym hadn't noticed before stood covered with food. "Go and eat your fill. I will leave you to it. I must see to other matters."

Nila walked swiftly across the water, around the little island, and out the door. Matt and Chloe headed straight toward the food, talking loudly about how easy their first day of training was. Kym stayed where she was, her eyes fixed on the little island. It was farther than she'd been able to walk all day. She looked longingly at the door, when suddenly her stomach growled loudly. So she gritted her teeth and stepped out onto the water, focusing on the table of food and not her trembling feet.

Kym reached the island, the water beneath her feet becoming more unsteady with every step. She went to step on the island, but was forced to stop after looking more closely at it. The island was only big enough for the table. Certain she would fall through the water any second, Kym grabbed a cheese covered roll from the tray closest to her and ate as fast as she could. But as she ate, her body didn't feel any heavier. Instead, she felt her strength and energy returning with each bite. Kym ate until she couldn't swallow another mouthful.

"I'm gonna go," Kym said to Chloe and Matt, who'd been chatting quietly on the other side of the table. She could hear Matt and Chloe laugh as the door closed behind her.

The next day, they started training by walking as far as they could around the edge of the water, where they could step back onto solid ground when they needed to. Finally, on her fourth attempt, Kym made it all the way around without stepping off. Ecstatic, Kym looked for Nila, but she wasn't even watching. She was talking to Chloe and Matt, who'd made it around the room during Kym's second attempt. Kym cleared her throat loudly.

"Good, you finished. We can now move onto today's lesson."

Nila stepped onto the water and turned to face Kym and the others. She held up her hand, closed her eyes, and inhaled. A glowing blue spiral appeared, like the ones Kym got during Nila's test and at Temple.

"These are the Marks. Notice their shape; the spiral follows the flow of energy through your arms to your hands. When you focus on your energy, they shall appear. Now, since you, for the most part, have mastered the basics of walking on water, you will learn to control it. Each of you will make an orb of water rise out of the surface. Project your energy from your hands, surround the water you wish to control and lift that energy out of the pool. The water will follow.

"But," Nila added sharply as an orb of water rose seamlessly from the surface, "you must be wary. Do not let your energy enter the water you control. That requires skill far beyond your capabilities. Simply surround the water and bring it to you. Begin."

Kym stared down at the water. Standing and walking on water was hard enough but levitating some like Nila had seemed nearly impossible. And everything Nila said about energy made absolutely no sense. She didn't even tell them where their energy comes from. Was the reason Kym felt so heavy and tired the day before because she'd run out of energy? For someone who'd been teaching magic for hundreds of years, Kym thought Nila was really bad at it.

She tried to mimic Nila's motions, picturing her energy flowing into the water in her mind. She focused as hard as she could, and she thought she could feel something, like a faint tingling running through her arms to her fingertips. But after an entire day of trying Kym only managed to make the water in front of her bulge slightly. Matt and Chloe succeeded after only a couple of tries. By the end of the day, they had orbs the size of a child's ball flying around the room.

The third day was no better than the first two. Supposedly having mastered making a single water orb, Nila told Kym, Matt, and Chloe to make several. They stood on the water and couldn't let any of the orbs they made fall while trying to make more. Nila left them alone for most of the day, only checking on their progress every couple of hours. And while Nila had nothing but praise for the other two, she barely spoke two words to Kym.

By the end of the day, Kym finally managed to make an orb rise from the water. Sure, it was the size of a grape and trembled as it wobbled through the air, but at least she did it. Nila didn't say anything. She was too focused on watching the others play a game of dodge ball with their numerous orbs. When Nila finally dismissed them, Kym ran straight to her bedchamber, which she could now find with ease. It was only six o'clock, but all Kym wanted was to crawl into bed.

Why did she think this new life would be any better than the one she left behind? Back at home, she was invisible and people only spoke to her when they had to. But now, she'd become something far worse. Matt and Chloe didn't even bother to hide how stupid they thought she was. She tried her best to learn and keep up, but it was never good enough. Even Nila seemed to have given up on her. Why should she waste her time on someone with no magical talent whatsoever?

Seeing Veronica and Isabel waiting for Kym with her new gown for the evening was the final straw. Kym walked straight past them and into the bathroom, slamming the door behind her. Her back pressed against the smooth door, she slid to the floor. She buried her face in her knees as the tears fell hard and fast. Her maids' soft voices drifted through the door, asking if she was all right. But Kym just kept crying.

When Kym finally cried herself out, she crawled forward, giving Veronica and Isabel enough room to squeeze into the bathroom. To their credit, they didn't say a word as they dove into their work. They washed and dressed Kym, moving around her like a silent storm of hands, brushes, and fabrics. They skillfully erased any signs of sadness from Kym's face. She looked just as stunning as usual in a blue gown that faded to white at the hem, the entire thing covered in glittering blue gemstones.

Kym waited as long as she could before going down to the dining hall. Matt and Chloe were already there, sitting at a table near the front of the hall and laughing with several other Favored. Not wanting to know what they were laughing about, she found an empty table on the opposite side of the hall. She stared so intently at her plate that she didn't notice the girl who sat with her the first night approach her table.

"Can I sit?" Kenna asked, flanked on either side by her maids.

"Sure," she muttered, looking up only long enough to give Kenna a quick nod before falling back into silence.

"All right," Kenna snapped after Nila finished thanking the gods. "What's up? Those other new Favored can't stop talking about how cool their magic is. But you've hardly said two words."

"It's…" Kym began, not really sure what to say. "It's just a lot harder than I expected."

"Of course it is. You're learning magic. It's not something that will just happen if you don't put in the effort."

"I am putting in the effort," she argued, taken aback by Kenna's harshness. "I'm just not getting the hang of it like they are."

"What did you expect?" Kenna demanded as one of her maids placed a beautiful white fish on her plate. "You're the oldest new

Favored I've ever seen. At your age, it's a wonder your magic manifested at all."

"So that's it?" Kym asked, her heart falling. "I'll always be bad at magic, no matter how hard I try?"

"That's not what I said. You're just going to have to work harder."

"But I'm already—"

"How much are you practicing before bed?" Kenna cut across her.

Before bed? Kym had been so exhausted from all the training that the second she got back to her bedchamber, she'd fall right to sleep. Practicing, on top of her normal training, was something that hadn't even entered her mind. But now that Kenna said it, it seemed so obvious. Hadn't Veronica and Isabel said the urns in her room were there for her to practice? Why hadn't she been using them?

"But what good will it do? I clearly don't understand this whole magic thing. I never wanted this. I never wanted magic or to be a Favored. Extra practice isn't going to help."

"Great Pheil! Will you stop complaining? This may not be the life you chose, but it's the life you have now. Accept it. Everyone learns magic at their own pace. Quit comparing yourself to those other Favored because it's obviously not working for you. Use that energy and try to improve yourself instead. Tonight before you go to bed practice everything you've learned so far. The more you practice, the easier this stuff gets."

Her meal finished, Kenna got up to leave, and even though her plate was still covered with food, Kym did the same. She walked around the table, and before Kenna could even open her mouth to protest, Kym wrapped her arms around her. She wanted to thank Kenna for saying what she said, even if it had been harsh. So Kym hugged her, even with Kenna only gingerly returning it.

Back in her bedchamber Isabel pulled several urns to the middle of the room while Veronica helped Kym change back into her training clothes. They refused to leave until they dressed Kym for bed, so they sat on the edge of one of the small couches to wait. For the next few hours, Kym focused solely on perfecting her water orbs. The first was small, just like the one she'd made earlier, so Kym tried to make it bigger. The difference was small from orb to orb, but by the end, they grew to the size of a large ball. And even though sweat ran down her face, she didn't stop.

She tried making more than one orb at a time, which was a lot harder than Matt or Chloe made it look. When she finally managed to make two orbs at once, water started dripping and falling off them until they finally splashed onto the floor. From that point on, Veronica and Isabel were on their knees, towels in hand, trying their best to mop up the nearly constant streams of water falling from Kym's orbs. She tried to stop it, but every time she shifted her focus to one orb, the other would start to fall apart.

Finally, the large urns nearly empty, Kym managed to maintain two small orbs with neither of them falling apart. She sent them flying around the room, and she couldn't help but smile as they followed Isabel and Veronica around while they tried to clean up. But she couldn't move them too fast since they'd start falling apart every time she tried. Satisfied with her work and on the verge of collapse, Kym returned the orbs to the urn.

"I think I can manage from here," she panted, leaning against the bedpost while Veronica retrieved her nightdress. "I'll see you in the morning."

Her maids left, and Kym slipped into the weightless dress. She walked over to close the balcony door, which she'd opened halfway through her exhausting practice. The sky was full of twinkling stars, and in the faint, silvery light of the moon, Kym could just make out something large and round crawling up the beach. She walked over to the balcony's edge, eager to get a closer look, and leaned over the small railing. Squinting through the darkness, she realized it was a turtle. Kym sat down in a chair and watched the beautiful creature slowly creep farther and farther inland until it vanished in the shadow of the palace. But as the turtle disappeared, Kym stayed where she was, her head resting on her arms, fast asleep.

CHAPTER FIVE

SPARRING AND HEADACHES

KYM TRIED HER BEST TO KEEP UP WITH MATT AND CHLOE AS THE weeks passed, especially since Nila hadn't taught them anything new since water orbs. Instead, Nila gave them single tasks, like building a floating pyramid out of water orbs, to complete as a team before the end of each day. Whenever Nila was actually in the training room, the three of them worked as a team, with Chloe and Matt involving Kym in the task. But the second Nila left, Matt and Chloe would take over, completely shutting Kym out.

"We're supposed to do this together."

"You're too slow," Matt said, his voice slightly strained from holding up the entire pyramid on his own.

"But I can help."

"Look," Chloe sneered, staring up at Kym. "You should thank us. If Lady Nila asked you to do this on your own, you'd never be able to handle it. At least this way you're not falling behind."

All Kym wanted was to tell Chloe to shut up and mind her own business. But she didn't, because deep down, she knew Chloe was right. She could do everything Matt and Chloe could, but it seemed to cost her much more energy. She practiced every night, but she still felt like she was falling behind. She even spent her weekends practicing while the other Favored played and relaxed in the ocean. But after running through the same drill for hours, Chloe and Matt laughed their way out of the training room while Kym, red-faced and sweaty, dragged her feet up the stairs.

Kym shook her head, trying to push the thought from her mind.

Her skills may not be as polished as theirs, but she'd improved every day. Nila even gave Kym the smallest of nods while she demonstrated her multitasking skills a few days before. So, since it was so important to Chloe and Matt, she let them build the pyramid. Kym would try it on her own before she went to bed.

Nila entered the room just as Chloe placed the final orb on the top of the pyramid. Kym quickly tried to make it look like she was contributing something to the exercise. Nila stared blankly at the pyramid and raised her hand. Her Marks glowed, and the pyramid fell silently back into the water.

"You will begin your study of combat magic next week. You will each spar against one of your fellow Favored at the end of each day."

"Yes!" Chloe said, excitement radiating from her eyes. "Who are we fighting? I hope I'm paired with Aidan."

Aidan had been at Wadita for at least five years. Since she spent the majority of her free time practicing in her room, Kym only ever saw him at mealtimes. But from the way she heard the other Favored talk about him, she knew his magic was exceptional. If Chloe fought him, she'd get beat in seconds. Kym couldn't help but smile at the thought.

"Why would Aidan spar against you?" Nila demanded. "A Favored of his skill would never bother with a novice like you. I will pair you with a Favored of your same skill level."

"Oh," Chloe sighed, looking crestfallen.

"Don't worry, Chloe. I'll go easy on you," said Matt cockily.

"I could take you with both hands tied behind my back."

"The three of you," Nila plowed over them, "will have your basic combat lessons in the mornings. You will join the other Favored for sparring in the afternoons. You will complete at least one sparring match per day. I will see you at dinner."

Kym left the room, uninterested in hearing Chloe and Matt argue over who was going to knock whom out. Her stomach twisted into one big knot as she climbed the stairs. Was she really ready to fight another Favored? She needed to relax. There was still time before dinner, and Kym wanted to lie down for a bit. She was almost in the entrance hall when she heard something behind her.

"Bet you five oratem she passes out before her match even starts." It was Matt, and Kym could hear the glee in his voice.

"Oh no," said Chloe, "I'd just be giving you gold if I took that bet. Besides, you still owe me seventeen argmus since she managed to keep up last week."

"Fine," Matt grumbled. Kym heard the tinkle of metal as the silver exchanged hands.

"I bet you she steps up to spar," Chloe giggled, "and gets knocked on her butt in the first five seconds."

"You're on."

Kym couldn't believe her ears. She knew Matt and Chloe thought they were better than her and never really wanted her around. If she were honest with herself, she didn't want to be around them, either. But she never bet on whether they'd fail. Suddenly, all of their laughter made sense. Hot tears welled up in her eyes. How much money had passed between them? She brushed the tear away, not wanting to know the answer, and ran the whole way back to her bedchamber.

"You're back early," Isabel's voice called from the depths of the closet.

"How was training today?" Veronica asked, not looking up as she embroidered Kym's dress.

"Fine," she lied. "We've mastered the basics, so Nila said we're ready to learn combat magic next week."

"Lady Nila, Miss Kym," Isabel corrected. "But that sounds interesting. Are the other Favored in your group excited?"

"They're excited to see me fail." The words burst from her before she could stop them. Kym flopped down on her bed.

"Why would you say that?"

"I heard them betting on how long I'd last in my match," she droned, not wanting to think about it. "And it was in seconds."

"That's horrible," Veronica gasped. "They shouldn't treat you like that. You should demand an apology at dinner."

But Kym knew no good would come from talking to them, so she didn't even bother looking for Matt or Chloe when she walked into the dining hall. Instead, she walked to the table where Kenna sat next to a tall boy with chocolate-colored hair. The boy left as Kym approached, and she sat in his empty chair, causing Kenna's face to fall. Usually, Kym could only sit with Kenna if she caught her alone, which wasn't very often. But Kenna was Kym's only friend at Wadita, so she tried to sit with her when she could.

"So, how're things?" Kenna grumbled, watching the boy join another table.

"Fine, I guess. I'm practicing every night like you said, and I'm not falling behind as much."

"Great," Kenna said, clearly uninterested.

"We're starting combat magic next week," she said as Veronica placed a heaping platter of food in front of her.

"Oh yeah?" Kenna said airily. "You'll have fun with that."

"I don't think so. I overheard the other two in my group betting on how bad I'll be."

"That's an easy fix. Just beat them in your first match," Kenna stated matter-of-factly.

"How am I supposed to do that? It takes me twice as long to nail the skills, and we only have half a day to practice before the first matches. There's no way I can do it."

Kym stared longingly at Kenna, who looked back at her through half-shut eyes, her head cocked slightly to one side. It was like she was struggling with some deep, internal conflict.

"I guess…I could help you a little if you wanted," Kenna sighed. "I'm pretty good at magic, after all."

"Really?" Kym asked, halfway rising out of her seat in excitement. "You'll help me?"

"Well don't get too excited," Kenna added, sliding her chair back a fraction. "I don't know if there's much I'll be able to do."

Even though Kym usually got up around nine on the weekends, she bounced out of bed before seven. She'd convinced her maids to stay away until six that evening, so she dressed herself in the first clothes she found. Kenna agreed to help Kym practice for her sparring match, although she wasn't sure if two days would be enough to get Kym ready. So Kym sat and waited until the clock finally read eight. There was a sharp rap on the door, and Kenna walked into the room before Kym could respond.

"Good. You're ready." Kenna didn't even look at Kym as she walked straight to her water urns. "Let's get started."

Kenna raised her arms, and both of her Marks appeared. The floor trembled, causing many of the delicate decorations on the small tables to rattle around. Kenna flicked her hands downward, and the floor between her and Kym sank several inches. Water rose from the urns, and Kenna guided it into the hole in the floor. Kym and Kenna now stood on opposite sides of a shallow pool.

"How did you do that?" Kym marveled.

"The palace is made out of solidified water," Kenna said, stepping onto the water, which glowed beneath her feet.

"I know." Kym gingerly stepped onto the water.

"Well, if you're strong enough, you can control it." Kenna pulled an orb of water from the pool, and Kym did the same. "You'll learn how…if you ever make it that far.

"So," Kenna continued, "I'm guessing Lady Nila told you to not put your energy into the water you control? You just surround the water with your energy and lift it. Well, now you're going to let your energy in."

Kenna's arms tensed, her eyes narrowed, and her orb began to spin. It spun faster and faster, emitting an odd, otherworldly ringing. Kym stared, transfixed, at the spinning ball of water. Suddenly, the ringing orb began to glow, filling the room with bright blue light.

"Energy makes the water denser, faster, and more powerful than it was before. The most your orb could do is knock me off balance, maybe. But this; knocking you off your feet is the least it can do. Try it. Let your energy flow into your water."

Kym stared at the center of her water orb, hoping something would happen. She focused on the tingling sensation in her arms, which she thought must be her energy. She pictured it like a cloud, surrounding her orb and keeping it aloft. She imagined that mist sinking into the water, and she could feel her energy flow from her hands.

Her orb began to spin and ring, and it was like Kym was back at her first day of training all over again. Her entire body shook as her arms dropped several inches. She could feel the orb, and it was like it was forcing her into the floor. She'd never felt her energy drain so quickly.

"Don't," Kenna shouted. Kym started, making her arms wobble even more. "If you stop now, you'll have wasted all that energy on nothing. You're nearly there."

Panting, Kym tried to double her efforts. Did Kenna think she wanted to drop it? Didn't she know how hard this was for her? The more energy she fed into the now-glimmering orb, the louder her heartbeat grew in her ears. But all she could do was hope it would be over soon.

Luckily, ten long seconds later, Kym's orb looked just like Kenna's. Her energy no longer drained from her, and she could even feel some of it returning, but only slightly. Her glowing orb floated just above her outstretched hands, and even though it was not touching her, she could still feel it in her palms. But instead of feeling the orb's weight, all she felt was a gentle throbbing; like a little heartbeat.

Kym sighed with relief. She'd done it, and on her first try too. She looked expectantly at Kenna, who just stared blankly back at her. Annoyed at Kenna's lack of enthusiasm, Kym tried moving the glowing orb through the air. It moved much faster than the orbs she'd made in the past, which would fall apart if they moved quickly. But this glowing one kept up with even the quickest flicks of her hands.

However, the orb seemed reluctant to leave her hand, and the farther away it got, the less it moved.

"I'll leave if you're going to mess around."

"Sorry," Kym mumbled, turning her attention back to Kenna. "What's next?"

"Take your orb in one hand, like this, and throw it at me."

"What?" she blurted. "You want me to throw it at you?"

"Would I have said to if I didn't? Throw it at me."

Nervously, Kym shifted the orb to her right hand. She glanced at Kenna, her orb glowing above her hand, and threw her orb as hard as she could. Kym's orb traveled about a foot in front of her, stopped glowing, and fell into the pool with a splash. Puzzled, she stared at the place where it fell. What happened? Why did it stop working?

"Again," Kenna said. She waved her free hand at her orb, and lowered the no longer glowing water back into the pool.

"Why didn't it work?"

"Did you even think about your orb after it left your hand?" Kym opened her mouth to respond, but Kenna barreled on. "Magic is all about intent. You can't just throw it at me and hope it makes it here. You need to concentrate on it the entire time, and push it with your energy. If you don't, the energy you put in the water will lose its connection to you, and without that, you'd be better off splashing me."

"You didn't tell me that part."

"I thought it was obvious," Kenna droned. "Go again."

Kym thought only of her orbs as she threw, trying to push them through the air and toward Kenna with her outstretched hand. Each new orb traveled farther than the previous before splashing into the pool, but none of them ever reached Kenna. But Kym didn't stop. She threw orb after orb for what felt like hours, all while Kenna stood examining her nails on the other side of the pool.

Panting, her entire body shaking from exhaustion, Kym threw another orb at Kenna. She pictured it striking Kenna in her mind, and miraculously, it did. The orb hit Kenna right in the stomach. It exploded in a flash of blue light, sending Kenna flying through the air and onto the floor behind her.

"Finally," Kenna huffed, jumping to her feet and giving her body a quick shake. "I wasn't sure you were gonna get it. You can finally move on."

"What happened to the orb?" Kym panted.

"The energy that's released when it hits a target consumes the water too," Kenna answered quickly. "The release knocks the target back. Now, if you don't have any more pointless questions…"

"Actually, could I take a little break?" Kym clutched at a stitch in her side. "I just need a few minutes."

"Fine."

Kym stepped off the water and collapsed onto a small couch while Kenna flopped down on Kym's bed. Leaning back, Kym breathed deeply through her nose, trying to alleviate the pounding in the middle of her forehead. She wanted to get back to training, even if Kenna wasn't too helpful. At least she was better than Nila, who'd never answer a question if Kym asked.

Frustrated, Kym tried willing herself into feeling more energetic. She stood up, having already rested as long as she dared. Luckily, her body wasn't trembling too badly. She stepped gingerly back onto the water, but it felt solid beneath her feet.

"Better? May I continue teaching?" Kenna asked as she got up from Kym's bed and stepped onto the water. Kym nodded. "Perfect. Now, like I was saying, you are finally ready to move on. This time, instead of throwing your water at me with one hand, keep it in both hands and shove it toward me."

Confused, but not wanting to ask any questions, Kym did as instructed. She quickly made a glowing orb, took it in both her hands, and pushed, like she was trying to knock someone over. The orb shot forward in one long, glowing blast of water. Surprised, Kym lost her concentration, and the blast fell into the pool with a splash.

"What was that?"

"A water blast. It's stronger than water bolts, which are what you spent all morning working on. Blasts require much more concentration, which is why yours died out. Water bolts," Kenna pressed on, anticipating Kym's question, "are mostly for knocking opponents around. You can use blasts for more…aggressive purposes."

If Kym thought water bolts were difficult, the blast was about ten times worse. Each blast felt like she was pushing a boulder across the room, even with using both her hands to guide the water. The blasts didn't even reach Kenna, and splashed into the water when they were halfway there.

Her headache returned after she'd only tried the blast a handful of times, but Kym didn't stop. She'd already taken a break, and she wanted to finish at least one blast before taking another. But after a few more tries, the aching became too unbearable. Kym fell to her knees, splashing into the shallow pool while she held her head in her hands. The throbbing was so bad Kym thought her head was going to explode.

"What now?" Kenna asked impatiently, walking across the water.

"My head," she grimaced, sweat pouring down her face. "It hurts."

"Get up," Kenna ordered. She grabbed onto Kym's upper arm as she half led, half pushed her off of the water. "Your body's out of energy. Rest until you think you can go again."

Kym sat huddled where Kenna left her for several minutes. When she could finally lift her head without it pounding, she saw Kenna seated on a couch, her arms crossed while she tapped her foot on the floor. Kym stood up, and even though every part of her body shook, she stepped back onto the water.

When her maids arrived, Kym wasn't sure how much longer she could last. Not wanting to upset Kenna, she only took about half the breaks she should have. She'd managed to shoot several feeble blasts at Kenna, but she easily stepped out of their way. Kenna restored the room with a great sweep of her hands. Barely able to keep her eyes open, Kym leaned against her bedpost on trembling legs.

She collapsed the second the door closed behind Kenna. Her head felt like it was about to split open, and every inch of her body screamed in agony. Veronica and Isabel tried to move her, but they quickly realized that was impossible. So, with Kym slumped against the side of her bed, they tried their best to coax some food and water into her. She was so tired she didn't even notice what they fed her.

When she could finally stand it, Kym removed her sweat-soaked clothes and crawled into bed. Kenna was returning the next morning for another day of practice, but Kym didn't know if she'd be recovered by then. Her eyes began to droop the instant her head hit the pillow, and she was asleep before her maids could extinguish all the candles.

"Wake up."

Kenna's words, along with a stiff shove to Kym's shoulder, jolted her from a dreamless sleep. Groggily, Kym looked around through half-open eyes. It was ten after eight.

"If you'd rather sleep," Kenna said, "that's fine. There are plenty of things I'd rather do with my free time."

Kym scrambled out of bed and joined Kenna on the already prepared practice pool. She spent the morning reviewing everything Kenna taught her the previous day. Tired of being Kym's punching bag, Kenna had Kym aim her attacks through the open balcony doors. They'd fly through the air for some time before finally fading away to nothing.

Even though it was only her second day, Kym found the attacks much easier now that she knew what she was doing. No wonder Kenna seemed annoyed with her yesterday; the attacks really weren't that hard after some practice. Finally satisfied with Kym's review, Kenna closed the balcony doors and stepped back onto the pool.

"There's one more thing you need to know before your sparring match. The two attacks I've shown you are just that; attacks. But tomorrow, you'll need to defend yourself. That's where shields come in. All you need to do is take a bolt and hold it out in front of you like this."

Kenna extended her arms, her hands facing Kym like she was telling her to stop. The bolt in her hands flattened out, expanding into a disk the size of a garbage can lid. She moved her hands around in unison, and the shield followed. It covered her entire chest and when she crouched down, it shielded her whole body.

"Throw a bolt at me."

Kym's bolt zoomed across the room, landing right in the center of Kenna's shield. The bolt exploded, and even though it should've knocked Kenna off her feet, she only slid back a few inches. Smiling, she lowered her shield.

"Just like everything else, shields require focus. Instead of making the shield move, you need to make it as hard as possible. If done correctly, nothing your opponent throws at you tomorrow will touch you. But if you lose focus, it'll shatter. Your turn."

Kym held her bolt out in front of her, praying she wouldn't mess up. It expanded slowly and was half the size of Kenna's when a water bolt tore through it. The shield shattered, and the bolt hit her right in the chest. She flew backward and landed at the edge of the pool. Fuming, Kym staggered to her feet and saw Kenna already had another bolt ready in her hand.

"What was that for?"

"To show you what happens when your shield isn't fully formed. It didn't hurt that bad, right? Destroying the shield took most of the bolt's energy. You can't make your shields at your own pace. Most of the time, you'll need to make a shield after an attack is already coming. You can't take your time. Some defense is better than none."

Kenna spent the rest of the day randomly firing attacks at Kym, testing her defenses. When her shield fully formed, it could withstand multiple attacks before showing signs of failure. Light blue cracks would appear in the shield, and on the final blow the shield would still block the entire attack before shattering. By six o'clock, Kym could make a fully formed shield in a second, and none of Kenna's attacks had touched her in over an hour.

"I have to admit," Kenna panted, nodding at Kym as she put the room back to normal, "you surprised me. From what you told me, I didn't expect you to get any of this. You might actually survive tomorrow."

Training the following morning was the first time Kym actually enjoyed herself since arriving at Wadita. Nila showed Kym, Chloe, and Matt the basic combat skills, which were all the moves Kenna had taught Kym. Chloe and Matt eagerly watched Kym, no doubt wanting to see her struggle. Kym just smiled to herself as she outperformed both of them; their faces red with fury.

When their practice time was over, Nila led them down the spiral staircase to another training room. It was almost identical to the one they normally used, except this room had rows of benches set along the curved walls and no island in the middle of the pool. Kym, Matt, and Chloe sat with the other Favored on the benches while Nila explained the rules. They were to fight until a Favored yielded, or one was knocked out by the other. Other than that, there were no rules.

Nila paired Kym with Chloe for the first match of the day. Chloe could hardly hide her excitement while Kym's stomach twisted itself into a knot. Maybe she should have toned it down a little during practice. No doubt Chloe wanted to make Kym pay for showing her up. Her heart pounding in her ears, Kym walked to her designated spot while Chloe stood opposite her. Across the large pool, little Chloe looked even smaller than usual. How could Kym fight someone so feeble?

Nila instructed them to assume their fighting positions. Kym turned sideways, not taking her eyes off of Chloe, and extended her dominant hand palm down. She could see a gleam in Chloe's narrow eyes, and an image of Chloe holding Kym beneath the water flashed through Kym's mind. She tried to shake it off, but she realized Chloe drowning her was actually a real possibility. Any reservations she had about fighting Chloe vanished. Nila sent a wave through the pool; the match had begun.

Kym invoked her Marks and started making a shield, but she was too late. Chloe's blast ripped through the shield, and Kym flew through the air. The water trembled slightly beneath her as she rolled across it, but she didn't fall through. Kym leaped to one side, narrowly avoiding Chloe's bolt, which exploded right where she'd been. Kym tried to stand, but Chloe's next bolt hit her shoulder, knocking her back to the ground. She frantically threw a bolt at Chloe, who fell back in surprise. Relieved, Kym staggered to her feet, two bolts ready in her hands.

WHAM! Chloe, wasting no time, fired a blast from the ground into Kym's side. She flew through the air, her bolts fading and falling back into the water. Pain radiated from the spot where Chloe's blast struck her; she soared across the water and smashed into the wall with a crash. Dazed, Kym tried to stand up, but she instantly fell back down. Her stomach felt like it had been turned upside-down, and little lights popped in her eyes. She lay on her side, watching Chloe's feet grow larger and larger.

"I don't know," Chloe whispered cheerfully, venom dripping from every word, "how you got so good. But it doesn't matter. You're not good enough."

Chloe smiled, created a bolt, and held it over Kym's head. Kym closed her eyes, preparing for the worst. Suddenly, Matt and Chloe's laughter, neglect, and bets pushed their way to the front of her mind. Kym's eyes snapped open, her entire body shaking while her skin felt like it was on fire. But it wasn't exhaustion. This was rage.

So while Chloe gloated to the cheering crowd, Kym formed a small bolt and threw it upward. It struck Chloe right under her chin, knocking her backward. Kym stood, forming two bolts as she walked toward Chloe, who was struggling to get back to her feet. Kym threw them at Chloe, one after the other, while making new orbs rise from the water, ensuring she always had one ready.

Chloe's shield withstood three of Kym's bolts before the fourth blew it apart. She reeled backward, knocked off balance by the force of Kym's attacks. Her head pounding, Kym combined her two bolts and shoved, imagining her attack blasting Chloe through the wall. The blast was larger than any she'd created, and launched Chloe into the air. She slammed into the opposite wall, which cracked while Kym's blast pinned Chloe there until it finally died out.

Chloe slumped to the ground in silence. Pride spread through Kym like fire. She'd done it. She'd won. Cheers from the watching Favored filled the air as Kym's body gave a violent shudder. The water gave way beneath her, and everything went black.

T H E
P L U N G E

KYM WAS ON FIRE. EVERY INCH OF HER SKIN FELT LIKE IT HAD A million needles jabbed into it. Her skull was a drum, pounding and beating against the inside of her head. Every little movement just caused more pain, pulling her deeper into never-ending darkness. Nothing made sense in this place of torment, and she just wanted it to end. She didn't even know how she got there. All she could remember was a lot of bright blue light and rage.

After a while, light broke through the darkness. Strange noises filled her ears, and the warmth surrounding her screaming body felt oddly foreign. It took several seconds before she realized she could see. The hangings of her bed fell around her, and even though every part of her body still ached and throbbed, she rolled onto her side. Lights popped in her eyes as her stomach gave an uncomfortable lurch. She retched, but luckily, nothing came up. Afraid to move any more, Kym stayed where she was, taking in all her new vantage point allowed.

Sunlight stretched along the blue floor, and a warm breeze, along with the sweet smell of the sea, wafted through the room. The balcony doors must be open. Out of the corner of her eye, she saw the enormous clock by the door, and realized she wasn't alone. Veronica and Isabel sat like guards on either side of the door, both fast asleep.

Puzzled, Kym just stared at them, the throbbing in her head making her brain move like a slug. What were they doing there? They'd never spent the night in her room before. The servants all slept in their own chambers on the ground floor. So why were they there? And why were they asleep?

Veronica and Isabel's eyes snapped open. They both sat up and looked directly at Kym, lying awkwardly on her side as she stared back at them. Veronica bustled silently to the bathroom while Isabel hurried to Kym's bed. She placed her small, cool hand against Kym's forehead, and pain radiated from the spot like an explosion. Kym moaned, and Isabel rolled her onto her back as Veronica returned with a pitcher of water. They smiled down at Kym, coaxing her into a semi-sitting position while every part of her body screamed in protest.

"Thank Pheil for you, dear," Veronica whispered, slowly tipping some water into Kym's open mouth. "I knew the Great Mother would send you back to us."

"We thought we lost you to Nothingness. You slept for so long."

Kym coughed, spewing water all over her sheets. Her pounding brain might work as well as a rock, but she was aware enough to understand Isabel's words. And they terrified her. Nothingness was where the banished god, Thed, God of Death, lived in exile. It was the place where lost people wandered, hoping to find peace. It was where people went when they died.

"You thought I was where?"

"We're sorry, Miss, but we didn't know what to think. We prayed to the gods for you all day and night. We begged them to return you to us."

"You prayed for me?" Kym croaked. "Why? What happened? And why does everything hurt?"

"Oh my," Veronica said softly. "You don't remember anything. Miss, you had your first sparring match against Miss Chloe. She beat you in the beginning, but you got a little overzealous. You won, but you passed out right after."

Images of Chloe flying through the air, her standing over Kym, and Kym falling into darkness filled her mind, and it felt like her head was going to split open. If she hadn't remembered doing all those things, she would've called her maids liars. But she did. She knew she should be happy she won; she'd felt that way just before blacking out. But as every part of her body throbbed, all she could feel was shame. Why did she take it so far?

"Is Chloe all right? I remember being a little aggressive toward the end."

"She's fine. Everyone's more worried about you. Apparently, you overexerted yourself and used more energy than your body had. You didn't even have enough energy to keep yourself on top of the water, which is why you fell through when you passed out."

"Lady Nila pulled you from the water and brought you up here," Isabel said, slightly in awe. "When she entered the room carrying you, we thought you'd died. But Lady Nila didn't seem too concerned. She was very pleased with your performance in the sparring match. She said she'd never seen a new Favored show that much raw power in their first match."

"Wait a minute. Just slow down."

Kym was having trouble keeping up with all her maids said. So Nila had paid attention to Kym during her match and even thought she did well. That was something that hadn't happened since she arrived at Wadita. But if she'd done so well, why did Veronica and Isabel think Kym had died?

"Why do you keep saying you thought I died? What happened? What was wrong with me?"

"Miss Kym, do you remember when Miss Kenna told you magic uses energy?" Isabel asked tentatively. "You nearly passed out this weekend when you pushed yourself too far, remember?"

"Um…" At the moment, Kym couldn't remember anything Kenna told her.

"Miss," Veronica said, stepping up to Kym's side. Her face was stern, like a grandmother ready to scold her grandchild. "Your magic requires energy. There's only a certain amount you can use before it runs out. Naturally, your body will reserve some just in case. But during your match, you used up all of your reserves and then some."

"How do…I thought you didn't know anything about magic?"

"Lady Nila explained what she thought happened. She thought you must have tapped into your life energy at the end of your match, which is very dangerous. There was a Favored about twenty years ago who tapped into his life energy to try and complete some very complicated magic. The act consumed him, and his body crumbled into dust."

Kym tried to speak, but no sound came out. Could she really crumble into dust if she pushed her magic too far? That didn't make any sense. If something like that could happen, Nila would have mentioned it. She thought back to her first days of training, and something Nila said stirred in her memory. She said to not put too much energy into the water when they first started because they needed to practice more before doing so. If that was Nila's version of a warning, it was a horrible one.

"Why didn't anyone tell us that could happen?"

"I don't know, Miss. I really don't know."

"What are you doing?" Veronica demanded, pushing Kym back into bed as she tried to sit up. "Lady Nila said you must rest until you've fully recovered."

"I feel fine," Kym lied, fighting against her maids as she struggled to get out of bed. "Can't I just sit on the couch?"

"Not until you're healed."

"C'mon, Veronica. The girl can stretch her legs. She's been stuck in that bed for the better part of three days."

Kym's feet slipped on the slick ground. She wrapped her shaking arms around the tall bedpost, but it wasn't enough. She slid down the pole, landing on the ground as pain radiated through her body. Her maids each offered her their hands, but she waved them away. Instead, her face dripping with sweat, Kym used the pole to pull herself to her feet. The inside of her head might still feel like a drum, but she knew she hadn't misheard Isabel that time.

"I've been asleep for three days?"

"Yes," Veronica answered, leading Kym to one of the couches. "But Lady Nila wasn't worried. We watched over you, and if you hadn't improved after five days, we'd send for Lady Zara at Crystal Palace."

"Why? What could she do?"

"As the Ruler of Life, Lady Zara controls life itself. She could restore the life energy you used up before it was too late. But thank the Great Mother she wasn't needed. You woke, and now everything is fine."

As the fiery pain faded slowly from her body, a new pain seemed to creep up inside her. It worked its way down to the deepest parts of Kym, filling her body with an unnatural cold. And as her mind cleared, her own actions in the sparring match became clearer. When she could finally bear to stand, Kym slowly got to her feet, causing identical expressions of puzzlement to appear on her maids' faces.

"Where's the Temple?"

Kym hadn't bothered attending Temple since arriving at Wadita. Back home, she only went because her parents made her, and even then she never really wanted to go. Attendance wasn't required at Wadita since all the Favored supposedly had a profound connection to the gods. So Kym really didn't see the point in attending. But she couldn't shake the match from her mind, and the Temple was the only place she could think to go.

Wadita's Temple was on the ground floor. It was small for a Temple and looked very different from Kym's temple back home. Two sets of benches, arranged in rows, faced the altar of Reta in the center of the room. The woman standing in the shallow pool was just like the one from Kym's memory, except this altar was made of solid water, not stone.

"Where are the other altars?" she asked as her maids helped her over the threshold. She'd only managed a few steps on her own before they needed to step in.

"They're there," Isabel whispered, pointing to the back of the room, where Kym saw miniature versions of the other gods' altars. "They don't get much use here. At Wadita, most pray solely to Reta."

"I need a moment," Kym said, holding onto the edge of a bench for support.

Silently, her maids backed out of the room and closed the door behind them. The Temple had no windows, but the walls, floor, and ceiling seemed to emanate a soft, blue light. Kym stumbled her way right up to Reta's altar, where she knelt before it. Wrapping her light shawl more tightly around her shoulders, Kym closed her eyes. The prayer her father made her say the first time he caught her sneaking out crept its way through the clouds of her mind, and Kym began to speak.

"Under the eyes of the ever-watchful gods, I have done wrong this day. I acted brutally against one who did not deserve it. I call upon Reta, bringer of water's purifying touch, to absolve me of this sin. Let my soul be free of this burden, and let me rise, cleansed by your touch. I offer myself to your purifying water."

Kym opened her eyes, placed her hands into the altar's warm water, and lifted her trembling arms over her head. Bracing herself, she let the water cupped in her hands trickle onto her face. Somehow, it felt hotter than it did when it left her hands, but it cooled as it trickled down the rest of her body. She was supposed to dry herself off, something about wiping herself clean, but there was no towel on the altar. Dripping, she struggled to her feet, and only made it to the first row of benches before she needed to rest.

The Temple doors burst open, and the sound of hurried footsteps echoed through the room. Startled, Kym turned sideways in her seat, wondering why her maids were making so much noise. They were always so respectful and quiet. But it was not her maids who walked down the aisle.

Kenna sat right next to Kym, her face softer than Kym had ever seen it. She wrapped her arms around Kym, pulling her into a tight hug that made Kym wince. The gesture took her by surprise, especially since Kenna only reluctantly returned the hugs Kym gave her.

"I was so worried about you," Kenna said gently. "After I heard about your match, I tried to come see you, but your maids wouldn't let me in. Are you all right?"

"I'm fine," she said slowly, pulling awkwardly away from Kenna.

"What you did is all over the palace. People can't believe it, especially with the rocky start you had. In all my time I've never seen such raw power in someone so new. Are you sure you're okay?" Kenna added, sounding concerned. "You look a little off."

Something was very wrong. Kym had to beg Kenna to help her over the past weekend, and the whole time Kenna looked like she'd rather be anywhere else. Kym was sure Kenna thought she was very annoying. But now Kenna was acting like she was Kym's best friend. She'd even tried checking on Kym when she heard about the match. What was going on?

"Why are you acting weird?"

"Weird?" Kenna asked, looking confused. "What am I doing?"

"Well, you've always acted like you don't want me around. But now you're acting different, like we're best friends or something."

"What?" Kenna gasped, a little too loudly. "I…you…you're just tired. I think you're confused. Anyway, what are you doing down here? I've never seen you in here before."

"Oh," she said, taken aback. "I…I just…"

"What are you doing in here?" Kenna's eyes raked over Kym's wet appearance. "You're atoning? What do you need to atone for?"

"Chloe," Kym murmured, glancing at Kenna before staring down at her hands. "I feel bad about—"

"You won your match. There's nothing wrong with winning."

"I feel bad about how it ended."

"Why? From what I heard the ending was the best part. What a show of power. And anyway, Chloe's fine."

"She is?" From what Kym remembered, Chloe should not be fine.

"Oh yeah. She's just got three broken ribs and a bruised spine. Nothing major."

"Nothing major? Those all sound pretty major to me."

"Like I said," Kenna said, smiling warmly at Kym, "don't worry about it. Most of the losers end up with that or worse after the first matches."

"That's horrible."

"That's how it works. Chloe and the other losers will sit out so they can heal, but it's what they deserve. They lost. Besides, I've heard she's not even mad about her injuries."

"Really?" Kym asked. That was harder to believe than Kenna's new friendly demeanor.

"She's mad she got beat, but what was she expecting, going up against a powerhouse like you? The fact that you beat her just made it worse. Everyone here knows the little squirt doesn't like you."

"Thanks," she said, not really sure how to respond.

"She's apparently demanding a rematch. She'll probably ask for one the next time you see her."

Kym got to the training room early the next day, hoping to arrive before Chloe and Matt. Nila was already there, setting up targets for them to practice with. She wasn't sure if Kym should train since she hadn't recovered completely. But Kym didn't want to fall behind after spending so much time catching up. Nila agreed to let her stay, but only after Kym promised to rest the moment she felt tired.

Kym took it slow. Her energy still felt low, and she worried how training would feel when she wasn't at her best. But by the time Nila took them to the sparring room, Kym hadn't taken a single break. Nila began dividing them into sparring groups when Chloe stepped forward, her entire torso wrapped in thick, white bandages.

"I want a rematch with Kym," she grimaced, her body shaking.

"No," Nila said, the faintest trace of a smile on her lips. "Your injuries are too extensive. You, and the rest of the injured, will not spar for the foreseeable future."

Steaming, Chloe stomped off the water and joined the other injured Favored, and her injuries were by far the most severe. Smiling, Kym looked at her new sparring partner. He was about a year younger than her and had been at Wadita for almost two years. Why had Nila paired them together? He had far more experience than she did, and in her weakened state, how was Kym supposed to win? When it was their turn to spar, Kym stepped gingerly onto the water.

But she did win, and quickly. The boy attacked first, but Kym easily deflected his blast with a shield. She threw two bolts at him, knocking him to the ground and sending him rolling across the water. He yielded before Kym could even make another bolt. Two other Favored pulled him from the water and helped him to a seat.

For the next several weeks, after working on technique in the mornings, Kym would spar against a Favored with more experience than the one she fought previously. And as the matches grew more challenging, Kym didn't just survive; she thrived. She started looking forward to her matches, no longer feeling like the weakling everyone thought she was when she arrived. But what she enjoyed most was winning. She'd won the majority of her matches, even against Favored who'd been at Wadita for over two years.

Since so much of Kym's training was focused on combat magic, she was sure she'd feel exhausted all the time. But she never did. In fact, her energy levels seemed to have doubled as the weeks passed. She never felt tired when she practiced in the evenings, and she could do things much faster; she could turn an orb into a bolt seconds after pulling it from the water.

"You don't have more energy," Kenna laughed, draped over Kym's sofa after the two of them spent the afternoon at the beach. "Your body can't make more energy than it had to begin with. You're just finally adjusting to the toll magic takes. And since you're practicing all the time, your magic requires even less energy. That's why you can do things so much faster now."

At first, Kym felt a little awkward spending so much time with Kenna. But after hanging out for a couple of days, she actually started to enjoy her company. Ever since her first match, Kenna always asked Kym about her training. She cheered and congratulated Kym after her wins, and even consoled her after her few losses. Kenna must just take a while to warm up to others.

After one particularly good day of training, Nila asked Kym to stay behind when she dismissed the others. Kym stood awkwardly to one side while the others left, most of them congratulating her on her victory against two other Favored. When the room finally emptied, Nila asked Kym to follow her. She expected Nila to walk up the stairs, but instead, she turned right and headed deeper than Kym had ever gone in Wadita.

Nila opened two doors as they descended. The first was full of fish swimming through the air, but they were unlike any fish Kym had ever seen. They glowed and made the same faint ringing sound as her water bolts. Were they even real fish? Kenna walked out of the fish swarm, and the door closed silently behind her. Nila continued farther down the stairs before stopping at the second door. Kym took several steps back, trying to avoid the hurricane raging inside the room. Nila raised her hand, her Marks glowing, and the storm died. A tall boy hurried out of the room and joined them as they continued still downward.

Finally, they reached the bottom of the staircase, which Kym had begun to wonder if it even existed. There was only one door leading off the dark landing, flanked on either side by torches. Nila opened the door, and the boy and a smiling Kenna followed her inside. Utterly confused, Kym hurried after them.

The vast, domed room was larger than any training room Kym had seen at Wadita. But the strangest thing about the room was not its size. There was no water, just a flat expanse of floor. Kenna shut the door behind Kym and joined Nila and the boy in the middle of the room, where they faced Kym.

"Kymbralyn, this is Aidan, and you already know Kenna. They are two of the most advanced Favored currently at Wadita. If something goes wrong, they are here to assist you. Shall we begin?"

Kym didn't know what to say. She had no idea what was going on, and she seemed to be the only one. Both Kenna and Aidan looked perfectly calm, like this was completely normal. What was Kym going to learn that Nila needed backup in case something "goes wrong"? Did Nila think Kym would screw up so badly that she'd need others to clean up her mess? But Kym hadn't fallen behind for weeks, so she slowly nodded her head.

"Good," Nila said briskly, "All Favored have unique abilities specific to their element. The Water Favored are capable of existing underwater. You will be able to breathe just as easily as you do on the surface. Since water will constantly surround you, your magic will be much faster, as well as enhanced. To use this ability, merely invoke your Marks whenever you are submerged. Are you ready?"

"Um…"

Ready? Ready for what? How was she supposed to breathe underwater? There was no air. And what if it didn't work like everything else did when she first started? Would she drown? Two near-death experiences in one month must be some sort of Wadita record. Why did Nila think Kym was ready for this? She didn't even understand what she was supposed to do.

"I guess," Kym croaked.

"Excellent. I will fill the room. Stay relaxed. If you have difficulties, Aidan or Kenna will assist you."

Nila raised her arms, her Marks glowing, and the room filled with the sound of rumbling stone. Kym turned wildly around and saw small sections of the curved wall sliding upward. Water sloshed into the chamber, covering Kym's shoes in seconds. Trembling, Kym looked to Kenna and Aidan and saw their Marks glowing too.

Kym closed her eyes, took a deep breath, and felt her energy flow through her. Opening her eyes, she saw her blue Marks glowing on her pale arms. The water continued to rise, and before she knew it, it was at her chin. Her heart racing, Kym took one last breath as the water rose over her head.

Her first instinct was to panic, and she did. Kym clamped her eyes and mouth shut, and could feel the air in her lungs growing smaller as her heart pounded in her chest. The pressure built in her ears as she knew the water continued to rise above her. She thrashed wildly, trying to find her way to some nonexistent air. Her throat began to contract, and Kym heard a soft whoosh as something moved past her.

Hands gently took hold of her own, and pulled them away from her throat.

"Relax, Kymbralyn." Nila's voice sounded perfectly clear through the water. "Open your mouth and breathe."

This was crazy, but she was out of options. So, going against her every impulse, Kym opened her mouth and took a deep breath. It was like breathing in on a cold winter day. She coughed, the first mouthful of water sending chills through her body as it washed down her throat. But, just as the water was going to fill her lungs, it vanished, replaced by crisp, sweet air.

The pressure in her ears vanished, and somehow, she no longer felt wet. Reluctantly, Kym opened her eyes and saw Nila, Kenna, and Aidan floating in front of her. They all beamed at her, and Kym saw them as clearly as she would have on land. Elated, Kym kicked upward, gliding around in a large arch. This was where she belonged.

C H A P T E R   S E V E N

I N   T H E
Z O N E

SHE WAS FREE. KYM'S MANY TRIPS TO THE RIVER HAD MADE HER A confident swimmer, where she held her own against the strong current and high water. But this swimming was something different altogether. She didn't worry about surfacing for air or going too deep to protect her ears. The slightest movement sent her through the water, propelled with the power and speed of a giant fish, all without really using her arms or legs.

She could see perfectly as she swam around the domed room. The water seemed to stop just before her eyes, and the usual blur it added to everything no longer existed, which just increased her overall feeling of confusion. She could breathe, see, speak, hear, and felt completely dry. If she hadn't seen Nila fill the room, Kym wouldn't have known there was any water in it.

"Kymbralyn," Nila's voice rang through the water. "Rejoin us down here. There are matters we must discuss."

Kym saw Nila, Kenna, and Aidan floating directly below her. She turned herself around and swam to meet them. But Kym overshot it, and couldn't slow herself down enough as she approached the floor. She flipped around just in the nick of time, and her feet slammed into the hard ground. The force of her landing was so powerful that she immediately began to float upwards. But after rising a couple of feet from the floor, she stopped, and Nila, Kenna, and Aidan rose to join her.

Kym gulped down several mouthfuls of water, and each breath sent a shudder of cold through her body. She looked expectantly at

Nila floating in front of her, her mouth slightly open while her shoulders rose and fell, all without a single bubble passing her lips. It was one of the most bizarre things Kym had ever seen, and it all felt perfectly natural.

"So, is it everything you expected?" Nila asked.

"I love it down here. It feels…right somehow."

"That is natural. A Water Favored should feel most at home in her element. If you are comfortable, you may remain here with Aidan to finish your training for today."

Kym didn't speak at once. Nila had never once asked her, or any Favored as far as she knew, for their input during training. They always showed up and did what Nila said without question. Why was she asking Kym for her opinion now? What changed?

"That's fine with me."

"Excellent. There is no time to waste then. Aidan, restore the room when you are finished. Come, Kenna."

Kenna gave Kym a quick thumbs up before swimming to the door behind Nila. Kym watched, her body tense, as Nila raised her hand toward the door and waited for something to happen. But nothing did. Kenna just swam up to the door and pushed it open. It was only then that Kym realized what Nila had done. Even though the door stood wide open, none of the water from inside the room rushed out of it, like Kenna hadn't even opened the door. Nila and Kenna stepped through onto dry land, and the door closed quickly behind them.

Kym turned to Aidan, getting her first proper look at him since Nila pulled him from the hurricane room. He looked older than Kym, maybe by two or three years, and had muscles larger than any Kym had ever seen. He was at least a head taller than her, and smiled at Kym with pearly white teeth. His short hair swirled around his face while he bobbed slightly in the water. Kym, unsure what to say, just floated there.

"This should be fun," he said in a deep voice. "Kenna's told me how talented you are."

"Well, she's helped me a lot."

"I hope I can make my mark as well. Ready to start?"

"Absolutely."

"Perfect. So Lady Nila gave me a brief overview of your training so far, and I'm impressed. Your sparring performances have been phenomenal, and you've picked up the basics of magic with relative ease."

Kym thought Nila's review of her skills glossed over the rough patches of Kym's training, which were numerous. What happened to Kym practically failing at everything Nila taught her during her first month? According to Nila, those failures never occurred. But with Nila finally taking notice of her, she didn't want to contradict her, even if her account wasn't entirely accurate. So, Kym nodded her head, her stomach twisting around itself.

"Kenna's told me the same," Aidan continued. "No wonder Lady Nila chose to accelerate your training. We'll start with basic combat magic and work on translating it to this new environment. When pools are your water source, the first thing you do is make an orb. Well, now that you are in the water, you can skip that step. If you tried to make an orb here, you wouldn't be able to see it. You'd just be holding water in more water. Kinda pointless. So, the first step in underwater magic is making an energized orb."

Kym did as Aidan said, but creating an energized orb in the water was much more complicated than Aidan made it seem. A lot more could go wrong in the water, like something Aidan called energy bleeding. On land, the only place Kym's energy could go was in the orbs she controlled. But with water all around her, Kym had to focus on sending her energy only into the water she wanted instead of letting it run off.

Her first attempt was a disaster. She succeeded in making a bolt, but she left a cloud of energized water floating in its wake. She tried a couple more times and found that if she imagined a circle in the water and focused her energy on a dot in the center, her bolts formed more easily. At least it solved the energy-bleeding problem.

Once her bolts were perfect, Aidan drilled her on all the combat magic she'd learned. She threw bolts at Aidan while he swam around the room, easily avoiding them. Apparently, underwater combat was just as hard as forming the attacks. Her bolts moved faster than they did in air, but she and her opponent were no longer on the same plane. While she could now attack from any direction, Aidan could swim all around the dome to avoid her. When they finished with bolts, they practiced blasts before moving to shields, which were by far the hardest. She'd drift backward when Aidan's attacks hit her shield, and wouldn't stop until her body ran out of momentum.

After that, Kym practiced dodging Aidan's attacks. She swam as fast as she could, but she had no real way of controlling herself. Once she got going, she couldn't change directions until she came to a complete stop, leaving her open and defenseless. Aidan finally stopped attacking after he'd hit Kym for what felt like the hundredth time in a row. She floated awkwardly upside down near the bottom edge of the dome.

"Focus on controlling yourself," he called. "Use your energy to guide your body while you swim. It's kinda like making an orb. And with concentration, you'll even be able to control your speed."

Aidan was by far Kym's best teacher. He actually explained how things worked and corrected Kym when she did something wrong. Not having to figure everything out on her own while Nila or Kenna just watched was oddly refreshing. She also didn't tire as quickly now that she wasn't wasting so much of her energy screwing up.

Once she'd avoided Aidan's attacks for ten straight minutes, they decided to call it a day. They'd both used so much energy that it took them a while to meet in the middle of the room. Aidan raised his arms, his face set, and sections of wall rose near the floor. Water poured out of the room, and Kym was only slightly surprised to find she was still dry. When the room was finally water free, Aidan closed the walls and fell to his knees, panting hard.

"Are you okay?" Kym stooped down, patting Aidan gingerly on the back.

"Yeah," he huffed, getting to his feet. "Clearing this room is harder than Lady Nila makes it look."

Walking on her legs felt almost unnatural after spending what felt like hours under water. Kym shook with every step, and each breath felt oddly dry and warm in her throat. The door to the water dome swung shut behind them as the reentered the dark stairwell. Aidan, instead of mounting the stairs with Kym, walked over to examine something set into the wall. It was a large, stone clock.

"What is it?" she panted.

"We need to hurry," Aidan huffed, rushing past her up the stairs. "Dinner starts in half an hour. Lady Nila will kill us if we're late."

Kym sprinted up the stairs and through halls, bursting into her bedchamber in record time.

"Miss, you're—"

"Please don't start," Kym gasped, collapsing onto her bed. "I know I'm late. It won't happen again."

But Kym underestimated Veronica and Isabel's ability to multi-task. They led Kym to the already-drawn bath, undressing her as they went. As they washed her, a continuous stream of etiquette and manners issued from their lips. Kym tried to speak a couple of times, but by the time she'd thought of a response, Veronica and Isabel were already four topics ahead of her. But, to their credit, their lectures to Kym never impeded their work, and twenty minutes later, Kym stood fully dressed and ready for dinner.

Kym looked for an empty table when she arrived in the dining hall, but Aidan and Kenna waved her over to join them. Slightly surprised, Kym sat next to Kenna, leaving only two open seats—one between Kenna and Aidan, the other between Kym and Aidan. A boy around Kym's age filled the chair between Kym and Aidan moments later. The boy, Ryland, had a thin face, sandy hair, and had been at Wadita since he was eleven.

The four of them chatted, waiting for Nila to arrive. Ryland moved his chair to the side and grasped Aidan's hand. They both smiled at each other, their fingers intertwined. When Nila finally arrived, she took the open seat at their table between Aidan and Kenna.

"So, Aidan," Nila asked after giving the opening prayer, "how did Kymbralyn fare in the water dome? Did she surpass your expectations?"

"She did," Aidan answered, beaming at Kym. "I've never seen someone so new do this well in such a short time."

"I agree," Kenna added. "Kym's raw talent is really without equal. She might even be moving faster than Lance did?"

"Who's Lance?" Kym asked, her face turning a bright shade of pink.

"Only the best Water Favored ever," said Ryland. "He mastered water magic in only four years. No one's ever done it that fast before."

"Well, Kymbralyn," Nila said, the corners of her lips twitching upward, "those are some rave reviews. You should be pleased."

"Thanks," she said, wanting to hide her face in her napkin. "But I really don't deserve all the credit. Kenna helped me a lot, and Aidan's a great teacher."

"Do not be foolish," Nila snapped. "It all comes down to you and your abilities. Based on what I have seen and heard of you since your arrival, training with novices such as Chloe and Matt is doing you a disservice. Therefore, I have decided to put you in a group with Favored more around your skill level, like Ryland here. Kenna and Aidan will instruct you for the majority of your training, while I will observe periodically to evaluate your progress."

"Are you serious?" she asked, joy spreading through her like fire.

"Of course," Nila said. "Is this arrangement suitable?"

"Yes," said Kym, unable to suppress her smile. "Of course. I'm honored you think so highly of me."

"Do not disappoint me."

When they finished eating, Kym and Kenna left the dining hall. Kym held it together until they reached the entrance hall. Unable to contain herself, she grabbed Kenna's hands, squealed, and pulled her into a hug. Kenna grinned just as broadly at Kym, and Kym knew she must be pleased. Kym would still be struggling with the most basic skills if it weren't for Kenna. This was as much Kenna's victory as it was Kym's. As they pulled apart, Kym heard footsteps echoing around the entrance hall. It was Aidan and Ryland.

"I want to thank Aidan," Kym said to Kenna. "But I don't want to interrupt—"

"Just do it." Kenna pushed Kym toward Aidan and Ryland. "We'll meet in your room after."

"Hi," she said, smiling awkwardly at the two of them. "Ryland, could I borrow…?"

"Sure." Ryland kissed Aidan on the cheek. "See you upstairs."

Kenna hooked arms with Ryland and steered him toward the bedchamber stairs. Laughing, Aidan led Kym through the door to the palace garden. She'd only been out there a handful of times since she spent most of her free time practicing. Ordinarily, Favored relaxed on the grassy lawn or the beach, but tonight, it was completely deserted. The setting sun flooded the sky with beautiful reds, oranges, and yellows. They stopped at the wall separating the garden from the sandy beach, watching the sky slowly turn indigo.

"What's up?"

"I wanted to thank you. Today was amazing, and I know Nila wouldn't be moving me up without you."

"*Lady* Nila, Kym," Aidan corrected, laughing softly. "And I doubt that. It's obvious you're a natural. If I hadn't told her how great you were today, someone else would have done so soon. So, is living at Wadita all you imagined it would be?"

"Um…" She didn't even know where to begin explaining the past month and a half. "It's been different. I think I'm finally starting to get the hang of this magic stuff. I really miss home, but the longer I'm here, the less it seems to bother me. Does that make sense?"

"Sure," Aidan said. "It's natural to miss home, especially getting here at your age. Most new Favored are a lot younger than you, so it's easier for them to forget their homes in all the fun they're having here."

"Why am I so much older?"

"Not sure. You must be a late bloomer. It happens."

"Ryland seems nice," Kym added, looking up as stars started to appear in the darkening sky.

"He is," Aidan said, and Kym could hear him smiling.

"How'd you two meet?"

"On one of our days off. He was sitting alone in the shallows away from everyone else. I walked over, and we just hit it off."

Smiling, Kym continued to watch the stars, focusing on a bright red one just above them. It was unlike any star she'd ever seen, but the cities were full of so much light, she'd probably missed a few hundred stars.

"Which star is that?" she asked, unable to take her eyes off of it. "It's beautiful."

"I…" Aidan's voice trailed off.

"Its like it's made of fire."

"It can't be," Aidan muttered, more to himself than to Kym.

"Is it getting bigger?" Kym asked, certain the star had almost doubled in size.

"What th—DUCK!" Aidan shouted as the star suddenly shot downward, straight toward Kym and Aidan.

Aidan grabbed Kym's wrist and dove to the ground, pulling her with him. The star was as wide as Kym was tall, and soared right where Kym and Aidan's heads had been. Looking frantically upward, Kym watched the star arch back around. It stopped over the middle of the beach, where it floated four feet off of the ground.

But this was no star, as Kym had first thought. It was a giant ball of flame. She stared at the fireball, which began to transform before her eyes. Two large wings sprouted from the ball, as did a tail, beak, and two long legs with razor-sharp talons. The ball twisted around, reshaping itself into a giant, flaming bird.

Aidan vaulted over the wall, running straight for the firebird, which was already preparing to attack. Pushing her fear down, Kym followed him over the wall. She sprinted to the water, stumbling slightly on the hem of her dress, and created two bolts the second she could. The bird, who had been occupied with Aidan on the beach, turned its head and charged Kym.

Panicked, Kym threw a water bolt at the bird, but it had remarkable speed for something so large. It swerved effortlessly around her attack, and the force from its wings knocked her back into the water, her remaining bolt vanishing as she flew through the air. She tried to get up, but the bird dove right at her. Its fiery talons pierced her hastily made shield, resting less than an inch from her chest. But miraculously, the shield did not shatter.

With all the strength she could muster, Kym tried to push the bird from her shield. Instead, the bird drove its talons deeper into the shield. Pinned down, Kym watched as the bird raised its fiery beak, preparing to strike. Her mind raced, but there was nothing she could do.

There was a bang, a flash of blue light, and the bird was blasted away from Kym, destroying her shield in the process. Splashing around, Kym saw the bird hovering several yards away as a bolt zoomed over her head. It exploded on contact, blasting the bird even farther backward, its wings flapping wildly around. Behind Kym, Aidan stood at the water's edge, both his arms directed toward the firebird. The water beneath the bird began to swirl and glow. With a blast like a cannon, the water shot upward, trapping the bird inside a raging cyclone of energized water.

Kym struggled back to the shore as the cyclone moved violently around the shallows. She could see the bird trying to escape the raging water, but it never did. When the cyclone was mere feet from the beach, Aidan directed his hands upward before bringing them quickly back down. The cyclone carried the firebird in an arch, slamming it into the beach and spraying Kym and Aidan with a mixture of sand and water. The firebird, still as fiery as ever, lay motionless on the ground.

"Is it dead?" Kym stammered as she approached the bird.

"I...I don't—"

The firebird thrashed wildly around, sending hot sand and water flying in all directions. Its long tail caught Kym and Aidan, knocking them both into the air. Kym's chest stung and burned momentarily before she landed with a soft thud in the sand. Propped up on her elbows, Kym watched as the bird's wings, tail, legs, and head pulled into itself. The bird seemed to be collapsing. By the time Kym reached the fireball, it was no larger than a pea. It disappeared a second later, leaving no trace of itself behind. The sand wasn't even warm.

"What was that thing?" She turned to Aidan, still lying in the sand.

"It was a fire construct," Aidan said darkly, getting slowly to his feet.

"A fire what-now?"

"A fire construct," Aidan repeated. He placed his hands on Kym's shoulders, and she realized for the first time she was trembling.

"What the Thed is a fire construct?"

"It's very advanced magic," Aidan explained. "Skilled Favored can turn their element into beasts to do their bidding. That one was created by a Fire Favored."

"Why was it even here?"

"Probably to spy on Lady Nila." His face grew stern the moment he spoke, like he'd said something he shouldn't.

"Why would a Fire Favored want to spy on Nila?"

Aidan glanced at Kym, looking her up and down before answering. "Look, I shouldn't tell you this; I'm not supposed to know myself. You know how the Rulers meet every month to run Princirum? Well, they always bring a Favored with them to the Summit, and last month, Lady Nila took me.

"When it was almost over, Lady Zara told the Favored to leave the throne room so the Rulers could speak in private. Well, all of us Favored wanted to know what was going on, so we listened at the door, and Lady Melana, the Ruler of Darkness, said the Rulers should overthrow the gods."

Kym's mouth fell open. "She didn't."

"She did," Aidan continued gravely. "It went really quiet, then all of the Rulers started yelling at once. It was crazy. I couldn't understand what was going on—but I heard at least a few voices agree with Lady Melana. Lady Zara called for silence and said she didn't want to hear another word about it. After that, the Rulers left the Summit in a hurry. I don't think any of them are speaking right now."

"Why?"

"Probably because they don't know whom they can trust. I don't know who supported Lady Melana's idea, but I know Lady Nila opposed it. And with Lord James being the Ruler of Fire, his relationship with Lady Nila has always been a little rocky. I bet one of his Favored sent that fire construct here to see what Lady Nila's up to.

"It's getting late," Aidan added. "We better get back inside."

Aidan hurried inside, and Kym stumbled behind him, trying to absorb all he said. She'd always viewed the Rulers as one whole unit. It never occurred to her that there might be some disagreements between them. But for their distrust to be so high that their Favored would spy on other Rulers seemed completely absurd. They were the most powerful people in Princirum, after all.

Kym was so caught up in her own thoughts she didn't even see Kenna waiting in her room. The second she stepped over the threshold Kenna practically tackled her, wrapping her arms tightly around Kym's neck.

"Are you all right? I saw the whole thing from the window. I was going to jump down and help but they—"she scowled at Kym's maids standing in the corner—"wouldn't let me."

"You would have hurt yourself, Miss Kenna."

"I would have landed on the water and been perfectly fine. Anyway," Kenna turned back to Kym, "are you okay? You did amazing down there."

"I think I'm okay, just a litt—."

"Miss, you really should get to bed," interrupted Veronica.

"Ladies," Kym said, trying and failing to hide her irritation, "you can go for the night. See you in the morning."

Bowing low to Kym, Veronica and Isabel walked swiftly out of the room. Kym waited until their footsteps faded away before she turned back to Kenna.

"What was I saying? Oh yeah, I'm okay; just shaken, really. I've never fought anything like that before."

"It's okay to be shaken after a fight like that."

"That's not what it is. Aidan talked to me before we came inside, about the Rulers not trusting each other because of something Melana said at a Summit, and how that fire construct thing was here to spy on Nila. That's crazy, right?"

"I don't know," Kenna said slowly, her brows furrowed. "The only place the construct could have come from is Inferon, the Palace of Fire. Did Lord James make it himself? I don't know. All I know is that Lady Nila is nervous. I've gone to many Summits with her, so she told me what Lady Melana said. She has at least some support for her idea, but Lady Nila doesn't know how much. I guess that's what it's like for the rest of the Rulers. They don't know who stands where on this, and it could end badly for those who are not on the right side."

"The right side?"

"The winning side," Kenna clarified. "It's no secret that they all love their power and will do anything to keep it. So, if Lady Nila backed Lady Melana, but they couldn't overthrow the gods and take power for themselves, what would the consequences be? The winning Rulers wouldn't waste any time taking power from the Rulers who opposed them."

"C'mon, Kenna," Kym said, throwing her hands into the air. "This is crazy. We're talking about overthrowing gods. Gods. Aren't they way stronger than the Rulers?"

"Not if the Rulers have an army of Favored behind them. Ever since Lady Melana's proposal, the Rulers have been recruiting Favored like crazy, going to the cities every month or more instead of a couple of times a year."

"And they expect us to follow them?" Kym asked, dumbfounded.

"If it comes to it," Kenna said blankly, as though Kym had asked her what time it was. "Anyway, it's getting late, and you need to recover your strength."

Slightly numb, Kym crawled under the covers while Kenna extinguished the remaining candles before climbing into the extra bed Veronica and Isabel had set up for her. So, that was how the Rulers found her so quickly. They hadn't been looking for Kym specifically. They'd been there to find any Favored they could get their hands on in order to grow their numbers.

But how could the Rulers overthrow the gods, even with an army of Favored behind them? The gods were all-powerful, or that was what every priest she'd ever met led her to believe. Besides, the gods knew everything that happened in Princirum, and like Kym's father told her, they always had a plan. But if they knew what the Rulers were up to, why hadn't they done something to stop them? What were they waiting for?

O L D   F O E S ,
N E W   A L L I E S

"Miss Kym, Lady Nila requests you join her in the garden."

Kym, midway through her breakfast, just stared at Isabel. Her brows formed one long line, and there seemed to be less color in Isabel's cheeks than usual. Her skin tingling, Kym turned to Veronica, hoping to glean a bit more information from her. But Veronica had already slipped into Kym's closet, no doubt retrieving an outfit more suitable for seeing Nila than Kym's pajamas. They dressed her in a simple blue gown, ignoring Kym's attempts for just one more bite of toast while Kenna demanded to know what was happening.

She ambled through the dark, deserted halls. As far as she knew, she hadn't done anything to warrant a summons by Nila on her day off. What could Nila want or need to tell her? She already knew about moving to the advanced group. Did Nila know about the fire construct? How could she? Kym and Aidan were the only ones who saw it. But that wasn't true. Kenna saw the whole thing from Kym's room, and if she saw it, anyone else could have.

Kym shaded her eyes as she staggered outside, jarred by the intense morning light after the shadowy halls. She could make out two people standing by the garden wall. She knew the taller of the two right away; Nila was the tallest person Kym knew. But as she drew nearer, Kym still couldn't make out the second person standing with their back to the sun, their face shrouded in darkness. She only realized who it was when she was right in front of them.

"Aidan," said Kym, slightly perplexed. "Why are you here?"

"Aidan's presence is necessary," Nila said briskly. "What we are discussing concerns you both. Late last night, Aidan came to my chambers and told me of a disturbance here yesterday. I need your account of these events."

Kym glanced at Aidan, who stared unblinkingly at Nila. What did he tell her? Kym recounted the events of the previous night as best she could; how she and Aidan went outside, the bird appearing, the battle, and finally the construct vanishing. But when she got to what Aidan told her about the Rulers, she stopped herself. Everything he told her he learned from a private conversation. And besides, Kym didn't know if she believed any of it. Even after thinking and dreaming about it all night, she still couldn't understand why the Rulers would overthrow the gods.

"Anything else?" Nila demanded. Her eyes narrowed as Kym's pause grew longer.

"No," she said, shaking her head slowly. "Aidan kind of explained what a construct was, and then we both went inside."

Kym saw Nila's face soften, but only slightly. She stared at Aidan and Kym, making Kym shift uncomfortably from one foot to the other. Finally, Nila said, "Well, I must say I am impressed. Most Favored of your experience would not have survived a battle with a construct. You should be proud. If you and Aidan had not intervened, the construct would have come and gone without anyone from Wadita noticing."

"Thanks," Kym said. She uncrossed her arms, and some feeling returned to her numb limbs. "Why was it here?"

Kym could feel Aidan looking at her. Glancing sideways, she saw his narrow eyes darting between Kym and Nila. What did he think was so wrong? Even if she and Aidan hadn't talked about it, she would have still asked. She wanted to know, especially after fighting the thing. Didn't she deserve to know what Nila thought about it?

"It…was nothing," Nila said slowly, her voice flat as the corners of her mouth twitched. There was something off about the smile; it looked almost painful. "Nothing more than a joke by one of Lord

James's Favored. I will deal with this matter personally. Focus on your training. Drive last night from your mind."

Kym wanted to forget; she tried to put everything that happened that night behind her and act like it never happened. She didn't want to think about spying Rulers, secret plots, and plans of revolution, especially since she didn't even know if any of it was true. But no matter how hard she tried to make things return to normal, she couldn't. She'd heard it all, and there was no going back.

Kym found herself watching Nila as the weeks passed, unsure what she was looking for. Maybe she wanted some sign that everything Aidan and Kenna told her wasn't true. But the more she looked for reassurance, the more confused she became. Nila left the palace several times a month, leaving Aidan and Kenna in charge of everyone else's training. She'd return, but never with any new Favored. Nila focused all her attention on a select group of Favored, which now included Kym. She'd dine with them, discuss their training, and ensure they were as happy as could be.

This left Kym with more questions. When she first met Nila, Kym thought she wasn't the warmest person, more adept at giving orders than comfort. She only showed interest in Favored when they proved themselves to be skilled or powerful, just like she did with Kym. Before her first match, Chloe and Matt had Nila's attention, since their magic was better than Kym's at the time. But the moment she proved herself, Nila forgot about Chloe and Matt in favor of Kym.

But that made no sense. If Kenna was right, and the Rulers needed the Favored to overthrow the gods, why would Nila only focus on a select few Favored? Wouldn't it make more sense if Nila ensured all her Favored were the best they could be? What good was an army if only a few of them were skilled enough to fight?

Kym decided Aidan and Kenna had to be wrong. Aidan must have misunderstood what he heard at the Summit. He admitted he really didn't understand what was said, and Kenna must have misunderstood what Nila told her too, and blew it out of proportion to fit Aidan's theory. They were probably just trying to impress Kym with how much they thought they knew. From where she sat, it just looked like Nila wanted as many Favored as possible, but didn't want to bother with them until they were worth her time.

Kym threw herself wholeheartedly into training, resolved to forget about the whole mess. She'd been so focused on figuring things out that she started falling behind again in training. Luckily, magic was so second nature to her that it was easy to pick up the slack. Her new group included Ryland and two others, and they spent most of their time in the water dome, though they'd practice in the ocean occasionally. They all mastered basic water control and combat magic, so they moved to more advanced methods of combat.

They started with something Aidan called the water wall, which was like a shield magnified by ten. Instead of making a large disk, the water wall was a dome that protected the creator from all sides. Kym preferred this method of defense over the shield, since it was stronger and could withstand more powerful attacks than the shield could.

However, there was a catch. To make the dome that strong, Kym had to stay where she was or risk it falling apart. She couldn't even attack while she was inside it. But Kym was able to find a way around this. She waited, protected by her dome, while her opponents wore themselves down. The second they'd stop, she'd drop her wall and take down her combatants with ease.

Next, they learned the water swipe, which created a long arch of energized water capable of knocking over multiple targets at once. It was very similar to a water bolt, and was not too tricky to master. But it was difficult to aim, and Kym had to focus on keeping the arch level while making sure it also reached the targets. Kym and her group tried to knock over as many targets as they could with one swipe. By the end of the day, Kym's best was six, coming in second behind Ryland's seven.

"Well done," said Kenna after Kym and the others demonstrated everything they knew. "You're doing well. There's one more skill to learn, and then you're finished with what Aidan and I call 'crowd control magic.' You've learned to protect yourselves from, and attack, multiple enemies. But you may face an enemy that is stronger than you, or you may be totally outnumbered. In that case, you can use a technique called compaction."

Floating next to Kym, Ryland was smiling just as broadly as she was. On Ryland's other side, Jax and Jean's eyes were wide with anticipation as they watched Kenna. After what happened with Chloe and Matt, Kym wasn't sure what to expect from her new group. But when she arrived on her first day, they'd all welcomed her with open arms, literally hugging her when they first saw her. With no more petty games and bets, Kym enjoyed the new arrangement, especially since they were all the same age.

Kenna, floating in the middle of the room, slowly moved her hands through the water. They moved in opposite, circular motions, and left streams of energized water in their wake. Writing this off as energy bleeding, Kym focused on Kenna's hands, but she kept repeating the motion, and more energized water appeared in front of her.

When Kym could only see Kenna's outline through the glowing water, she finally did something different. Kenna quickly pulled her hands inward, and all the energized water she created followed them, rushing into a single spot. Moments later Kenna floated before them, a bolt floating in her hand. But there was something off about it; first, it was way too small. Kenna's energized water could have easily filled Kym's bathtub, but her bolt was smaller than an apple. It also acted strange; bolts didn't normally quiver or jerk like that.

"Compaction," Kenna continued, her voice strained and tense, "occurs when you force more water into a space than would naturally fit there. The water in a compact bolt is actually working against you, so it requires more energy and concentration than the attacks you've learned. It wants to expand into its natural state. You must prevent that from happening until it hits its mark."

Kenna turned slowly and faced the targets Kym and the others used to warm up. She threw her bolt, and it shot through the water faster than anything Kym had seen. When the bolt hit the target, it was like a bomb had gone off. All of the targets were blasted back from the force of the attack, while a large scorch mark replaced the intended target. The strength of the explosion sent waves rippling through the water. Kym quickly made a shield, tucking behind it while the others flew through the water. Her shield slowed her down, but she still ran into the wall behind her with the others.

"All right, who's ready to try?" Kenna said as she swam in front of them. When no one responded, Kenna turned to Kym. "Why don't you give it a try?"

Kenna reset the targets while Kym swam into the center of the room. Deciding this wasn't the time to show off, Kym chose to make a bolt the size of Kenna's, but with only one-third of the water. Energizing the water was easy, but forcing it all together was the hard part. As she started pushing it together, her hands actually stopped, the force from the water preventing them from moving any farther. When she finally succeeded in getting all the water into one small bolt, her hands trembled and shook as much as the bolt did.

She threw the bolt, and it felt like a million tiny hands were pressing from the inside of it, trying to break free. She focused her energy, but when the bolt was inches from her hand, it exploded. Unable to do anything, Kym threw her arms over her face to protect herself. But when the explosion passed, she didn't feel anything. Lowering her arms, Kym saw she was inside a bubble of energized water. Next to Kym, Kenna lowered her arms, and the protective sphere around Kym vanished.

"Good try," Kenna said. "This move is tough, and takes a lot of practice to get right."

"Why is it so powerful?" Jax asked. He smiled at Kym as he took her place.

"The release of energy from the element gives any attack its power. So the more water you have, the more energy you can put into it, and the more energy is released. Compact bolts are so powerful because the energy is released so quickly. That much energy is not meant to be in such a small space. Go ahead, Jax."

They practiced compact bolts for the rest of the day. By the time they finished, no one's bolt made it farther than a few inches before exploding. Luckily, Kenna was always paying close attention and shielded them from their own exploding attacks. Kym ran all the way up to her room, her stomach growling louder with every step. Once dressed and in the dining hall, Kym sat with Kenna, Aidan, and Ryland. Kenna praised Kym and Ryland as she filled Aidan in on their training. As Aidan congratulated them, Nila, sitting a couple of tables away, stood. The hall fell instantly silent. This was odd, since Nila usually never addressed the hall after blessing the food.

"Tomorrow marks a crucial day for you all. The yearly evaluation of the Favored at Crystal Palace is upon us.

Evaluation? No one told Kym about any evaluation. She'd only been at Wadita for a few months. Did she even know enough to be evaluated? Her heart racing, she turned to Kenna, Aidan, and Ryland, hoping to see her anxiety mirrored on their faces. Instead, they looked almost bored.

"The carriages are already waiting on the front drive. When you have finished eating, make your way down to them and load as quickly as possible. Only four per carriage, and no need to worry about packing. Your maids and servants have already prepared your luggage for the five-day trip."

Her stomach one big knot, Kym stared at her plate while the others finished eating. After what felt like hours, though it was only a few minutes, Kenna, Aidan, and Ryland stood and started to leave the dining hall. Her mind full of a million questions, Kym barely noticed them leave. She hurried after them, catching up as Kenna climbed into one of the blue carriages. She sat next to Kenna on the cushioned bench, across from Aidan and Ryland. The carriage jerked forward after a few minutes, and they were off.

"Is Crystal Palace far from here?"

"Like ten hours," Kenna said, trying to find a comfortable place to lean her head. "We'll get there around sunrise if the drivers know what they're doing."

"What's the evaluation like?" Kym asked, pulling her feet onto her seat and wrapping her arms around her legs. "Is it hard?"

"Nah," Ryland yawned, leaning back onto Aidan's chest. "Well, not really."

"What?" Kym asked, thoroughly confused.

"You just have to show the Rulers everything you can do."

"That sounds kinda hard to me."

"It's not. Just hold back, and you'll be fine."

"Hold back?" Didn't holding back go against the whole idea of evaluations?

"Nila's orders," Aidan said, reaching up to dim the lamp.

"Why?"

"I dunno," Aidan grunted, his eyes already closed. "Something about saving something for next year's evals. If it means we don't have to work as hard, I'm cool with it."

Kym didn't remember falling asleep, but she must have. The next thing she knew she was opening her eyes, her cheek pressed against the cold window. Trying her best not to wake Kenna, who was sprawled over her half of their bench, Kym worked herself into a more comfortable position. She looked out the window, trying to rub some feeling back into her arms. The sky was a pale gray, but besides that, the only thing Kym could see was a massive, black mountain growing larger as their carriage approached. The mountain looked oddly familiar, but Kym couldn't figure out why.

With nothing else to think about, the evaluations invaded Kym's thoughts. If they were staying at Crystal Palace for five days, how long did the evaluations take? Her nerves rising, a shiver ran across her skin. Would it be better to go first and get it over with, or last so she knew what to expect? She guessed it didn't matter since Nila wanted them to hold back. But that didn't make sense. Nila only paid attention to Favored who showed real promise, so why wouldn't she want them to show off to the other Rulers when they could?

The sun rose higher into the sky, flooding the small carriage with red and orange light. Now able to get a better look outside, Kym squinted up at the black mountain, which they were headed right towards. Something vast and white twinkled on the mountain's high peak. Narrowing her eyes even more against the sun, she realized why the mountain looked familiar. She'd seen it in the paintings of the palaces at her old school. They'd arrived at Crystal Palace.

The carriage rattled up the winding mountain roads, waking Kenna, Aidan, and Ryland. Both Ryland and Aidan looked out the windows, while Kenna stayed where she was, her eyes closed.

"Oh goody. We're here."

"Don't be such a crab, Kenna." Aidan prodded her with his foot.

"Shut the Thed up," Kenna snapped, swatting Aidan's foot away.

"Someone's not a morning person," Ryland muttered, leaning over so only Kym could hear.

"I know." Kym smiled, thinking back to when Kenna had first helped her train.

Crystal Palace looked just like Wadita, except it had an additional wing on each side and many more towers. And while Wadita was blue, Crystal Palace was white, and every inch sparkled in the sun, like someone had covered it in glittering gems. Kym guessed that was why it was called Crystal Palace. The long, curved front drive was already full of carriages and led to a grand staircase. They were just like the one Kym rode in, but while Kym's carriage was blue, the ones they passed were green and gray.

"Good," Ryland said, also looking out the window. "We beat the Fire Favored here."

"Is that a good thing?"

"Yes," Kenna said, finally sitting up and sounding serious. "They don't like us, and we don't like them."

"You…you're serious?" Kym laughed. The whole thing seemed ridiculous.

"Very," said Aidan, and the seriousness in his voice was crystal clear.

Their carriage stopped, and Kenna, Aidan, Ryland, and Kym climbed out onto the graveled drive. Aidan and Kenna led the Water

Favored up the steps and through the front doors, which opened on their own. The entrance hall was already full of people dressed in green and pale gray, all standing according to color. Kenna and Aidan led their group to a space in the hall away from the others. They chatted among themselves for half an hour, while Favored dressed in yellow and violet joined the now-packed entrance hall.

The Fire Favored, all dressed in red, arrived last. They sneered and laughed as they marched past the Water Favored, and one of them even made a rude hand gesture toward Kenna. The front doors closed themselves with a soft thud, and everyone turned to face the opposite side of the room, where two sets of curved staircases led up to the vast landing of the next floor. A tall woman dressed in a flowing white dress glided forward. She placed her hands on the high banister, and looked down at the assembled Favored.

"Welcome to our courageous Favored."

Kym had never seen Lady Zara, the Ruler of Life, before. Why hadn't she ever visited Kym's school like all the other Rulers had? She remembered how odd the Rulers looked at her school, dressed in gowns and strange suits, wearing the enormous crowns. They always seemed so out of place. But in a palace, standing over people dressed not quite as finely, was where they belonged. The other Rulers joined Zara, flanking her on either side.

"Another year has come and gone, and once again we gather for your evaluations," Zara continued. "You shall be divided into smaller groups this year, with one member of each element in a group. However, since your numbers are not equal, empty places within the groups shall be filled with the Favored who remain. You will dine, and get evaluated with, the Favored in your group during your stay here."

Zara clapped her hands, and several servants dressed in white togas entered the crowd. They each grabbed a Favored and led them to different parts of the hall. Separating the Favored took a lot less time than Kym expected. An elderly woman with a kind, wrinkled face took her hand and led her to stand next to a large pillar. She reentered the crowd and returned moments later with a boy dressed in gray. He was slightly taller than Kym, with dark-brown hair that fell in waves to his shoulders. The woman left to find another Favored, and the boy smiled at Kym, but she looked away.

"Hey," he said, his eyes widening slightly as he looked at her. "I know you."

"I don't think so."

"I do. We went to school together. The Rulers chose us on the same day. I'm Tomark."

Kym looked up at him, and after a couple of seconds, she realized he was right. The day Nila chose her was a blur of sadness, so the details were hard to recall. But the more she looked at Tomark, the more she remembered him. He'd sat next to her in the gym teacher's office as the headmaster said the words Kym thought marked the end of her life. He hadn't said a word.

"Oh, yeah," she smiled. She'd never thought she'd see a face from her old life again. "I don't remember much about that day."

"Me either." Tomark nodded understandingly. "And everything since has been so bizarre. I never thought anything like this would ever happen to me."

"Neither did I. It took a while, but I think I'm finally starting to get the hang of all this."

"That's great."

The elderly woman returned with a short girl in a green dress. She leaned against the pillar, looking up at Kym and Tomark. Kym shifted uncomfortably as the girl stared, several small lines forming in the girl's forehead. Kym glanced at Tomark, who smiled softly at the girl. She looked a little younger than Kym, who thought one good wind would blow her right over.

"Nice to meet you," Tomark said warmly.

"Really," the girl said thoughtfully. "I bet I'll change your mind in two minutes."

"Wow," Kym chuckled, unable to stop herself. "That's a little harsh."

"C'mon," the girl droned, rolling her eyes and smiling. "Everyone here is so stuck up it's driving me crazy. Crack a smile once in a while, why don't you?"

The girl's words instantly brought a smile to Kym's lips. "I'm Kym, and that's Tomark."

"Kat. I can't wait to hate you on principle because that's how stupid everyone here is. Please tell me she's not part of our group?" Kat added, looking at a tall girl dressed in red standing at the edge of the Fire Favored.

"How can we know?" Tomark asked, frowning at Kat. "Why? Do you not like her?"

"Ha ha," said Kat. "It's not a Favored thing. I've heard stories about her. Her name's Amber, and apparently, she thinks she's *sooo* much better than any other Favored who's ever lived. Just look at her, standing with her nose in the air. She's getting on my nerves from all the way over there."

"Why?" Kym asked, glancing sideways at Amber.

"Not sure. She probably wants to feel better than everyone else."

To Kat's dismay, Amber joined their group. As she walked over, Kym couldn't help but agree with Kat. At the very least there was something different about this Amber girl. From the way she almost glided across the floor, her hands behind her back, and her lips, which were pursed slightly as she held her nose in the air. It reminded Kym of Nila, or how Zara looked just minutes before.

"Well," Amber asked slowly, her narrow eyes darting between Kym, Kat, and Tomark. "Aren't you going to introduce yourselves?"

"You first," Kat demanded, stepping toward Amber, who towered over Kat by at least a foot.

"Cute," Amber replied, her eyes glued to Kat. "Very witty. But if you insist, my name is Amber, and you are?"

"Kym."

"Tomark."

"Kat." Hers was more of a grunt.

"Hi." A girl in a yellow dress joined them, smiling as she tucked her long, red hair behind her ears. "I'm Ashlyn."

Ashlyn's timing couldn't have been better, even if her smile was a little much. They lapsed into silence, Kym and Tomark standing back while Kat and Amber glared at each other. The more she watched, the more Kym thought there was something between Kat and Amber they weren't saying. It was plain the moment Amber spoke, and the way they kept staring at each other. There had to be more to the story.

A Darkness Favored dressed in violet was the last to join their group. He looked around the same age as Tomark, but this boy was much larger. Tomark's thin arms were half the size of the newcomer's. They tried asking his name, but he wouldn't say anything at first. Finally, he told them to call him Pupil.

"Pupil?" Kat spluttered. "Seriously? What kind of a name is that?"

"The Darkness Favored are all called Pupil," Amber said superiorly, inclining her head slightly in Pupil's direction.

"Now that you are sorted into groups, the evaluations can begin." Zara's voice rang through the hall, which immediately fell silent. "We will evaluate eight groups a day, each following the same evaluation order: Light, Darkness, Fire, Water, Air, and Earth. Missing elements will be skipped, and the next element in line will proceed with their evaluation. The attendants who formed your groups will inform you of your evaluation time, as well as answer any questions you may have. Good luck, and may the gods bless you all."

"Your evaluations," their attendant wheezed, "are this afternoon. I will show you to your prep room, where you may change into something more functional while you wait."

Her body tingling once again, Kym and the others followed the attendant through one of the doors around the hall. The room was large, with several benches set in two sections in the middle of the room. Another door stood opposite the one they entered, which Kym thought must lead to where the evaluations took place. The only other things in the room were six large trunks, each the color of an element.

Kym tentatively opened the blue one, unsure what to expect, and found it full of beautiful gowns, shoes, and jewelry. But it was not the finery that brought a smile to her face. A plain blue shirt, leggings, and worn, flat shoes sat on top of Kym's other clothes. The sight of her favorite training outfit was enough to slow Kym's heart. Kym pulled the clothes from the trunk, making a mental note to thank her maids when she got back to Wadita.

"Feel free to practice before your evaluations begin," their attendant said. "You have some time before the other groups finish."

"Could I get some earth?" Kat called from the floor, jamming her foot into her shoe.

"Of course, Miss." The attendant bowed and started backing out of the room.

"Excuse me," Kym called, hurrying over to catch the attendant. "I'll need some water when you can."

"My pleasure, Miss."

With no way to practice, Kym and Kat sat and watched the others warm up. They didn't do much, but it was enough to take Kym's mind off her evaluation. Ashlyn made small birds of light soar around the room, which sang softly before returning to her, where they vanished with a flick of her hand. The shadows cast by the benches slid eerily around the floor under Pupil's direction. Amber made small fires bloom in a line on the ground, while Tomark sent blasts of air at those she left behind, extinguishing them. Kym stared at everyone's Marks, which looked like Kym's, except the colors matched their element. They also wrapped differently around their arms, all ending in different places.

The attendant returned with bowls of water and earth, allowing Kym and Kat to practice. But Kym, still a little shaky, decided to make a small water orb, which she weaved slowly between her fingers. Next to her, Kat condensed the earth in her bowl into little rocks, which she sent flying around the room. These rocks flew very close to Amber, and when one finally hit her on the head, Kat claimed it was an accident. Kym thought the smile on Kat's face said otherwise.

Several hours later, their attendant brought in large, covered trays and set them on a table near the door. After removing the lids, she announced it was time for lunch.

"So," Kym said to Kat, joining her and Tomark on a bench. "Have you done this before? This is Tomark's and my first evaluation."

"Oh yeah," said Kat, her voice trembling. "I feel like I'm going to throw up because I've done this before. Of course it's my first time."

"You can't have been a Favored for too long, then?"

"Why? Conducting a survey?" Kat asked before smiling. "It's been a few months."

"That's about when they found Kym and me," Tomark said. "Guess we're in the same boat."

"They're ready for you," the attendant announced when she reentered the room. "If our Light Favored would please step through the door, you may begin your evaluation."

Ashlyn stood, her face set, and walked over to the evaluation room door. This was clearly not her first evaluation. Kym tried to see inside the room, but all she saw was blackness. The door shut behind Ashlyn, and silence filled the room. Kym sat there, her nerves building like a boiling kettle, ready to burst at any second. But they never did. Kym tried tapping her foot, hoping to work some of it off, but it didn't help.

So she sat there, waiting for her turn, watching both Ashlyn and Pupil leave and return. She tried getting a sense of the evaluation from their body language, but they just sat in silence with the rest of the group.

"Water, they're ready for you," Amber said, the door bouncing loudly off the wall as she returned from her evaluation.

"Good luck," Tomark whispered.

Kym stood, and Kat punched her softly in the arm. Startled, Kym looked at Kat, who just smiled and winked. Laughing slightly from nerves, Kym walked up to the door and turned the knob. The room looked just as dark as it had for the others. Sneaking one last glance over her shoulder, she stepped into the blackness.

CHAPTER NINE

THE
EVALUATION

Darkness surrounded Kym. She turned to the door, which had provided some light, but it too was swallowed by the blackness. But that was impossible. She couldn't be more than a few feet from the door. Was she even walking in a straight line? Fear bubbled up inside her, and she couldn't stop her body from shaking. She'd never been so nervous for a test before. How was she supposed to take a test she knew nothing about in the dark?

Kym turned to face what she thought was the middle of the room, but the blackness was so uniform there was an equal chance she was staring right into a wall. She needed to see, but there was no sign of a lamp or torch. She would have been grateful for even a candle. If she just started walking, what was the worst that could happen? She needed to do something, and soon. Then it dawned on her.

She closed her eyes, which made no difference in the blackness, and focused her energy. She'd never tried invoking her Marks for no reason, and wasn't even sure it would work. She opened her eyes and saw her hands, and everything for about a foot around her, illuminated by her glowing blue Marks. The light was dim, but it was enough for her to move forward.

Kym returned to the door and started walking toward what she now knew was the middle of the room, which she thought was enormous. She tried to walk in a straight line, and every step sounded like a cannon blast. Since she always trained in the middle of the room at Wadita, that's where she thought she should be. After what felt like several minutes of very slow wandering, she finally saw something different in the darkness. A small circle, about an inch taller than the rest of the floor, enclosed what Kym thought was the room's center. Unable to think of any better ideas, Kym stepped into the circle.

The moment Kym stepped inside, a bright spotlight shone directly down on her. It illuminated the area inside the circle, but everything outside it remained shrouded in blackness. Startled, Kym staggered backward, covering her face with her arms, until her foot hit the edge of the circle. The ground beneath her jerked, and Kym fell forward as rumbling filled the vast room. Crouched on all fours, she looked this way and that, trying to see what was happening in the darkness, but still couldn't see beyond the light.

Everything around Kym stopped as suddenly as it started. She struggled to her feet, trying to rub the throbbing from her palms. She walked to the circle's edge, hoping to see something, anything. The darkness seemed to melt away as the light from the spotlight faded out into the blackness, finally revealing her surroundings.

Kym stood on a pedestal of white, glittering stone, but as far as she could see, that was the only solid surface in the room. The floor she'd walked on was gone, replaced by gently rippling water. Kym looked down into the water, wondering how deep it was, but couldn't see any bottom to the pool. Water lapped around the pedestal's edge, but never actually landed on the surface. The droplets of water fell right back into the pool.

"Demonstrate your knowledge of elemental skills," boomed a strange female voice.

"Elemental skills?" Kym muttered, looking around for the source of the voice.

She'd never heard magic called that before. Everything she'd learned had been called "basic" by her teachers; basic control, basic offensive, and basic defensive. The only other category Kym knew was the crowd control magic, but she was sure that wasn't an elemental skill. It had to be something simple. But after focusing on advanced magic for so long, everything seemed simple to her. Then it hit her; what were the skills that formed the foundation for all other magic? The ones that took her the longest to get right.

Kym stepped onto the water, which glowed brightly beneath her in the darkness. She walked around the pedestal, feeling a little foolish demonstrating her ability to walk. Once she made it all the way around the pedestal, she broke into a sprint, focusing on the water beneath her, ensuring not a single drop left the surface. Deciding she had plenty of time to hold back later, Kym rolled across the water, and slid across the surface before popping back up to her feet. Her clothes stayed dry the whole time, and Kym couldn't help but smile to herself.

Kym walked closer to the better-lit center of the room, directing her hand at the water. A large orb rose into the air, which started zigzagging around her. Once the orb settled on the path she wanted, Kym made a second and sent it following the first. She continued this until a line of ten orbs zoomed around her like a giant, watery caterpillar. Kym turned both her hands to the line, bringing it to a halt. She flicked her wrists, concentrating on what she wanted each orb to do, and they all went flying in different directions. She moved her hands like a conductor, and the orbs flew around her, circling her at many different heights. Kym lowered her hands, and the orbs sank back into the water, barely disturbing the surface.

"Return to the pedestal," the female voice said.

Smiling, Kym did as instructed. She'd either done something right or screwed the whole thing up, but she was more inclined to think the former. When she stepped back onto the glittering white stone, darkness filled the room, pressing right up to the light surrounding Kym. Unable to see past her circle, she strained her ears, trying to gain some insight into what was coming next. But aside from some faint rumbling around the room, there was nothing else.

"Demonstrate your knowledge of basic, offensive combat."

The darkness melted away, and the spotlight expanded, this time flooding the whole room with light. Kym blinked several times before her vision adjusted to the sudden change. She was inside a dome much larger than the one at Wadita. The walls were made of white stone like the pedestal, and the water came right to the edge of the curved walls. She looked up, trying to see where all the light was coming from, but there was nothing—just the smooth, curved ceiling.

Tall, square pillars rose from the water, each marked with an X, though the position varied from pillar to pillar. Kym made two orbs fly out of the water, which turned into bolts a second later. Picking the closest pillar, Kym threw a bolt at the X in its center, and it exploded, filling the air with a lot of white dust.

Kym turned and threw a bolt in the general direction of her next target. But, she overshot it, and the bolt hit the pillar at the top, nowhere near its X. A bright yellow disk appeared in front of the pillar, shielding the area not marked with an X, leaving the pillar intact. Curious, Kym threw a bolt at the bottom of the pillar next to it, whose X was at the top, and a bright green shield deflected her attack.

Kym began attacking, taking careful aim at each pillar before doing so. She started slow, building her speed until her attacks became almost continuous. New pillars rose to replace those she destroyed, always in new locations. At first, she relied solely on her bolts, but that quickly became too boring. This part of the evaluation was too fun for her not to give it her all. She'd have plenty of time to hold back later.

Seeing three pillars in a line, their X's in the same place, Kym shot a blast at them. It blew right through the first and second, finally stopping when it reached the third, but it was enough. The pillars crumbled, and she turned to the rest of the room, eager for more. But before she could attack again, the pillars sank silently beneath the water.

"Return to the pedestal," the female voice said again.

Kym walked back to the pedestal, disappointed she couldn't do more as the darkness once again pressed in on her. The room rumbled and shook, and she wiped the sweat from her forehead, bending over slightly as she tried to catch her breath. This wasn't so bad, she thought. If the rest of the evaluation was like that, holding back was going to be a challenge. And what was the harm in showing off a little anyway? She'd finally gotten the hang of this magic stuff, and breaking the pillars was oddly satisfying.

"Demonstrate your knowledge of basic, defensive combat," the voice said as silence and light filled the room once again.

Kym practically leaped onto the water, excitement pounding through her, but nothing happened. No pillars rose from the still water, leaving the room completely empty. She walked around, hoping to trigger something, but still, nothing happened. Thinking she must have misunderstood the directions, Kym turned back to the pedestal.

There was a flash of white light, and a high pitched whirring as something flew through the air. Kym barely turned around before the bolt hit her in the stomach. She slid back across the water, leaving a trail of rippling water in her wake. Grimacing, Kym looked up to see who attacked her, but it was not a who at all. The pillar was like the ones from before, but instead of an X, this new pillar had a niche, and inside the niche was what looked like an energized element. In this pillar's case, the element was water. But that made no sense. She'd never heard of a pillar holding an energized element before, let alone firing it.

But Kym had no time to worry about logistics. She was almost on her feet when the pillar fired another bolt at her. She barely blocked it with a poorly made shield, which shattered after stopping the bolt. The pillar shot again, and this time Kym was ready. The pillar's bolt bounced off her shield, ricocheting into the ceiling as she moved out of its line of fire. But even though she was no longer standing directly in front of it, the pillar still managed to shoot a bolt right at her. She blocked it, but before she could take a step in any direction, the pillar fired a blast at her.

It was unlike any blast she'd ever encountered; no Favored could hold a blast indefinitely like that. They always died out at some point, usually when the element was all used up, but the blast from the pillar just kept coming. Kym gritted her teeth and channeled all her energy into her shield, which was already cracked. The blast pushed her backward, her feet unable to keep a grip on the water.

There was another flash of white light. A second pillar appeared on Kym's left, this one housing energized fire. It shot a blast at Kym, who hastily formed a second shield. But, with her attention now split, both her shields shattered in seconds. The collective blasts from the two pillars knocked Kym across the room. There were more flashes of white light, and three new pillars appeared.

Kym stood, her arms extended, and spun on the spot, creating a ring of energized water beneath her. She raised her arms as the pillars began to fire, and energized water rose around her. The water wall formed seconds before the blasts reached her, protecting her from all sides, but she was pinned down. More pillars appeared, blasting Kym's dome along with the others, causing her whole body to tremble. Kym redoubled her efforts, focusing all her energy on her dome. She wasn't going to let those pillars beat her.

But after more than two minutes of attacks, Kym's dome started to crack as the water beneath her feet began to give way. With no other way out, Kym gave in, sinking beneath the surface, where the pillars did not follow. The sounds of attacks stopped, and the female voice rang through the water, telling her to return to the pedestal. Kym struggled over to it, barely registering that the pedestal was actually a giant stone disk floating on the water.

Exhausted, she climbed out of the water, thankful she still had enough energy to keep herself dry. Kym lay sprawled on the stone, not wanting to get up as the room filled with darkness and rumbling for the third time. At the very least, she'd broken the rules of the evaluation by using the water wall. It was part of Kenna's 'crowd control' magic, and wasn't basic at all. But what other choice did she have? Her shields would have done nothing against all of those pillars, especially once there were more than ten of them. How were people supposed to pass that part of the evaluation with only shields?

"To demonstrate any advanced techniques or skills, remain on the pedestal. If not, exit the chamber at this time. You have thirty seconds to decide."

Slowly, Kym sat up. She knew this was when Kenna and Aidan

would choose to leave. She'd shown all she needed to, so she should go and not let the other Rulers see everything she could do, just like Nila wanted. But she'd already messed that up; she'd already performed magic that was more advanced than she needed to. The Rulers already knew there was more she could do. So shouldn't she stay? She'd already come this far. She might as well finish what she started.

"By remaining on the pedestal, you are obligated to demonstrate your knowledge of advanced elemental forms."

The room filled with light and before Kym could even stand, water rose above the pedestal. Luckily, Kenna and Aidan always filled the water dome when Kym and the others weren't expecting it. She invoked her Marks and rose with the water, floating high above the pedestal as the room filled. No longer holding back, she dove downward, hoping to see the bottom of the room, but ran out of light before she could see any sign of it. Leaving it as a lost cause, Kym swam at her top speed, looping her way through the vast room.

Kym saw the flashes of white light on the edge of her vision. She turned, registered the swarm of pillars floating behind her, and didn't wait for them to attack. Her bolts flew through the water, breaking pillars no matter where she struck them, while the others began to attack. She swam through their attacks, dodging this way and that, narrowly avoiding them. She sent attacks in all directions, smashing pillars with bolts and blasts, and even managing to slice four cleanly in two with a well-placed swipe. She considered trying a compact bolt, but decided against it. She didn't need to show the Rulers that attack exploding in her face.

The number of pillars dwindled as the water filled with dust and chunks of stone. Kym tried to get back to the pedestal through the gloom, breaking every pillar she came across. When she reached the pedestal, the dust and debris vanished, the water began to drop around her, and the light focused back on the pedestal. The woman's voice rang over the din as the blackness rumbled and shook.

"Your evaluation is complete. Send in the next Favored for their evaluation."

"How'd it go?" Tomark asked as Kym walked back into the prep room.

"Good, I think. I'm not really sure. You're up."

With a smile that looked more like a grimace, Tomark stood, walked past Kym and through the door. Kym took his empty seat next to Kat, who seemed to have transformed since Kym left for her evaluation. She held tightly onto her legs, a look of intense concentration on her face, her eyes wider than normal. It was like she was trying not to blink, or even breathe. Kym scooted a little closer to Kat, but she didn't seem to notice.

"It's okay to be nervous."

"Nervous," Kat said, jerking her head violently toward Kym, making her jump. "What are you talking about? I'm not nervous. I'm going to rock the Rulers' world."

"Uh-huh," Kym smiled.

"Seriously, I'm fine," Kat snapped, convincing no one. "What was it like in there?"

"Um…" she trailed off, trying to think of the right words to describe it all. "Intense. There were these pillars that I've never seen before. They shot attacks—"

"I've heard about those," Kat interrupted, sounding both excited and wary. "An older Favored at Terradon told me about them."

"They did?" Kym asked, feeling slightly crestfallen. Her friends at Wadita never even told her there were evaluations, let alone what was in them.

"They didn't want to at first," Kat said, her set face cracking into a faint smile. "I had to…um…persuade them a little."

"How'd you do that?"

"Made it worth their while. Said if they didn't tell me, I'd be on their cases until I got bored, and I don't bore easily."

"Geez. You put the fear of the gods in them."

"I can have that effect on people," Kat nodded.

Kym sat back, looking at the ceiling while Kat fell into silence, staring at the evaluation room door. It was done. She'd finished her evaluation, and the first day wasn't even over. For the next four days, she could just sit back and relax while everyone else stressed, or in the case of Kenna and Aidan, not stress, about their impending evaluations.

They waited in silence for Tomark to finish his evaluation. Kat became more like a statue as time stretched on, not taking her eyes off of the door. Kym looked around for a clock, but the smooth, white walls were bare. She looked back at the door, which she thought should have opened by now. Her evaluation hadn't taken this long, had it? It couldn't have. Even after choosing to stay for the advanced part, there was no way it took this long.

"Your turn, Kat," Tomark said after finally walking back into the room, looking tired but pleased.

"Let's do this!" Kat's voice trembled as she wrenched open the door and ran into the evaluation chamber.

Tomark took Kat's empty seat, a relieved smile on his lips. Kym smiled back and was about to ask him how his evaluation had gone when Amber walked gracefully over to them. She stood over them, looking down her nose at Kym and Tomark while they both stared up at her.

"Do you want something?" Tomark asked, his voice stern.

"Well, I can see Kat already got to you," Amber said, her pristine voice rolling slowly through the silent room.

"What does that mean?" Kym asked.

"I'm sure she's told you about me. How I'm this horrible person whom you shouldn't even bother with, am I correct?"

"She didn't exactly put it like that," said Tomark.

"And I'm sure she exaggerated," Kym added, not wanting to offend Amber.

"If there's one thing you can count on, it's Kat exaggerating," Amber said, her lips curling. She took the open seat next to Kym. Even sitting, she still seemed to tower over Kym and Tomark. "Before you write me off, I ask that you keep this in mind; the two of you, along with Kat, are new to the world of magic. I'm sure you have found Favored to help guide you through this new world, but those Favored are not me. I have been a part of this world longer than any Favored in this palace. I grew up here. Magic is all I know. So, before you side with Kat, based on her minimal knowledge of me, imagine what I could offer."

"Offer?" Tomark asked, sounding offended. "What could you offer us? We'll probably never see you again once the evaluations are over."

"Perhaps," Amber said. "Remember, there are many days of evaluations left; days we will spend together."

"So we're supposed to pretend to be friends?" Kym asked.

"No. But in the time we have left, there may be a thing or two I could teach you. Like I said, I've been doing this for a very long time. Consider it," Amber said, rising gracefully from her seat, "and consider what you could gain by giving me a chance."

When the evaluation door finally opened, Kat looked very pleased with herself. But instead of walking back into the room, she stood leaning against the doorframe.

"The Rulers want us back in there," she announced to the room. "They're ready to give out scores."

Everyone stood and walked back into the evaluation room. Amber led the way, gliding across the floor while Tomark hurried behind her, followed closely by Pupil and Ashlyn. For a moment Kat looked at Kym, then the two of them walked silently after the others. Finally, words seemed to explode from Kat's lips.

"Okay, what's going on?"

"What? Nothing."

"Something's wrong. It's all over your face."

"It's Amber. She talked to Tomark and me during your evaluation."

"Was it as bad as I said?"

"I don't know. She's just so…"

"Yup," Kat agreed.

"She asked us to give her a chance, though."

"But you're not?"

"I…" Kym wanted to say she wanted nothing to do with Amber, but she couldn't. Hadn't people written her off back home because of what they heard about her family? Wouldn't she be doing the same thing to Amber if she took Kat's side now?

"So, you choose her?" Kat asked flatly.

"No," she replied, looking down at Kat. "I'm not choosing anybody. I think you and I have a connection, but I don't want to turn my back on Amber just because you don't like her."

She waited for Kat to say something, who studied Kym's face as they joined the others in the middle of the evaluation room. Finally, Kat smiled.

"All right."

"You're okay with this?"

"It's fine with me. I'm not a fan of people changing who they are to make friends. Get to know Amber if that's what you want. You saying you would stay away from her because of me would have been worse. You stuck to your guns; I like that."

"Why don't you like her?"

"We have… history," Kat answered slowly.

Kym couldn't help but smile. She'd expected Kat to be angry, declaring their short-lived friendship over because Kym wanted to give Amber a chance. But that didn't seem to be who Kat was. She may be sarcastic and blunt where Kym might use a gentler touch, but Kat always spoke her mind, even when she probably shouldn't. Wasn't that what she just did to Kym—to see whether she would tell Kat the truth or hide it to preserve their friendship?

They waited silently in the center of the room, which was now completely lit, for the Rulers to give them their results. No longer nervous, all Kym could feel was a sense of excitement, which buzzed through her body like an electric shock. Sure, she'd shown more than Nila had wanted her to, at least according to Aidan and Kenna, but there was nothing she could do about that now. She'd done her best, and the fact that she didn't back off made her even prouder.

The wall directly opposite the prep room door split open, and the seven Rulers glided gracefully out into the room. The Favored quickly formed themselves into a line, so that when the Rulers reached them, each Ruler stood in front of their respective Favored, with Zara standing just behind them. But something was off. The Rulers' blank, regal expressions were gone, replaced with mingled looks of discomfort and impatience.

"The Favored," Zara began, "are rated on a seven-point scale. Each Ruler can award a single point to your score if they were impressed by the skills you demonstrated. If you receive seven points, your performance was exceptional; six, advanced; five, above average; four, average; three, below average; two, mediocre; and one, horrendous. The Rulers will now present the Favored with their scores."

"I award Ashlyn a score of five for her above-average performance," Evanna said.

"My Pupil," Melana said dryly, "has been granted a six for his advanced performance."

"Amber has received a seven for her exceptional performance," said James.

"Katarein," Kai said, "has been awarded a five for her above-average performance."

"Kymbralyn has received a five for her above-average performance," Nila said.

"Tomark has been granted a five for his above-average performance," said Stailin.

Relief rushed over Kym like cold water. She turned to Kat, and could almost see the tension physically lifting off her narrow shoulders. They did it. It was over. And to top it off, Kym did better than she expected. She thought she performed well, but she hadn't expected to get an above average. She stepped forward and, without hesitating, wrapped her arms around Kat's small frame.

"Nice going, Kymbralyn," Kat chuckled as they pulled apart.

"Back at you, Katarein," she said, her eyebrows raised as she tried to stop herself from laughing. It didn't last too long.

"Bravo," Zara said over the continued congratulations of the group. Tomark seemed just as pleased with his score as Kym and Kat were, and Ashlyn returned Kym's smile with a warm one of her own, her eyes full of shining tears. Amber just stared at Kym, though Kym thought she saw something flicker in Amber's golden eyes. Pupil stood a little ways apart from the rest of the group, staring vaguely at the opposite wall, not saying a word.

"You have done well," Zara continued. "You should be proud of what you accomplished today. Before we join your fellow Favored for dinner, there is something I must discuss with my fellow Rulers. The Favored will please wait here. We will send for you when we have finished. We will need only a moment."

Zara led the Rulers, who looked more surprised than Kym, across the room. She smiled broadly at each Ruler as they stepped into the Favored's prep room. Kym and the others stood in the middle of the evaluation chamber, completely at a loss as to what was happening. Zara stepped into the prep room and closed the door sharply behind her.

CHAPTER TEN

LISTENING IN

"I DON'T UNDERSTAND," ASHLYN SAID, WIPING A TEAR FROM HER cheek. "Why do the Rulers need to talk? They've been together all day, but they need a private word now?"

"Isn't it obvious?" Amber drawled, her superior tone cutting through the silence. The sound made Kym flinch. "Some of the Rulers have been humoring the idea of overthrowing the gods, and Lady Zara probably wants to discuss it. Didn't you notice how on edge they were?

Nobody spoke. Instead, they just stood there, staring at Amber. Kym felt like someone had kicked her a hard in the stomach. She'd spent so long convincing herself that the Rulers overthrowing the gods couldn't possibly be true. But now she was hearing the same things all over again, and from someone who had no reason to lie to her.

"How do you know what they're talking about?" Tomark asked, not even bothering to hide his skepticism. "They have Princirum to run, and could be talking about literally anything."

"Because, my dear Tomark, I've heard it before. I've joined Lord James at the Rulers' Summit for the past several months. Lady Zara ordered the Favored to leave at the end of the last two so the Rulers could discuss something in private. Naturally, we wanted to know what was going on, so we listened at the door. It was hard to make it all out through the thick doors, but I heard Lady Zara loud and clear: 'How dare any of you suggest we overthrow our parents? If any of you speak of this again, I will strip you of your rank and banish you from Princirum.' "

Kym's heart raced at this new information. Aidan hadn't told her that part of the story. But was it true? She knew the Rulers would do everything they could to protect their power. But if they'd listened to Zara, what could they be talking about now?

"They're still on this?" Kat asked, sounding a little annoyed.

"You've heard this too?" Tomark asked.

"Oh yeah. It's all the important Favored at Terradon will talk about, but I don't know why they bother. It's never going to happen."

"Why do you say that?" Kym asked, her curiosity piqued.

"Because the Rulers are cowards. Sure, they talk a big talk, but they'll never do anything if they think it could pose a threat to them. They'll never take the risk."

"I don't know," Kym said slowly. "Like you said, the Rulers love power. Wouldn't they do whatever they could to get more?"

"Not if they had to put their own necks on the line to get it."

Kym looked at Kat, her brow furrowed in annoyance. She could tell Kat wanted her on her side, but she just couldn't see it. From where Kym stood, the Rulers' lust for power outweighed any possible danger that could stand in their way. Why wouldn't they take more power if the opportunity presented itself?

"You believe this too?" Tomark asked.

"I'm not sure what I believe. Some of the Favored at Wadita told me the same story weeks ago, and now Amber brought it up here. It's hard not to believe something when several different people are saying the same thing."

"I can't listen to this." Tomark threw his hands in the air. "How can any of you believe this? This could lead to an all-out war with the gods. And you know what will be left standing when it's over? Nothing."

"This is ridiculous," Ashlyn said, her soft voice shaking. "How could the Rulers even think about fighting the gods? They're the gods, after all. They'd lose in an instant. What good would the Rulers' power be then?"

"They could win," Amber shot back silkily, "if the Favored fight alongside the Rulers."

"Is that what you want, Amber? To overthrow the gods and have the Rulers take their places? I should have guessed."

"Take it easy, Tomark," Kym said slowly, sensing his anger boiling just below the surface. "Amber didn't say that."

"Finally," said Amber. "Someone who can see sense. I never said I want the Rulers overthrowing the gods. I was merely suggesting that if the Rulers were going to go through with it, they would be stupid not to use the Favored to their advantage. We do have the numbers of a small army, after all."

"And Amber's not alone," Kym added, her mind flying back to her conversation with Kenna. "Some of the Favored at Wadita have talked about fighting with the Rulers."

"But they'd never ask us to do such a thing," Ashlyn said, shaking her head. "How could they?"

"If you're through arguing," a deep voice said, "we can easily find out the truth."

Pupil hadn't spoken a single word since the Rulers left. He stood slightly apart from the others, who had gathered in a tight group as they spoke. There was something about the way the corners of his mouth twitched that made Kym feel uneasy. It was like he knew something the others didn't.

"Why don't you listen at the door?," Pupil continued. "You'll hear most of what they say. And while you do that, I'll slip inside and poke around."

"And how are you going to do that?" Ashlyn asked, and there was an added edge to her voice. "The Rulers will notice if you open the door and try to sneak in."

"Who said anything about opening the door?"

Pupil took a deep breath, and his Marks shimmered like neon violet string around his arms. For a moment he just stood there, his eyes closed, then, slowly, Pupil began to change. His whole body, including his clothes, grew darker until he was no more than the silhouette of a teenager. He'd transformed into something between liquid and gas, like a dense cloud of black smoke.

But Pupil didn't stop there. The black mass sank to the floor, forming a dark circle. But the circle's edges were fuzzy, and depending on how Kym tilted her head, it appeared darker or lighter. The circle began to shift, stretching and reshaping itself back into a human silhouette. Astounded, Kym couldn't take her eyes off of it. It was unlike anything she'd ever seen. Pupil had become a shadow.

The shadow glided smoothly across the floor and slid underneath the prep room door. Jolted into action, Kym hurried to the door with the others. They surrounded the door, each pressing an ear to the various gaps around it. Through the small space between the wall and the door's right edge, Kym heard the Rulers, clearly in the midst of an argument. There were so many voices that she really couldn't make out who was speaking.

"Are you scared, Evanna?" a cruel voice taunted. "Too scared to take on the old and weak gods? This is our chance to take what is ours."

"Of course I am scared, Melana. What you suggest will be the ruin of all we have built over centuries. Why risk everything we have on a venture I am sure will get us all killed. Facing our parents will be our undoing."

"Our parents have had plenty of time to act," Melana said, and her icy voice sent chills down Kym's back. "I have voiced my plans several times, and the gods have done nothing with that information. Their leniency shows us their weakness. They care for us, their children. We must use this weakness to our advant—"

"Melana! It is one thing to want more power, but to drag all of us down with you is madness."

"Our parents are weak, Stailin, and we all know you take after them. They have proven their weakness time and time again. They have let our power grow without acknowledgment."

"If you wish to face them," Stailin said quickly, "then, by all means, face them. Leave the rest of us out of your mess."

"Think about what you are saying, Melana." Kym recognized Nila's voice. "What would a fight with our parents achieve?"

"What would it achieve?" Melana sounded almost amused. "If we win, we would gain everything. We would be the gods!"

"Melana," said a soft, quavering voice. The speaker sounded almost frightened. "Think of Princirum. What do you think will happen while you battle our parents? It will destroy everything. And when all is said and done, there will be nothing left for the victor to rule. Do not let your pride be what brings everything crumbling down."

"Well, I must say I am impressed with you, Kai. Who knew you had a backbone after all these centuries? But it's a wasted effort, you stupid fool. It is clear that Melana is going to pursue her, um, unique venture with or without our support. Let her do what she wants. We will all benefit if she sucs—"

"Silence, James." Kym heard the authority in Zara's voice as the Rulers obeyed. "I am sick of this endless arguing and debating. I thought you would come to a sensible decision on your own. But it seems, like children, I must make the right decision for you. I have heard enough from both sides of the argument over the past several months."

Decision? What was Zara talking about? Hadn't Aidan and Amber said Zara stopped the conversation before it had gotten too far? Kym looked at Tomark, who was listening below her, and saw her confusion reflected on his face. To her left, Kym saw Amber and Ashlyn, listening through the same crack on the other side of the door, and Kat, who was listening awkwardly from the floor. Ashlyn and Kat both looked just as confused as Tomark and Kym, but Amber's brow was knit, her eyes narrowed in concentration. And even though no one spoke, it was clear that they all were wondering what Zara was going to say.

"After careful consideration of the variables, and perceiving all the options, I have reached my decision. There is no viable reason for us to overthrow the gods. Doing so would cause untold damage and plunge Princirum into chaos. This ruling is final, and I never want to hear this subject mentioned again."

Relief spread through Kym like cool water. All of the tension that had built up inside her faded away at Zara's words. For the shortest of moments, she thought Zara was going to back Melana's plan and declare war with the gods. But she needn't have worried. It wasn't going to happen.

"Lord Stailin, retrieve the Favored from the evaluation chamber. We are needed in the dining hall."

The relief Kym felt moments before vanished as Stailin's footsteps approached the door her ear was still pressed firmly against. Kym scrambled away from the door and took two steps before her feet ran into something hard, and she tumbled to the floor. Not even bothering to look back, she sprang to her feet and sprinted to the center of the room where Tomark, Amber, and Ashlyn already stood, panting hard. Her heart racing, Kym looked back at the door and saw what had tripped her. Kat, who'd been lying on the floor to listen, ran to join them as she clutched her side, her eyes narrowed at Kym.

As Kat ran toward them, Kym saw a dark shape slip under the door. The lone shadow reached the group when Kat did, sliding over her shadow as it took its place next to her. Kym could feel Kat, who stood almost on top of her, shudder. Kym turned and saw Kat rubbing herself like it was the middle of winter and she wasn't wearing a coat.

"That was so weird."

"What?"

"Pupil," Kat said, jerking her head toward him as he returned to normal next to her. "I felt all cold when his shadow thing slid over mine."

Beside Kat, Pupil stared forward with the same bored expression he'd worn before sneaking into the prep room. However, Kym thought she saw a glint in his eye that had not been there before. At the other end of the line, she distinctly heard Ashlyn whisper, "Show-off."

Before anyone could speak, the prep room door opened, and

Stailin walked into the evaluation chamber. This was Kym's first time seeing him up close, and she couldn't help but think of Nila. He was just as tall as she was, with a thin frame and a long neck that seemed to work perfectly for looking down at them. However, as he drew closer, Kym noticed his pale face was flushed, and his brows formed one severe line.

"We appreciate your patience," Stailin said. His deep voice reminded Kym of a large frog. "We need to join the rest of the Favored in the dining hall."

Stailin turned on his heel and walked back the way he'd come. Kym and the others hurried after him, forming a line as they walked into the now-empty prep room. They joined the other Rulers as they mounted the stairs in the entrance hall and continued to the dining hall in silence.

Kym's mind felt like it was going to burst open if she didn't speak soon. She wanted to know what the others thought about what they'd heard, and what it all meant. But with the Rulers right in front of them in the vast, deserted corridors, there was never a chance. So Kym walked in silence as they turned around another corner and saw two large, white doors. These doors swung open as they approached, and they all walked into the already-packed dining hall.

The dining hall was much larger than the one at Wadita. Torches hung in ornate brackets all along the walls and the grand fireplace set into one wall could easily have fit Kym's whole bed. The hall was full of circular tables draped in white cloth, each ringed with six chairs. A single long table sat on a raised platform at the far end of the hall in front of a wall of windows. The table was set for seven and draped in a shimmering white cloth, and the Rulers all took their seats behind it. Kym and her group quickly sat at the only open table in the hall, right in front of the Rulers' raised one.

"We thank the Gods," Zara began, standing from her place at the middle of the Rulers' table, gazing up at the pure white ceiling, "for their everlasting guidance as we determine the skill of their chosen few, their Favored. Your power knows no equal, and we are humbled by the gifts you grant us."

Kym couldn't help but laugh at Zara's words, but luckily only those at her table could hear her. Zara thanking the gods and praising their power was just too ironic after they'd discussed going to war with them not five minutes before. Kat wasn't as good at hiding her amusement, but she managed to turn her snort into a semi-convincing coughing fit.

"We thank you, Pheil, our Great Mother," Zara said after all the other Rulers gave thanks to the other gods in turn, "for the ever-abundant life in the wondrous world you created. May the glow of your life never fade, as we replenish our own lives with this great bounty."

"So," Kym asked a little louder than she normally would have while the tables around them talked loudly, "what's your training like, Kat?"

"What?" Kat, who had been staring at the Rulers with her mouth slightly open, jumped slightly in her seat as she turned to look at Kym. "What about tanning?"

"Not tanning," she corrected, rolling her eyes as Kat struggled to follow her train of thought. "Your training."

"Training? It's like any other element, I guess. We learn control, how to fight with it, how to move through it. What?" Kat added after seeing the look on Kym's face.

"There has to be more than that," Kym said pointedly.

"What's wrong with you? Why are we talking about training? We should be talking about what they—ow!"

Kat turned to glare at Tomark, who sat next to her. Her nostrils flared, and it looked like she was ready to wrestle him from his seat and throw him to the floor.

"You kicked me."

"I know," Tomark whispered calmly, tilting his head gently toward the Rulers. "We shouldn't talk about that nonsense here."

"Nonsen…oh," Kat said slowly, finally catching on. "Right. How's your training going, Tomark?"

"It's good. I think we all learn the same basic stuff at the beginning, like controlling and fighting with our elements. But my favorite part has been learning to fly."

"You can fly?" Ashlyn asked, like she'd never heard of the concept.

"Of course he can fly," Amber sneered. Her superior tone seemed to have intensified since entering the dining hall. "All of the Air Favored can fly. Haven't you been a Favored for several years now? How do you not know that?"

"Amber," Kym snapped, finally fed up with her. "That's enough. So what if she didn't know? I didn't know. I bet there's one thing you don't know about one of the other elements. They're all different, after all. Just because the Rulers gave you a seven doesn't make you an expert."

Amber looked like she was about to retort, but Zara stood at the Rulers' table, and silence fell over the hall.

"Once again, I would like to welcome everyone to Crystal Palace. I hope that you are enjoying your meal and getting to know each other. We do not get the opportunity often, so take this chance to learn something from the Favored of the different elements. Each of you will be sharing a room with one other Favored. Once you have chosen your roommate, please let an attendant at the head table know, and they will sort everything out."

Kym and Kat immediately stood and walked to the nearest attendant, and informed her they'd like to room together. Up at the head table, Kym saw Nila, seated between Melana and Kai, stare at Kym with a look she couldn't quite place. It wasn't anger, though Kym was sure Nila wasn't thrilled about her rooming with Kat; it was more like disappointment.

They followed their attendant through a maze of stairs, doors, and passages before finally turning into a small hallway lined with identical doors. The attendant stopped at one about halfway down the hall and stepped aside to let Kym and Kat enter the room. It was just as large as Kym's bedchamber back at Wadita, but looked smaller thanks to the second large bed. Their blue and green trunks arrived less than a minute after they did, each carried by two servants, who placed them at the foot of each bed. Kym opened the curtains, eager to see the view, but all she could see was blackness.

After quickly washing and changing into their pajamas, Kym and Kat sat on the foot of their beds, facing each other. They didn't speak, but Kym knew they must be thinking about the same thing. Finally, after glancing at the door like she thought someone might burst in at any moment, Kat spoke in a soft voice. It was like she thought the walls were listening to them.

"What do you make of it?"

Kym sighed, and she was a little surprised to find herself whispering too. "Honestly, I don't know what I think. I didn't believe the Rulers would consider doing something like this when I heard it at Wadita. All I wanted was to forget it, but how can I forget it when I heard them say the words?"

"It seems crazy, but does it really shock you after getting to know them? Is this so out of character for them?"

"I buy them wanting more power. I would've believed that even before I was a Favored. But all this craziness about overthrowing the gods…"

"To be fair, that's Melana's craziness. And you heard them. Most of the Rulers are too afraid they'll get their butts handed to them to do anything anyway. It's a fight they can't win."

"But what if the Rulers use the Favored to even the odds?" Kym asked. "Like Amber said?"

"It'll never happen," Kat said dismissively.

"But what if it does? Amber's not the first person I've heard say that?"

"Kym, c'mon," Kat said, her tone a little gentler. "They can't force us to fight for them, even if it did come to that. And if they do ask me to fight, they can count me out. I'd never be caught dead in a battle with the gods, especially since the gods are gods, and we aren't."

"Yeah," Kym said, laughing softly, looking at the small clock on her bedside table. "It's getting late; we should get some sleep."

"I guess so," Kat sighed. "Night."

"Goodnight."

Kym extinguished the lamps and climbed into her bed, which felt like cool air on her hot skin. Her body ached with exhaustion from the day, and all Kym wanted was to sleep, but her head buzzed with the Rulers' conversation. It played over and over in her mind, and Zara's decision was the highlight of the show. For one frightening moment, Kym thought Zara would declare war on the gods. Images of battle flashed through her mind as the war that might have been invaded her thoughts. No matter who won, all that was left was destruction.

Her mind finally starting to quiet, Kym remembered what Kat said about not fighting if it came to it. Could she turn her back on everyone she cared for at Wadita if they marched into battle? Would she really defy Nila if she asked her to fight? Many more questions flooded Kym's mind as she eventually fell into a restless sleep.

L E A R N I N G   T H E   R U L E S

SOMETHING LARGE AND SOFT LANDED ON KYM'S FACE, JOLTING HER awake. She thrashed around, entangling herself in the sheets as she rolled onto the floor. She emerged, spluttering, her hair flying wildly around as she tried to discern what hit her. She found her answer in the form of Kat, who stood on her bed, a pillow held over her head.

"Finally," she said, dropping the pillow as she bounced into a sitting position. "I thought you would never get up."

"What time is it," Kym groaned. The curtains were drawn and the lamps unlit, leaving the room dark.

"Not sure," Kat shrugged. "I woke up a while ago."

"And you thought the best thing to do after that was wake me up?" She couldn't stop herself from chuckling.

"Waking you was already a done deal. The real question was whether I used a pillow, or tackled you."

"Oh…well I'm glad you went with the first choice," Kym smiled.

Kat hopped down from her bed and offered Kym her hand. She took it gratefully, but still slipped on the sheets wrapped around her feet. Once upright, Kym opened her trunk to look for something to wear. Aside from the training clothes she'd worn the day before, the trunk was full of dresses and gowns. Even with them so far away, the controlling reach of her lady's maids was inescapable as she extracted the simplest dress she could find.

Kym and Kat talked the whole way down to the dining hall, resulting in their getting lost numerous times before finally stumbling through the door. The room was full, with most of the tables already occupied with anxious-looking Favored. Relieved she didn't have to worry about anything for the next several days, Kym sat at the same table they used the previous night, where Tomark sat alone.

"How'd you sleep?" Tomark asked, gesturing at them with a forkful of scrambled eggs.

"Fine. Until a pillow attacked me," Kym tried to sound serious, but couldn't stop herself from laughing.

"A pillow?" Tomark asked, his eyes darting between Kym and Kat, who was also laughing.

"It didn't attack you," Kat said, plopping down into an empty chair. "It flew through the air really fast and landed on your face."

They continued to laugh as two servants arrived with trays of food, and soon the sound of forks scraping against the glittering silver plates replaced their laughter. The rest of their party trickled in as they ate, looking oddly relaxed in the sea of stressed and anxious faces. Kym couldn't understand why they all looked so scared. The evaluation wasn't even that difficult. Sure they got scored, but that was no reason to look like they were marching to their deaths.

"Ugh," Amber moaned. "We have only been here a day, and I'm already sick of this place."

"I wouldn't mind going home," Pupil said, staring blankly around the packed room. "It's not like they let us do anything fun while we're stuck here."

"Would they let us go?" Kym asked.

"As if," Pupil snorted, apparently thinking her question was an obvious one.

"We have to stay," Ashlyn said, her tone gentler. "But don't worry. We won't be stuck here for long."

"Well I've been here countless times," Amber said superiorly, "and there's absolutely nothing to do."

"I'm sure we'll find something," Ashlyn said.

And find something they did. The Rulers announced which groups would be evaluated that day, and the hall emptied in a matter of minutes. Those getting evaluated went to their prep rooms, while the rest returned to their bedchambers, some looking even more nervous than those being evaluated. Kym, Kat, Amber, Ashlyn, Tomark, and Pupil sat alone in the now-empty dining hall. They sat there for a while, then Kat slammed both her hands on the table, making the rest of them jump.

Kat stood silently, her head moving slowly from side to side as she looked around the hall. Perplexed, Kym just watched Kat until suddenly, her head stopped moving. She marched from their table to one right next to the doors. The utensils and dirty dishes had been cleared away, leaving only the long tablecloth on its surface. Kat grabbed a fistful of the white fabric, yanked it off the table, and continued to march out of the dining hall.

Kym and the others stayed in their seats, seemingly unable to move. What was Kat doing? Suddenly, her loud voice rang back into the dining hall.

"Hey, slowpokes. Let's move!"

They raced after Kat, who was already at the other end of the corridor, dragging the tablecloth behind her. They caught up with Kat as she struggled to open a locked door at the end of the hall. Undeterred, Kat rammed the door with her shoulder, and it burst open onto a vast garden that stretched to the very edge of the mountain. Kat walked to the middle of the field, where she stopped and roughly tore the tablecloth in two.

"What the Thed are you doing?"

"Well, Princess, if you must know," Kat shot back at Amber, sounding annoyed, "we're going to have fun. We're stuck here until the evals are over, so we might as well enjoy ourselves."

"And how does ripping a sheet do that?" Amber snapped. Apparently, she didn't like being called *Princess*.

"We are going to play a game," Kat continued, talking over Amber. "I assume everyone except Miss Priss knows what capture the flag is?"

"That's it!" Amber invoked her Marks, and a fiery red orb appeared in her hand.

"Calm down, Amber," Kat said, apparently sensing she'd taken it too far. "I was joking."

Kym stepped forward and put her hand gently on Amber's shoulder. She felt Amber's shaking body relax as she lowered her hands, her fire fading away. Kym's body shook too, but it was mostly because of the laughter she was trying to suppress. Kat could make Amber go from zero to a hundred in the blink of an eye.

"So we're playing capture the flag?"

"Not exactly, my young Pupil. We're playing capture the flag, but we're gonna do it Favored style. We'll use bolts, blasts, and shields, and you're out if you get hit when you are not on your side of the field."

"Sounds like fun," Ashlyn grinned.

"How do we get back in once we're out?" Pupil asked, his usual air of boredom replaced by something resembling excitement.

"How should I know?" Kat shrugged. "I can't make up all the rules."

"Are we really gonna fight each other?" Tomark asked.

"C'mon. It's just for fun."

"I guess," Tomark said slowly. "I say wait a couple of minutes after you're out, then come back in."

"Are we really doing this?" Amber muttered so only Kym could hear her.

"It sounds fun. At the very least you'll blow off some steam."

They hung the two halves of the tablecloth in a tree and over a very large bush after dividing into groups. The two teams lined up to face each other on either side of a thin line Kat made across the entire field. Kym, Kat, and Amber stood on one side, while Pupil, Ashlyn, and Tomark faced them, all waiting for Ashlyn to signal the start of the game.

"Go!"

Kym raced back toward the bush with their flag while Amber and Kat stayed at the line. There was a small pond peppered with stones and several fish halfway between the flag and the center line. By the time Kym reached their flag, she had two bolts ready in her hands. Amber and Kat were already attempting to reach the other flag guarded by Ashlyn. They split apart, trying to take on Ashlyn from both sides.

A bright-violet bolt whizzed past Kym, blowing her hair back. Pupil stood before her, another violet bolt floating in his hand. Tomark stood a little behind him, his silvery shield already formed. Kym threw her bolts at Tomark, but his shield easily blocked them, and they ricocheted off to the side. Another darkness bolt flew toward her, but she deflected it with a shield. Smiling, Kym divided her shield and threw a bolt at each of them. This was easier than she thought. It was just like sparring with another Water Favored.

But that wasn't entirely accurate. Kym was so focused on keeping Tomark at a safe distance, she didn't notice the long, dark shadow sliding across the ground.

"Boo," Pupil whispered from behind her.

Kym whipped around, startled by Pupil's sudden appearance. She lost her concentration, and the bolt floating in her hand vanished as she fell to the ground. Laughing, Pupil took the flag from the bush and raced back to his side of the field.

"Cheater!" Kym called, scrambling back to her feet and chasing after him.

"Cheater?" Pupil asked, trying and failing to sound innocent.

"Yes. You cheated. It doesn't count. Give it back."

"What's going on?" Amber demanded as the others joined Kym and Pupil in the center of the field.

"Pupil cheated."

"Don't be a sore loser," Pupil smiled. "It doesn't look good on you."

"I'm not," she said. "You broke the rules. We agreed on basic combat magic only. I'm sure that shadow thing you do is about a million miles from basic."

"Seriously, Pupil?" Tomark asked. "Should we just stop?"

"Maybe he forgot?" Ashlyn offered.

"Yeah, and I'm a bunny rabbit," Kat said, rolling her eyes. "We all know Pupil didn't forget, but it's just a game, guys. We're just trying to have fun. We can't do that if we're stopping every five seconds to debate the rules. So, we're all sticking to the basics so we can actually have some fun."

And they did have fun. Even Amber looked like she was enjoying herself by the time the sun began to set. She walked next to Kym, both red-faced and sweaty, back to the palace. Recalling Amber's words from the prep room, and the exceptional score she received from the Rulers, Kym had to admit Amber was right. Even though they were all doing basic combat, Amber's attacks were more precise and faster than anyone else's. She really was the best Kym had ever seen.

"You are really good at this."

"As are you," Amber conceded, "for a beginner."

"No one's better than the Fire Princess," Kat said, appearing on Kym's other side, dragging the tattered remains of the tablecloth behind her. "At anything. Isn't that right?"

Kat ran ahead before Amber or Kym could say a word. Kym looked at Amber, and she could almost imagine the flames flickering behind her golden eyes.

"Don't let her get to you. She's just trying to be funny."

"She called me Fire Princess," Amber sighed, and for the first time since meeting her, Kym saw Amber waver.

"Is that bad? She's been doing it all day."

"You don't know anything, do you?" Amber stopped walking. She looked up to the sky, and it was like she was struggling to say something. Finally, she seemed unable to hold it in anymore. "All of the Favored, even those who live with me at Inferon, think I am this cruel, unkind, ruthless person who thinks I'm better than everyone else. Well, I am all of those things, and there's no sense denying them. But I'm more than that, more than the 'Fire Princess.'

"My father's a Fire Favored, and when I was born, Lord James sensed the magic already inside me. They sent me to Inferon, and I've lived there my whole life. I've been waited on hand and foot, and nothing was ever out of my reach. For as long as I can remember, I've been told how special I am—the only Favored chosen from birth. I was told I was better than everyone around me, and I listened.

"My father didn't help. Whenever he visited me at Inferon, he brought me gifts and started teaching me magic when I was very little. I was only allowed to visit my mother when I turned nine. She doesn't have magic and is a teacher in one of the cities.

"My mom doesn't like the Favored lifestyle, and she wanted me to see how normal children acted. So for ten days, I went to regular school and dressed in the normal clothes my mother picked out for me. She tried her best to influence me, but she couldn't override what I'd been told for years. One day, I was walking into the classroom and Kat, who was a student of my mother's, accidentally bumped into me. 'How dare you?' I yelled at her. 'Don't you know who I am? Apologize at once, or I will end you.'

"She ran away in tears. My mom tried to explain I did something wrong, but I didn't understand. How could I? Anyway, Kat's never forgiven me for what I did, for not knowing any better."

"So why do you still do it?" a voice asked quietly. Kym hadn't noticed Tomark standing a few feet away from them. "That's exactly how you've treated us. Why don't you change?"

"I…" Amber trailed off, apparently struggling to find the right words. Her whole body seemed to deflate, the constant perfection she always exuded melting away. It was like seeing a whole new person appear before Kym's eyes. "It's what's expected of me. Most of the Favored know who I am, or have heard of me. They expect to meet the person they've heard about."

"The Fire Princess," Kym breathed. She knew a thing or two about living with other people's expectations and could tell Amber wanted none of this.

Kym stood there, waiting for Amber to do something, anything. She glanced sideways at Tomark, who stared at Amber like he'd never seen her before. Kym felt like she should say something but couldn't think of the right words. Amber sighed, and her body regained its usual demeanor. Without saying a word, Amber walked back to the palace, gliding off like nothing happened.

"You need to lay off Amber," Kym said, closing the bedroom door behind her.

"What?" Kat asked, rolling over on her bed to face Kym.

"Amber told me what happened when you were kids."

"She did? Wow."

"Yeah, she did. And she seems really upset about it. Could you just let it go?"

"The Fire Princess got upset. I deserve a medal."

Kym couldn't believe her ears. Didn't Kat feel anything for Amber? She directed her hand at the water pitcher on the table. The water rose out of it and flew right at Kat. It wasn't energized, but still hit her with enough force to knock Kat off her bed. Kat spluttered, crawling to her knees, her wet hair hanging just low enough to cover her eyes.

"What the Thed was that for?"

"You need to forgive Amber. And stop calling her Fire Princess," she added, walking over to where Kat knelt on the floor.

"For the record, I forgave Amber for all that crap years ago. We were kids, and kids do stupid things, especially when one of them believes they're an untouchable 'fire princess' who's better than everyone. I haven't exactly told her about the whole forgiveness thing yet, but I'm over it."

"You don't have to tell her," Kym sighed. "But you need to act like it. Deal?"

"Deal," Kat laughed.

They met in the castle garden for the next three days to play capture the flag. They switched teams each day, so by the end of the last day, Kym had fought with and against every person in her evaluation group. Since they used different elements, Kym thought their magic would be different as well. But as the days passed, she realized she was wrong, at least on a fundamental level. All of the different-colored bolts, blasts, and shields worked exactly the same.

By the end of the evaluations, Kym felt quite close to her group. Sure, Ashlyn's constant positivity was a little much and Pupil and Amber were harder to read than rocks, but seeing them sitting next to Tomark in the morning always made Kym smile. Kat even stopped goading Amber, and after a couple days, Amber began to thaw again. It was like they'd all become friends, and she was actually sad to leave them.

Everyone gathered in the entrance hall after the final evaluation, once again organized by element. Kym craned her neck, trying to spot her new friends in the multicolored sea before her. She couldn't see them but noticed a disturbance in each colored group. It was like someone was trying to move through each of the tight crowds. Kym pushed her way through the Water Favored and found her new friends all standing in the middle of the room. For a moment they stood there in an odd, multicolored huddle, then all at once, pulled each other into one giant hug.

The Rulers led their Favored out to the carriages, which sat ready on the front drive. Each step felt like Kym was waking from a very good dream. Just like on the journey there, Kym road in a carriage with Kenna, Aidan, and Ryland. She'd spent so much time with her eval group, she'd hardly spoken to any of them since they arrived. The carriage lurched forward the second the door closed, heading back to Wadita.

"So," Kym said, trying to break the odd silence that filled the carriage, "how were your evaluations?"

"Who cares?" Kenna yawned, leaning back in her seat.

"Aren't the evaluation scores important?"

"Not really," Ryland sighed, lying longways in his seat, resting his head in Aidan's lap. "The Rulers give the scores because the gods say they have to. It honestly doesn't matter how well we do or not."

"Weren't you listening when we told you Nila wanted us to hold back?" Kenna asked.

"Then why do we even do them?" Kym asked, slightly annoyed by their blatant indifference.

"It's part of the deal," Aidan said. "We have to do them, but like Ryland said, they don't really matter."

"You hung with the Favored from your eval group a lot," Kenna said after a few moments of silence. "Was it horrible?"

Kym looked at Kenna, her eyes trained on the carriage roof. She knew what Kenna wanted to hear: that Kym had a horrible time with her group and was happy to be free of them. But why would she? She'd felt more at peace and like herself over the past five days with Tomark, Kat, Ashlyn, Pupil, and Amber than she ever had at Wadita. Why did Kenna, Aidan, and Ryland care if Kym enjoyed herself?

"It was great, actually," she said, turning her back on Kenna to stare out the window.

At Wadita, life returned to normal, at least on the surface. Kym trained with Ryland, Jax, and Jean under Kenna and Aidan's guidance, with occasional appearances by Nila. However, Kenna and Aidan stopped teaching them anything new. They spent their days practicing what they'd already learned while Kenna and Aidan critiqued their most minimal mistakes. All that mattered was how powerful their magic was.

Kym found herself longing for her friends from Crystal Palace. Besides Amber, none of them cared about how powerful she was. In fact, she'd learned more about them in five days than she knew about Kenna, Aidan, or Ryland after months. The more time she spent at Wadita, the more she realized she had nothing in common with the Favored there. So while she focused on her training, she secretly wished for a way to see Kat, Amber, and the others again.

An opportunity presented itself three weeks later. Kym ate her dinner in silence while Kenna, Aidan, Ryland, Jax, and Jean droned on about the various magical advances made by the Favored who'd left Wadita—their favorite topic. Uninterested, Kym got up and left. However, she stopped when the sound of footsteps filled the entrance hall. Turning around, she saw Nila walking straight toward her.

"I have a request," Nila said, looking down at her.

"Of course Nila—Lady Nila. What is it?"

"Tomorrow, I leave for the Summit of the Rulers at Crystal Palace. Each Ruler brings one Favored with them to listen to the discussion. This month, the opportunity is yours if you want it."

"I-I'm honored," Kym stammered.

Nila always took her top Favored to the Rulers' Summit, which usually meant Kenna or Aidan. But Kym? Was this a joke? But Nila wasn't the joking type, so she must believe Kym was ready for this. This could be precisely what Kym was waiting for. The chances were slim, but Tomark, Kat, Amber, Ashlyn, or Pupil could be at the Summit. She wasn't sure how the other Rulers picked who went with them, but if they were anything like Nila, there was a chance Kym could see one of them.

"We leave in the morning. I expect you will make me proud." Nila turned to address Kym's maids. "We depart before sunrise," she barked. "Ensure Miss Kymbralyn sleeps well."

Nila awkwardly patted Kym's arm, then disappeared through one of the many doors around the entrance hall. Kym stood where she was, unable to move, like Nila's touch had turned her to stone. "I expect you will make me proud." What did that mean? Did Nila think Kym would embarrass her in front of the other Rulers?

"What did Lady Nila want?" Kenna appeared at Kym's side, pulling her out of her stupor. "I saw her talking to you."

"She asked me to attend the Rulers' Summit."

"Oh! That's a big honor," Kenna said, pulling her into an uncomfortably tight hug. "What's wrong?" she added, seeing the concerned look on Kym's face. "You look like you're going to throw up."

"Nila said she expects me to make her proud. Does she think I'll make a fool of myself or something?"

"Tell you what; meet you in your room in ten minutes. We shouldn't talk about it here."

Ten minutes later, Kym sat cross-legged on her bed while Kenna paced in front of her. She spoke very quickly, barely pausing to breathe. She might not be the most genuine person, but at that moment, Kym was happy Kenna was there.

"First, you must always stand on Lady Nila's right side. When she sits, you need to take one step back, so you're behind her. I don't know why, but you need to keep your hands behind your back. Finally, and most importantly, only speak if a Ruler addresses you specifically, or if they open the topic for Favored input. Otherwise, keep your mouth shut. Even if they're talking about throwing all the babies in Princirum into the volcanoes in Igmonis, don't speak. If you want to speak, step forward so you're level with Lady Nila's throne. If Lady Zara thinks it is okay for you to speak, she will tell you. If not, step back."

"How the Nothingness was I supposed to know this?" Kym asked, rubbing her face in her hands. "I'd have been screwed if you hadn't told me what to do."

"Calm down," Kenna said smugly. "You know now. Just do everything I told you and you'll be fine. Trust me. I've done this loads of times."

Kym had barely slept when Veronica woke her. She led Kym into the bathroom while Isabel opened the curtains, which seemed pointless since it was still pitch black outside. Trapped in the groggy state between sleeping and waking, Kym hardly noticed her maids washing and dressing her. The first thing she was really aware of was walking through the entrance hall and out to the front drive, where Nila stood waiting next to a massive blue carriage. Kym climbed in after Nila and fell asleep as the carriage lurched forward.

The carriage jerked to a stop and Kym's eyes snapped open. The door opened, filling the carriage with blinding light as Nila silently exited. Kym hurried after her, stumbling over the hem of her dress as she squinted against the high sun. There were five other carriages parked along the drive, meaning all the other Rulers had arrived. Kym followed Nila into the entrance hall, where all the other Rulers, besides Zara, stood waiting.

Kym looked around the room, and excitement surged through her body like electricity. Kat, Ashlyn, Tomark, Amber, and all three of the darkness Pupils stood beside their respective Ruler. They were dressed more elegantly than she'd ever seen them, and Kym realized her own dress was fancier than usual. She only had time to give Kat a small wave before Zara stepped out onto the balcony above.

"We are ready to begin."

Zara turned, and the Rulers walked up the curved staircase to the second floor. The Favored hurried behind them, trying to keep up with the Rulers' giant strides. Panting, Kym realized Zara was leading them to the heart of the palace, which she hadn't explored during the evaluations. They walked for about five minutes when the hall opened into a vast, rounded room. Its tall, white walls were completely bare, supported by massive pillars, and an enormous pair of wooden doors stood closed opposite the hallway. The Rulers and Favored approached the massive doors, and servants dressed in white togas silently pulled them open.

The throne room was perfectly round with a vast domed ceiling. A skylight illuminated the single throne in the middle of the room. Kym assumed this must be Zara's, and she was right. The other Rulers sat in thrones positioned about two-thirds of the way between Zara's and the wall, forming a hexagon. Nila's throne was closest to the door, with Kai seated to her left and Melana on her right. The floor in between Zara's throne and the others' was set a couple of inches lower than the floor next to the walls.

"This Summit shall now officially be called to order," Zara began. "First, we must decide which Ruler shall host the Festival of Creation. Lady Melana, Lord Stailin, and I have all expressed interest in hosting the glorious event, which takes place in sixty days' time. We must also discuss the state of the four cities. Finally, we need to decide on law enforcement within the cities."

The Summit seemed to drag on forever. The Rulers took over an hour to decide who would host the Festival of Creation. Most thought Zara should host the event, but Melana and Stailin dug in their heels. They each spoke for at least twenty minutes about why they were better suited for hosting the festival. Zara's throne turned to face each speaker, who pled their case directly to her. Finally, they agreed to let

Zara host the event since it hadn't been held at Crystal Palace in seventeen years. Stailin's disappointment was nothing compared to Melana's, whose cold fury made her look even more frightening.

Next, the Rulers debated whether they should increase the size of the four cities. Nila, Evanna, and Kai were all for it, but everyone else seemed to think it was a bad idea.

"The people in the cities are cramped and crowded," Evanna said. "They deserve more space to grow. The Favored I have received the past several years clearly bear the signs of the lack of space. Providing them with more space should help with this issue."

"I'm not sure it would be wise," Stailin said. "If we give them more space, they will ask for even more, and the cities will become too large for Princirum to maintain. This lack of space is just a product of the current city ideals and will likely return to normal before long."

"Lord Stailin," Nila said, "they cannot help it if their populations rise. The people in the cities have always been loyal to us, and we should reward their loyalty. I'm sure we could spare some of our lands to give the people room to flourish."

Kym knew all too well what the Rulers were talking about. The cities were all planned to be a uniform size, and everyone needed to fit into the four of them. Initially, the cities were full of large parks, gardens, and open spaces, which were all converted into apartments and cheap houses to accommodate the rising population. From what she could remember, her parents' house had one of the few yards left in the city. She hoped the Rulers would decide to make the cities at least a little bigger.

"Why do we even bother helping the detested?" Melana asked, her voice emotionless. "Their value is of little importance."

Melana's words sent a tingle running down Kym's spine. *Detested?* What did that mean? It sounded like Melana meant those who lived in the cities. Kym's skin continued to shiver, and she knew that's exactly what Melana meant. The people in the cities might not be Rulers or Favored, but they were still human beings. They deserved to be treated with respect. Much to Kym's delight, the other Rulers stared at Melana, their shock clearly visible on their faces.

"The detested have no real use to us," Melana continued. "The gods have forsaken them. If they had not, they would have magic like the Favored. Their only redeeming quality is that they are a decent breeding ground from which the best can be collected and groomed. They deserve their current conditions."

White-hot fury boiled up inside Kym. The last time she'd felt this angry, she'd blasted Chloe into a wall. She couldn't believe what she was hearing. Somehow, her aunt and uncle drifted to the front of her mind. They were killed, tossed aside because the priests feared the Rulers would find out they'd spoken against them. But the Rulers didn't seem to care about the people in the cities at all.

Her hands balled into fists. Kym tried to stay put, but her anger propelled her forward. She stepped past Nila's throne and stared directly at Melana, flanked by her three Favored. When she spoke, her voice trembled with suppressed anger and rage.

"Lady Melana, that's the most vile, disgusting thing I've ever heard."

N O T   Y O U R
P L A C E

EVERY SINGLE PERSON IN THE THRONE ROOM, BOTH FAVORED AND Ruler, stared at Kym, their eyes wide with shock. But their shock was nothing compared to Kym's. She wanted to take the words back the moment they passed her lips, but she couldn't. She'd broken one of the Summit's most important rules; she'd spoken out of turn, and insulted Melana. One transgression may be forgivable, but the other certainly wasn't.

But strangely, Kym didn't care. She was sorry she broke the rules, but not for speaking up. No one, not even a Ruler created by the gods, had the right to talk about people the way Melana did. And if the other Rulers wouldn't stand against her, Kym would. She'd fight for her people, for her family, all treated horribly in the name of the Rulers and gods. No one should suffer the way her aunt and uncle did. So she stayed where she was, staring into Melana's dark, cold eyes.

"I have never," Melana said, her silky voice dripping pure venom, "been more insulted in my life. How dare you, a tiny speck, speak to a Ruler of Princirum that way? I expect more from your Favored, Nila. Are you not always preaching loyalty to the rest of us? Your mother might be the goddess of purification, but I doubt even she could wash the stains of this speck away."

Kym spoke before Nila could make a sound, her voice shaking with anger. "It's your job to look after the people of Princirum. You're supposed to guide us in the ways of the gods and protect us, but you act like we're dirt on the bottom of your shoes. I won't let you treat your people this way."

"Kymbralyn," Nila snapped. "Step back."

"No. I'm sorry. I'm sick and tired of you only caring about those with the greatest power. When I was little, I heard stories about the Favored protecting the cities from danger, but I'd hardly ever seen a Favored before becoming one. You've cut yourself off from the people and talk about them like they're less than human, but you have no idea what life in the cities is really like. There are no maids or servants, no giant palaces, or clothes covered in jewels. People get by with what they have, which is not a lot, but they manage. And no thanks to you."

Kym finally looked away from Melana's icy face, her eyes full of fiery anger, and turned instead to Nila. Her face was rigid as stone, and she stared at Kym through narrow eyes. Kym braced herself for the retaliation she was sure would come, but Nila remained silent as she continued to stare at her. Confused, she turned to the rest of the room. Most of the Rulers still wore shocked expressions, and Evanna's thin face was so white she looked like she might faint.

"Even though," Zara said slowly, finally breaking the silence, "it was not her place, I am touched by this Water Favored's words. When the gods left the world of men, they created us to stand in their place. They charged us with the sacred duty of protecting their greatest creation: Princirum. After hearing this young woman's words today, I realize we have failed in our duties." An angry swarm of muttering broke out at these words, but Zara pressed on.

"We have spent centuries attempting to maintain our great status, but we have forgotten the purpose of our creation. The people of Princirum, whether they live in the cities or grand palaces, deserve our equal attention and respect. Those residing in the cities have counted on us, and I now see that we have failed them. But how can we know of their struggles since, as this young woman stated, we have never lived in the cities ourselves? I call upon the Favored to step forth and speak now, for they know of life in the cities in a way we never shall."

Kym couldn't believe her ears. She'd expected Zara to punish her, like sending her to fall off the edge of the world. But instead of punishing her, Zara agreed with Kym. Relief spread through her body, extinguishing some of the fire Melana's words had ignited inside her. Zara wanted things to change, and she also wanted to hear the full story before making a decision.

The rest of the Favored stepped onto the sunken portion of the floor. She'd been so focused on the Rulers' reactions she didn't even notice her friends'. On her left, Kat merely stared at Kym, her mouth slightly open, and for the first time since Kym met her, seemingly lost for words. Kym looked to Tomark, standing on the other side of the room, slightly to Kym's right, and saw the shadow of disappointment flash across his face. Before she could even think about what that could mean, Zara instructed them to begin.

"I think," Ashlyn said, her voice cracking slightly, "the cities need more protection. Sure, they're surrounded by walls, but those are centuries old and even crumbling in places. When death demons attack, crumbling walls don't do any good."

"I agree," Tomark said, standing a little straighter as Zara's throne turned to face him. "Walls are nothing when death demons are involved, and the city patrols are not equipped to handle them. I grew up in the City of Contellus, and when I was little, a death demon attacked. It went on a rampage, running through the streets and destroying everything it touched. The patrol tried to stop it, but there was nothing they could do." Tomark stopped, and Kym could see the pain etched across his face. "So many people died...in-including my parents."

Kym wanted to run across the room and pull Tomark into her arms. The urge came from out of nowhere, but seeing Tomark in so much pain made her entire body ache. She didn't know he'd lost his parents. Having also grown up in the City of Contellus, Kym remembered that day like it was yesterday. The death demon attacked the opposite side of town, but Kym and her parents still stayed inside for days, afraid another demon would appear after the first finally vanished.

"Where were you?" Kat asked, her voice uncharacteristically

quiet. "Like Kym said, it's your job to protect the people. You told all of us it was our duty to defend the cities from death demons when we became Favored. But I've never seen any Favored sent anywhere, and I've been a Favored for months."

"Well," Zara said, "the death demons have never presented any real threat."

"To whom?" Pupil asked, stepping ahead of the other Darkness Favored. "The Rulers? The demons attack the cities because they aren't mindless beasts. They know they'd be crushed if they attacked the Rulers on their own turf. But in the cities, death demons are a real threat. They're not prepared to defend themselves against a demon attack."

"What would you do, my young Pupil?" Pupil seemed to shrink several inches as Melana spoke. "Send the Favored to deal with every little problem the cities cannot face?"

"Well, like we said," Ashlyn piped in, "death demons are not little problems—"

"Was I speaking to you?" Melana snapped.

"If we aren't going to use our magic to protect people, why even bother to train us?" Kat asked harshly. "What's the point of just having us around?"

Kym saw the Rulers exchange quick looks with each other before turning their attention back to the Favored. Judging by their expressions, she was sure they were all thinking about their now-banned plan to overthrow the gods. Apparently, the theory of a Favored army wasn't too inaccurate after all.

"You are trained," Evanna said quickly, attempting to cover up the awkward moment, "so you do not waste your divine skills."

"But we're wasting those 'divine skills' by not using them," Kym said. "You've taught us so many incredible things, and all we do with them is get evaluated once a year."

"I agree with Kym," Amber said slowly. "I was never raised in the cities like the rest of the Favored here, and I don't fully understand their struggles, but I do feel it is our duty as Favored to protect them if they are incapable of doing it themselves. We must use the gifts the gods gave us."

"You train us to fight," Tomark said, his voice still shaking. "Everyday, without fail, you have your Favored fight one another to determine who's better. You told us we're preparing to defend Princirum, but we never have. Instead, we just battle each other, and I don't see the point in that. Train us to fight the demons, not each other."

Silence followed Tomark's words. Kym wanted to say more, but every time she thought of something, she realized someone else already said it. Affection for all five of them rushed through her. They backed her up and even validated her outburst with their testimonies. When Zara finally spoke, Kym felt oddly small as Zara looked down on everyone from her raised throne, bathed in golden light from the skylight above.

"The Favored will step out into the hall. We need a moment to discuss these matters privately."

The doors to the throne room swung inward of their own accord, creaking slightly. Feeling like the wind had been knocked out of her, Kym led the way out of the throne room and into the hall. Once all the Favored were outside, the throne room doors shut with a soft thud. The two Darkness Favored Kym didn't know stepped to one side, leaning silently against the smooth white walls. Pupil walked over and joined Kym and the others in the center of the rounded hall, and they all began to speak in hushed whispers.

"Holy Nothingness, Kym," Kat gasped. "I didn't know you had a death wish. What the Thed is wrong with you? I'd never say that to any Ruler, not even if you paid me a hundred oratem. And you said that to Melana, of all people. Did you see her face?"

"I'm happy you said it," Tomark said. "But I don't think you thought this through. You know we can't speak unless instructed to, right?"

"Of course I do," Kym said sheepishly. "A Favored at Wadita told me all about the rules before I left. But I- I couldn't...didn't you hear what Melana said?"

"Of course we did," Ashlyn said, accurately sensing Kym's rising temper. "But what could we do? We weren't allowed to speak."

"Well, I couldn't stand there. Hearing her call them 'detested'; it just set me off. I'd stepped into the middle of the room and told Melana to shut up before I even knew I wanted to speak."

"Well," Pupil said, and Kym was shocked to see him grinning, "if it's any consolation, she took it better than I thought. Most people don't speak to Lady Melana like that and walk away without a scratch. She doesn't like it when people make her look like a fool, and you just did that in front of the Rulers and their chosen Favored. I'd watch my back if I were you."

"Melana will need to get in line," Kym huffed. "Nila's going to kill me."

"I wouldn't be so sure," Ashlyn said. "She was smiling by the end of our little debate. She actually looked pleased."

"Pleased?" Kym was certain Nila was about as far away from pleased as she could be. "Why would she be pleased?"

"Are you really that thick?" Amber asked dryly, and when Kym didn't respond, she pressed on. "Lady Nila finally has a Favored with some fire. She usually just brought that one guy. What's his name? Allan?"

"Aidan."

"Yes, him. Well, anyways, I doubt he's said two words in all the Summits he's attended when Zara opened the discussion to us. But with you, she finally has someone who will speak her mind and won't back down, even when it may not be your place."

Kym hadn't thought of that. She knew Aidan had been to many Summits, and Kenna must have attended a few since she already knew the rules. Aidan and Kenna, who always did whatever Nila asked without question. They'd never speak out at a Summit, and if they did, they'd probably say what they thought Nila wanted to hear. Kym couldn't stop herself from smiling, even knowing the mountain of trouble she still had to face. Amber was right. It was time for the Water Favored to show a little backbone.

Before anyone else could speak, the throne room doors opened, and Zara's voice rang out from inside it.

"Enter."

Kym hurried back in with the others, where they quickly took their places behind their Rulers' thrones.

"After careful evaluation and considering the variables, we, the Rulers of Princirum, have reached a decision regarding the duties of the Favored. The Favored have lost their purpose as the centuries have passed. Therefore, we offer the following remedy: Those Favored who have shown the most skill from each element shall be responsible for Princirum's death demons. We Rulers can sense when they appear, and will send our chosen Favored out to vanquish these threats."

There was a moment's silence, then Zara's throne, which turned slowly while she spoke, stopped with its back to Nila and Kym.

"Is there something you wish to say, Favored of Fire?" Zara asked. Amber, blocked from Kym's view by Zara's throne, must have stepped forward.

"There is, my Lady Zara," Amber's voice rang through the room. "How will Favored be chosen for this great task?" To Kym's left, she heard Kat's snort of suppressed laughter.

"The manner of choosing shall be left to the discretion of each Ruler. If there are no other questions, we must continue our discussion of the size and protection of the cities."

The Rulers took over three hours to decide on the cities, during which time Kym and the others were not called to speak again. She tried her best to pay attention, but the Rulers' debates were so boring that she felt herself drifting off. But finally, the Rulers made a decision; they wouldn't give the cities more land since that would take land away from the Rulers themselves. However, they agreed to increase the size of the city patrols, which after everything, felt like a victory to Kym.

With the Summit finally over, the Rulers walked out of the throne room, followed closely by their Favored. Nila stayed silent as she led Kym through the various hallways and stairwells to the entrance hall, Kym jogging to keep up with her lengthy strides. The silence made Kym's sense of imminent danger, which was high enough when they left the throne room, grow into a full-blown panic. No matter what Amber said, Kym knew she wasn't going to get out of this unscathed.

Nila didn't stop walking until she reached her royal blue carriage, where she nearly knocked over the driver in her haste to climb inside. Kym clambered in after her, and as she looked over her shoulder, a vibrant green carriage sped past her and down the drive. Apparently, all of the Rulers wanted to get away from Crystal Palace as fast as they could. Kym closed the door and took her seat across from Nila, who sat in silence as the carriage began to pull away from the palace.

"Nila—Lady Nila," Kym corrected herself, her voice trembling slightly. "I…I know I messed up, and I'm sorry for speaking out of turn. I know I wasn't supposed to, but I'm not sorry for what I said. I couldn't just stand there and listen to Melana talk about people that way. No one was doing anything to stop her, so I felt I had to."

She stared into Nila's cold face, wishing she'd understand why Kym did what she did. She spoke out to stop Melana, not to make Nila look bad or weak in front of the other Rulers. Nila knew that, didn't she? If she did, Nila's cold, impassive face wasn't too comforting. They rode along in silence for several minutes before she finally spoke. Surprisingly, Nila's voice was calm.

"Kymbralyn, I do not blame you for defending the people you love and where you grew up. It shows me I was right to bring you today. However, your actions were inexcusable, no matter how noble your intentions. Lady Melana, though harsh at times, is the Ruler of Darkness and deserves your respect. When Lady Zara asked the Favored to leave the throne room, you were the first thing we discussed."

"Me? I thought you discussed the death demon problem?"

"We did. But first, your behavior warranted a discussion. As you may have expected, Lady Melana was furious. She wanted you executed," Nila said flatly, "but all the other Rulers objected. She then demanded we strip you of your magic and banish you from Princirum."

"Strip me of my magic," she repeated slowly. "You can do that?"

"Indeed, we can," Nila said, and for the first time since Kym met her, Nila seemed uncomfortable.

"How do you take a Favored's magic away?"

Nila took a deep breath and closed her eyes, and it looked like she was in pain. Finally, she said, "Only the combined might of the Rulers can reach inside a Favored and rip the magic from them. We only use it when the vote to remove the magic from one who no longer deserves it is unanimous. It has only ever been used once."

"Who'd you use it on?" Kym asked in almost a whisper. She wasn't sure if she wanted to know.

"A Fire Favored five centuries ago. He meddled in things he should not have; very dark things that have been forbidden ever since. We took his magic, but the strain was too much for his body to bear. He rolled around on the ground, thrashing and screaming, begging for mercy while he clawed at his flesh. He died before the process was complete."

Kym's entire body shook, and her stomach lurched as Nila's words sank in. She couldn't imagine the pain that man endured as his magic, which Kym always imagined as something living deep inside her, was ripped away from him. From what Nila described, the man had been using very evil magic. But did that even deserve such a fate? She doubted if anyone could survive having their magic ripped from them. Stripping a person of their magic was not a punishment; it was a death sentence.

"This," Nila continued, "was the fate Lady Melana wanted for you. And I must admit that she had support from a few of the other Rulers. However, I argued that your actions, though horribly out of line, were noble, and with the help of Lady Zara, we swayed the other Rulers to our side. They chose to forgive you, but only just."

"Thank you," Kym sighed. It was like a giant weight being lifted from her chest.

"I cannot guarantee the same outcome another time. I was able to defend you, as Lady Zara's approval of you was on my side. However, I may not be able to save you next time. You have shown such promise these past several months, promise I would like to reward with your continued presence at these Summits. But you must learn to hold your tongue. If you would like to speak, step forward and Lady Zara will allow it if she sees fit. But whatever you do, do not speak against Lady Melana again."

With nothing more to say, Nila settled back in her seat, gazing out the window at the passing countryside. Kym just sat there, her body numb and her mind buzzing. She'd expected to be told off, to be yelled at, or even punished. Images of Nila locking Kym in some dungeon for her actions swirled through Kym's mind. She didn't even know if there were dungeons at Wadita. But none of it mattered, because Nila wasn't punishing Kym. Instead, in her own way, Nila had complimented her. Unless Kym was mistaken, Nila actually seemed a little proud.

The ride back to Wadita seemed to take no time at all. The view from her window quickly transformed from magnificent, tall mountains to a sea of palm trees, the vast blue palace shimmering in the distance. Kym climbed out of the carriage and followed Nila up the front steps. Once in the entrance hall, she started walking toward the bedchamber stairs when Nila called after her. Kym froze. She knew she'd gotten off too easy.

"Did you need something, Lady Nila?" she asked, bracing herself for the blow.

"Yes. I have decided you will be the Water Favored I send to vanquish the death demons."

"Really?" With everything else going on, Kym had completely forgotten about the Rulers choosing Favored to fight the demons. "Are you sure you want to pick me?"

"I am. If you had not spoken out, there would be no need for me to choose anyone. This all started because of you, so it seems fitting that you are the one to protect Princirum from these beasts."

Unable to speak, Kym just stood there as Nila glided through the door that must lead to her chambers. Numbly, not even daring to believe her luck, Kym walked blindly up the stairs, not even aware of where she was going until she stumbled through her bedroom door. She undressed and breathed a sigh of relief. She'd worn the same tight dress since that morning, and she hadn't realized how uncomfortable it was until it was lying in a heap on the floor. She pulled on her favorite nightclothes and crawled under the cool covers. Happy the day was finally over, Kym gratefully shut her eyes.

C H A P T E R T H I R T E E N

V A N Q U I S H E R S

"H OW'D THE S UMMIT GO?"

"Huh?"

"C'mon, Kym. Tell us."

"What?"

Kym had been trapped in a daze the whole morning. The events of the Summit buzzed through her mind like a hive of angry bees. Half the time it felt like the entire thing had been a dream, then in a flash it became all too real. She didn't even remember walking into the dining hall with Kenna. They sat in silence until Aidan and Ryland joined them, and then the interrogation began.

"My maids said you and Lady Nila didn't return until late last night," Kenna pressed on, disregarding Kym's silence. "Why? What took so long?"

"It couldn't have been the Summit," Ryland said, turning to Aidan. "You're always back before dinner when you go."

"Must have been some Summit," Aidan said, his eyebrows raised. "What happened?"

"I..." Kym couldn't quite figure out where to begin. "Some unexpected things came up that the Rulers needed to discuss."

"That's a load of crap," Kenna burst out. "Holy Nothingness, Kym. Tell us what happened."

Luckily for Kym, Nila entered the dining hall at that moment, forcing Kenna and the rest of the hall into silence. She sat silently at Kym's table while everyone began to eat. In fact, Nila didn't say a word the entire meal. When the clink of cutlery started to die, Nila stood, and the low hum of chatter that started to fill the hall faded away. Anxious, Kym tried to gauge what Nila might say, but her face was just as stony and impassive as ever.

"Before you begin your training, there is something I need to tell you. At this month's Summit of the Rulers, we made a decision which affects one among you."

Kym turned to look at Nila so fast her neck cracked. A decision made at the Summit that was about one of them? Was she talking about Kym's outburst toward Melana? Absentmindedly rubbing her sore neck, Kym gripped the edge of the table so tightly her knuckles turned white.

"At the Summit," Nila continued, "it was brought to our attention that the Favored are not being used to their full potential. Therefore, each Ruler will choose one of their Favored to battle the death demons that appear in Princirum. These Favored shall be the Vanquishers, and the first Vanquisher of Water is Kymbralyn Collins."

Every pair of eyes locked on Kym, her face turning bright red as polite applause filled the hall. Kym couldn't help but let out a bit of nervous laughter. Everything just felt so ridiculous, from thinking Nila was going to call her out for what she did at the Summit, to the name the Rulers chose for those fighting the death demons. Vanquishers? Seriously? It was bad enough the Rulers felt they needed a name but calling them Vanquishers was even worse.

Nila glided from the hall, and the applause died the second she stepped over the threshold. Kym stayed in her seat, staring blankly at the table, while several people came up to wish her congratulations. When she thought enough people had left the hall, Kym lifted her head and found Kenna, Aidan, and Ryland all staring at her. She tried to make her face look normal, but the burning in her cheeks told her they were still bright red. Did they have to stare?

"Well," Kenna said, her words clipped, "that was something."

"Was it?" she asked, flustered. "Nila told me last night that she picked me." For some reason, Kenna's stare made Kym feel like she needed to defend herself. "The whole thing was kinda my fault, I guess. Nila said it should be me because of that."

"Oh," Aidan said, exchanging a not-so-subtle look with Ryland. Both his and Ryland's faces were set, unable to hide their scowls. "Well then, congratulations" Aidan continued, standing quickly. "We need to go. Jax and Jean are probably waiting for us."

Kym spent the rest of the day in what felt like a forced silence. Aside from their preliminary greetings, neither Jax nor Jean said one word to her the entire day. Ryland and Aidan were no better. Ryland seemed determined to make her know exactly how mad he was. They practiced evasive movements together, and all his attacks flew a little too close to Kym for her liking. Was he actually trying to hit her? Aidan didn't even notice what Ryland was doing. He spent the whole time critiquing Kym's swimming.

Kym skipped dinner that night, happy to find the peace and quiet of her room. That day had gone from strange to unbelievable to downright crazy. She climbed into bed before her maids arrived, wanting to just put the day behind her. It wasn't like she had asked to be a death demon fighter with a stupid name. Maybe after a good night's sleep, the others would realize that.

The next day started no better than the previous. People talked to her a little more, but Kym could tell from their forced tones that they were still mad at her. She decided to ignore it and focus on her training. This was the right call since they were practicing compact bolts, a skill no one in her group had mastered. As her tenth bolt blew up in her face, the door to the water dome opened and a Favored Kym only knew by sight swam in.

"Get out before you drown," yelled Kenna, who was instructing today.

"Kym's needed in the entrance hall at once," the young boy stammered.

"Well Kym's training," Kenna snapped. "She can't—"

"Lady Nila said it's urgent," the boy cut across Kenna, his voice cracking.

Kym burst into the entrance hall, where Nila stood waiting for her. "Kymbralyn, it is time."

"Um," Kym panted, not entirely sure what Nila was talking about. "Time? Time for what?"

"Time to fulfill your duty as Vanquisher of Water. I sense a death demon in the mountains of Contellus. It is not particularly powerful, and the Rulers agree two Vanquishers should be sufficient to handle it. Since Terradon is in Contellus, we will, of course, send an Earth Favored. The demon is close to the Contellus, Undarunci border, so you are the natural next choice."

Kym's head spun with questions, and she blurted out the first one that came to her lips. "How can the Rulers talk about all of this? I thought technology wasn't allowed at the palaces?"

"We have our ways."

More confused than she had been a second ago, Kym pressed on. "Is a carriage taking me? Are there roads in the mountains?"

"A carriage?" Nila laughed. "They are far too slow. You shall travel by water. The mountains are full of rivers, lakes, and streams, which all connect to the sea in one way or another. You will head west toward Contellus. Your magic will lead the way. The Vanquisher of Earth has already set out from Terradon. I suggest you do the same."

Nila turned and left Kym standing there, her mind so full of unanswered questions that she couldn't move. So she was just supposed to go out into the sea and start swimming west towards Contellus? She wasn't even sure which direction west was. She then needed to pick a river at random, and somehow find the death demon, all by letting her magic guide her? She had no idea what Nila was even talking about.

But, realizing there was nothing she could do about it, Kym ran through the halls. She burst into the garden, vaulted over the small wall, landed gently on the sandy ground, and sprinted towards the water. She invoked her Marks and dove straight into the sea. Unsure of which way was west, Kym turned right and began swimming up the coast.

She stayed near the sea floor, giving herself plenty of space as the water around her slowly rose and fell with the waves. She focused her energy on herself, and sped through the water while everything around her became bluish blurs. After about fifteen minutes, she passed through a current that didn't follow the typical rise and fall of the waves. She doubled back and rose to the surface for a better look.

Squinting in the bright light above the water, Kym tried to find the source of the strange current. She scanned the beach and noticed water pouring into the sea from the mainland. Nila said the rivers in the mountains all led back to the sea, but was this the right river? She still didn't even know if she was heading in the right direction. Deciding to just go with it, Kym dove back beneath the water, swam right for the river's mouth and started inland.

Swimming upriver was more exhausting than Kym ever imagined. Even at her top speed, the powerful current made her much slower, like she was pushing a giant boulder through the water rather than her slight body. At this rate, she thought she'd run out of energy before she even reached the death demon. All her worry was for nothing though, since as she swam, Kym never felt genuinely drained. Apparently, all her training in the water dome was paying off. But it would be pointless if she was going in the wrong direction, which was a real possibility.

Nearly half an hour later, Kym still couldn't tell if a death demon was near her, although she wasn't entirely sure what she was supposed to be feeling. She must have gone the wrong way after all. Frustrated, she began to turn around when she suddenly stopped. It was like a tiny spot inside her turned to ice. The feeling was faint and deep, somewhere around the area of her stomach. Confused, Kym looked down but couldn't see anything out of the ordinary. Was this her magic telling her she was on the right track? How could she tell? Kym decided to keep swimming upriver, though she moved a little more cautiously.

As Kym moved farther inland, the cold feeling inside her slowly spread through the rest of her body. The new places felt cold, while the older spots became clammy and stiff. She wriggled around as she swam, trying to rid herself of the growing discomfort, but it didn't work. Was this what death felt like—this cold, clammy stiffness? If it was, Kym decided she was never going to die, no matter how childish the idea sounded. Not if this awfulness was what it felt like.

She continued upriver, and the colder Kym felt, the darker the water became. Confused, Kym looked at her arms and stopped dead in her tracks. Her Marks, which always glowed so brightly, were dimmer than she'd ever seen them. She focused, and her Marks glowed brighter for a moment before fading once again. Could death demons make her magic weaker the closer she got? If so, she must be very close.

The cold feeling inside Kym suddenly lessened, and her Marks shone brightly in the water. She rose cautiously to the surface, barely letting her eyes rise above the waterline, where she saw something that made her gasp but also question why. Lying about fifty feet from the river, in the middle of a mountain valley, was a giant. A boulder the size of a small car sat on its chest, pinning it to the ground. The giant, which was at least thirty feet tall with pale, white skin and cold, black eyes, flailed its arms and legs around like a large, overturned bug.

"Nice of you to show up!" a harsh voice called from the edge of the river.

Looking around, Kym saw a short girl dressed in green crouching behind a boulder even larger than the one pinning the giant. Kat. Kym's face broke into a grin as she yelled back, laughing slightly.

"Oh, sorry. I took my time. I wanted to take in the views. Who beat up the giant for you, by the way?"

"Haha. Very funny," Kat said. "I did that"—she jerked her thumb toward the giant—"all by myself, thank you very much. Your services are no longer required. Run along n—"

The ground rumbled beneath them, and a deep roar filled the air, cutting Kat off. Looking around for the source of the noise, Kym saw the giant throw the boulder from its chest and clamber to its feet. It squinted at the ground like it was looking for something. Kym quietly emerged from the water and crept over to Kat, who was preparing to attack.

"Make a large hole in the middle of the field," Kym whispered, making Kat jump. "The giant's too far from the river, and there's no water for me to use over there."

"Right," Kat stretched one of her hands toward the field, her green Marks glowing, and a large cloud of dust rose into the air behind the giant. "It doesn't seem that smart, does it? I'll distract it so you can get water out there. Go."

Kat ran toward the giant while Kym faced the river. She made a column of water rise out of it with one hand, then used her other to direct it into the hole Kat had made with a loud splash. Making two bolts to take with her, Kym ran for the giant, ready to fight. But there was no fight. The giant just stood there, its head jerking this way and that at odd intervals. Kym looked frantically around for Kat's distraction, and when she saw it, her heart missed a beat.

Kat's idea of distraction was far different from Kym's. If Kym were going to distract a giant death monster, she would've kept a safe distance between her and the giant, throwing bolts at the ground near its feet, trying to knock it off balance. But Kat was not Kym. She stood right in front of the giant, throwing small earth bolts at its head while she screamed at it. Her voice carried back to Kym on the wind, and she didn't know whether to laugh or cry.

"Come on, ugly! You want a piece of me? Let's go! Come on, you big, fat baby! You're a sorry excuse for a giant! I've seen scarier butterflies!"

Kym didn't know if the giant understood a word Kat said, but it clearly didn't like the sound of her voice. The giant let out a roar that shook the nearby trees, causing several birds to take flight. It swiped down at Kat, who just laughed and sank straight into the earth. Kym stopped in her tracks. Where'd Kat go? The giant seemed to be struggling with the same question. It slammed the ground with its fists, like a baby throwing a tantrum.

Giving up on Kat, the giant whirled around and saw Kym standing in the middle of the field. It charged at her, the ground rumbling with each of its massive steps. She noticed the grass the giant stepped on, which had been a vibrant shade of green, now looked blackened and dead. Making a mental note not to let it touch her, Kym turned her attention back to the giant, and just in time, too.

The giant swung one of its massive arms down at Kym, and she dropped to the ground, quickly rolling out of its way. While the giant looked groggily around for her, Kym threw one of her bolts at the giant, hitting the underside of its massive chin. She then shot a blast at the giant's bulging stomach, hoping to knock the tottering beast to its back. But the giant merely took a few staggering steps before righting itself. It bared its blackened teeth at Kym. All she seemed to do was make the giant angrier.

Kym ran for the little pond Kat had made for her, and the slams of the giant's massive feet crashed behind her. When she was close enough, she made two more bolts and threw them blindly over her shoulder before diving headfirst into the shallow water. The giant's roars shook through the water as one of its massive hands plunged into the pond. The pure, bright water turned green and murky the moment the giant touched it, and Kym swerved to avoid the filthy sludge as it sank to the bottom of the pond.

Kym racked her brain, trying to think of something she could do as more clouds of green sludge sank around her. None of her attacks had made the remotest difference and only seemed to make the giant angrier. She needed something stronger, and then it hit her; a compact bolt. But that wouldn't work. She couldn't make one of those without it exploding in her face. But at the word exploding, she had an idea. She compacted as much of the pond water as she could, using more than half the water and making a bolt the size of a watermelon.

"Hey ugly!" she called above the water in a strained voice, struggling to keep the bolt from exploding.

The crashing behind her told Kym the giant was running for her again. She redoubled her efforts on the compact bolt, which pulsed wildly as arcs of energized water blasted from it. She couldn't hold it much longer. She waited until the giant was feet from her. As the giant's roars filled the air, Kym released her grip on the compact bolt and braced herself.

The explosion knocked her back through the water and into the shallow wall of the pond. Her ears rang, and she gingerly shook her head as she rose to the surface. The giant's large body smoked slightly as it swayed from side to side. Then, as though in slow motion, the giant fell forward. With an almighty crash it hit the ground, where it lay motionless.

Relieved, Kym climbed out of the now-nearly-empty pond. Chunks of stone and rock littered the ground behind the giant. Had her bolt caused all this damage? It couldn't have. Kym looked around, searching for the source of the rubble. Kat stood in the middle of the earthy wreckage, a wide grin on her face, her arms raised in an unmistakable sign of victory.

"Where the Thed did you go?" Kat demanded, sounding very annoyed. "I phased into the ground so I wouldn't get my head knocked off, but when I came up, you'd left and the giant was playing in your pond."

"Where did I go?" Kym laughed. "Where'd you go? All you did was yell at it and vanish. I did all the hard work by actually beating the thing."

"*You* beat the giant? I'm the one who hit it with a compact bolt. Well, kinda. I'm not good at them, to be honest. It sorta blew apart when it hit the giant. Where'd you think all of this rubble came from?" Kat asked, gesturing to the chunks of rock surrounding her.

"I hit it with a really bad compact bolt too," Kym laughed. "It was more like a poorly controlled explosion. We must've hit it at the same time. So what now?" she added glancing sideways at the still-motionless giant. "What do we do with it?"

"Not sure. But we should have a look at it. You know," Kat said, smiling broadly, "to make sure it's dead."

They walked over to the giant, Kym following a little behind Kat.

She didn't want to get near the demon, even though she knew it was probably out cold.

"Don't touch it," Kym snapped, grabbing tightly around Kat's outstretched hand, which was inches from the giant's shoulder.

"If I wanna touch it, I'm gonna touch it," Kat retorted as she tried to pull her hand free.

"Look at the grass." Kym pointed at the grass under and around the giant, which was blackened and dried like everything else it touched. "It's a death demon, remember? It must kill anything it touches."

Kat jerked her hand back, her eyes wide with shock. They stared at the giant's lifeless body on the ground, unsure of what they were supposed to do next. Thick, black smoke started rising from the giant, causing Kym and Kat to jump back several feet. The giant's body disintegrated into a mound of pure black ash, which sank slowly into the ground, leaving only the blackened grass in its wake.

"Thanks for that," Kat said, absentmindedly rubbing the hand she'd almost touched the giant with.

"No problem."

Kym turned away from the blackened grass, not wanting to look at it anymore, and took in her surroundings for the first time. They were standing in a valley covered in thick, green grass and peppered with little bushes. Small trees, no taller than fifteen feet, lined the river while wild flowers in a variety of blues, yellows, and whites littered the ground.

"So, what do we do now?" Kat asked. "Go back?"

"I guess," Kym shrugged. "Unless you want to hang and talk for a bit. I'm in no hurry to get back to Wadita."

"Sounds like a plan to me," Kat said, making two stone stumps rise from the ground for them to sit on. "Why don't you want to go back?"

"I dunno," Kym huffed, though that wasn't entirely true. "Everyone's been really weird the past few days. They wanted me to tell them about the Summit, but I didn't want to talk about it, and so they got mad at me. Then Nila told them about the whole Vanquisher thin-"

"Stupid name."

"I know, right? Anyway, Nila told them about it, and everyone just acted funny, like I'd done something wrong."

"You did nothing. They're just jealous because you're the Ruler's favorite and they're not."

"I'm not Melana's favorite. I know that much."

Kat waited a moment, then said, "Are you going to tell me what you mean or am I just gonna sit here and wonder?"

Kym told Kat everything Nila told her during their carriage ride; Melana wanting to take her magic away, the last time the Rulers took magic from a Favored, and Nila's warnings about not being able to protect her the next time.

"So," Kat said slowly. "Melana wanted to take your magic, and potentially kill you, just because you made her mad? That lady needs a serious reality check."

"It wasn't because I made her mad; it's how I spoke to her. Nila said several Rulers didn't like that I spoke my mind."

"It must have offended them somehow," Kat said, feigning puzzlement. Kym laughed and felt relaxed for the first time in days.

"But I don't see why," Kat continued. "She had it coming. If you hadn't said anything, I'm sure I would have. Melana loves power way too much anyway."

"I know," Kym said, thinking back to what everyone had told her about Melana. "And she always seems to want more."

"I know, right? Actually, I can't believe I forgot," Kat added. "Melana showed up at Terradon yesterday and wanted a private word with Kai. Kai's servants guarded the door, so I couldn't hear what they talked about, but when she left, she didn't look happy."

Puzzled, Kym looked at Kat. "Why was she at Terradon? I thought Kai was against Melana's ideas. She should know he won't go to her side."

"I think," Kat said, "she was looking for fresh meat. After the

Summit, Amber told me Melana has been going to Inferon a lot to talk to James. But he must not be interested in her ideas, so she switched to Kai instead. He's against Melana, but he's also the world's biggest pushover. She knows if she pushes him hard enough he'll fall onto her side."

So, Melana was trying to make friends with the other Rulers. But why? There was nothing she wanted that required backing from the rest of the Rulers, not unless she… Kym didn't have to think hard to find the answer. Melana was still trying to overthrow the gods. But Zara had made her plan illegal at the evaluation, so Melana must be trying to get support without Zara knowing. She must be meeting with the other Rulers to see who would back her in private before stepping out into the open. But it wasn't going well if both James and Kai refused her.

Even with the death demon gone, Kym's stomach once again felt cold and clammy. She'd thought the Rulers put overthrowing the gods behind them after the evaluations. But Melana seemed determined to get the power she somehow thought belonged to her, no matter what it took to get it. It was only a matter of time before this whole mess exploded around them.

O U R   O W N   S E C R E T   S U M M I T

"Can we just stay here forever?" Kym sighed, sprawled on the soft grass, her arms tucked behind her head.

"Well, I can," Kat said matter-of-factly. "This land belongs to Kai, so I can stay for as long as I want. You, on the other hand, are out of luck."

The sun crept steadily lower along the horizon, and the sky was a collage of pinks, reds, and oranges. They'd defeated the death demon hours before, but neither Kym nor Kat wanted to leave their unexpected paradise.

"Kai lets you leave Terradon and explore Contellus on your own? Nila would freak if I made it to the front drive without permission. She'd never let me explore Undarunci."

"You think I asked to leave that green prison?" Kat snorted. "That place drove me crazy after a grand total of two weeks; all the gowns, and crazy training, and the people. The people. I had to get out."

"So you sneaked out?" Kym asked as something stirred within her. Hadn't she felt just as overwhelmed when she arrived at Wadita?

"Don't be judgy," Kat said, and seeming to read Kym's mind, she continued, "I know you don't like it there. If you didn't, you would've left hours ago."

Wadita was the last place Kym wanted to be, especially with Kenna and Aidan acting like jerks. But sooner or later, she'd have to go back, and what then? She'd explode if the last few days turned into the norm. Why would she want to be around that? This day with Kat had been a break from the insanity, and even though it had only been a few hours, Kym already felt much better. Maybe a break from Wadita was exactly what she needed.

"Let's do this again," she said slowly.

"Fight a death demon? Yeah, it was oodles of fun, and I'm dying to do it again."

"No," Kym laughed. "Let's hang out. You said you sneak out all the time. So let's do it. Let's sneak out together."

Their plan needed to be simple, but careful. They'd do it on Saturday, no matter what was happening. After everyone fell asleep, they'd sneak out, and meet in this valley for a night of what Kat called "carefree laughs." Kym bid Kat good-bye at the river's edge, already eager for next Saturday to come. She dove in and began her long swim back to Wadita.

The full moon glowed in the cloudy sky as Kym resurfaced on Wadita's beach. The palace windows were dark, and the only sound was the rustling of the palm fronds in the breeze. She crept out of the water, trying to be as silent as possible. The moon drifted behind a cloud as she reached the garden, blanketing the entire palace in shadow.

A chill ran over Kym's body as she hurried to the back door, her heart racing. She grasped the cold knob, but when she tried to turn it, the door didn't move. Confused, she grabbed the knob with both hands and turned it, but the door still wouldn't budge. It felt like someone was pushing against it from the other side, keeping it closed. Kym turned it a third time, wanting to escape the oddly chilly air, and threw her shoulder into the door. It burst open and she fell to the floor, the door slamming into the wall with a crash.

Sprawled on the floor, her shoulder throbbing, Kym scrambled to her feet and quickly shut the door. She looked around, searching for who'd held it shut, but the hall was empty. Even more confused, her body still covered in that odd chill, she raced to the bedchamber stairs. Something cold and soft slid against her leg, and she spun around, clinging to the railing for support. But again, she saw nothing as she squinted through the dark. She continued up the stairs and felt the cold and slick something every couple of steps.

Kym was running by the time she reached the first landing, no longer worried about the noise she made. And as her speed increased, so did her discomfort. She looked around wildly, trying to see what was now grabbing her legs as she ran, but she still saw nothing. She rounded the corner and entered a hall filled with tall, thin windows as the moon drifted from behind a cloud, filling the hall with silvery light.

She hurried through the now-shadow-filled hall, and something unusual caught her eye. Her shadow was acting very strange. It didn't move in sync with Kym; doing everything a beat after her. Taken aback, she stopped and faced her shadow, which was cast along the wall in front of her.

Kym studied her shadow, waiting for something strange to happen, but it looked perfectly normal. She stepped to one side, but her shadow stayed where it was, firmly planted on the wall. Curious, and somehow unable to look away, she stepped toward the shadow, which started to bulge. Kym froze as the shadow pressed itself off the wall and, like a dark, formless mannequin, lunged at her. She scrambled backward, tripped over a rug, and fell shrieking to the floor.

"Calm down," hissed a harsh yet familiar voice. "Or you'll wake up the whole palace."

Confused and winded from her fall, Kym looked wildly around for the source of the voice. He stood right in front of her, his arms crossed as he stared down at her.

"What the Nothingness was that for?" she demanded, pushing herself into a sitting position. "You nearly scared me to death."

"Well," Pupil said dully, his face blank, "that was the plan."

"What? You wanted to terrify me?" Kym panted.

"Hey, it wasn't my idea. I'm just following orders."

"Oh," she said, realizing what Pupil meant. "Melana told you to do this, didn't she?"

"Lady Melana thought you deserved something after your stunt at the Summit."

"Well I'm honored," Kym said dryly. "You didn't have to do it, you know?"

"Didn't I? You may refuse requests from your Ruler, but I do what I'm told. Lady Melana only keeps three Favored, and if we don't do what she asks or meet her standards, she gets rid of us. So like I said, I do what I'm told."

For some reason, Pupil's statement struck a chord with Kym. Why would he do whatever Melana asked without question? If she asked him to jump off a bridge, would he do it? Kym would follow Nila's instructions, but only if she were comfortable with them. And terrifying someone for revenge was not something she was okay with. Especially when that person was supposed to be her friend.

"How'd you even know where I'd be?"

"Lady Melana knew you'd gone to fight the death demon, so she sent me here to wait until you got back. What kept you, anyway?"

"I took my time coming back," Kym said evasively. She didn't know why, but she didn't want Pupil to know about her and Kat's plan. But Pupil's face softened as she looked him up and down, and she decided to tell him. "Kat and I hung out for a while. We needed a break from all of this." Kym gestured around the hall.

"Sounds like fun," Pupil said, and though he didn't look it, Kym heard the longing in his voice. "Well, I guess my work here is done."

Pupil transformed into a shadow, sinking to the floor like he did during the evaluations. He glided slowly to the closest window, where he stopped, looking like he was midway through climbing out. It was like he was waiting for something. Kym hurried over to the window and, unsure where to look, addressed the middle of the shadow.

"Look, I know you did it because Melana asked you to, so don't worry about it. Tell her I fainted for all I care. But if you want to get away, Kat and I are hanging next Saturday. We're meeting in a mountain meadow near the Contellus-Undarunci border. Come, if you want a break."

Kym unlatched the window, filling the hall with crisp night air and the smell of the sea. Pupil stayed where he was, a shadow perched on the windowsill, showing no sign of leaving. The shadow of his hand slid over Kym's, which felt like she'd submerged it in a tub of icy water. Then, quick as a shadow, he slipped out into the night.

The week passed with the speed and excitement of a dead slug. Each day Kym hoped Nila would announce the arrival of another death demon, allowing her to escape from the prison-like palace. Kenna and Aidan's continued frostiness didn't help, and Kym avoided them whenever she could. But each day ended with no word from Nila, and Kym felt a mingled mixture of sadness, guilt, and happiness. She was disappointed about not leaving the palace but glad a death demon wasn't attacking. And to top it all off, the guilt from wishing one would appear just made everything more confusing.

Saturday passed in silence, so Kym quietly prepared her escape. This was harder than it sounded, since she was always surrounded by other Favored or accompanied by her maids. Insisting they should prepare her bedroom, something she'd fought against since arriving, her maids eagerly left her in the emptying dining hall. When she was the only person left, she ran into the entrance hall and grabbed a long rope from the cupboard, hiding it in the folds of her gown. Kym threw the rope under her bed just as Veronica and Isabel walked out of the closet.

Once her maids left, Kym changed into her training clothes, grabbed the rope, and hurried out onto the balcony. She tossed one end of the rope over the banister, praying no one would notice as it landed on the sandy ground with a thunk. She started to tie her end of the rope to the railing, her hands shaking with excitement. A loud knock echoed through her room. Kym jumped, and her trembling fingers lost their grip on the rope. It slithered out of her hands, and before she knew what happened, the rope vanished.

Another, more urgent knock rang through the room, making Kym jump again. Who could it be? Most Favored were in their rooms by this time, even on a Saturday. Someone must have seen the rope slide past their window. But how did they get here so quickly? Kym took a deep breath, trying and failing to calm her nerves, and hurried to open the door.

"What kept you?" Nila demanded, pushing past Kym without even waiting for a response. "Lord Stailin has sent word that a death demon has been attacking the coast of Silvaura, his realm, for the majority of the day. He thought a single Favored from Alfonburg could handle things, but the situation has escalated. He has requested I send a Water Favored at once."

Kym's entire body, which had been so tense moments before, relaxed. There was another death demon attack. She wasn't in trouble for trying to sneak out mere moments ago. She didn't even think Nila knew. She closed her eyes and felt her heart rate slow. She was in the clear, so long as she hid the rope lying on the beach before anyone found it.

"I see you are already dressed," Nila said. Her eyes narrowed as she surveyed Kym, already dressed in her training clothes.

"Yes, um…" Kym said, thinking fast. "I was…going to train tonight. Before bed," she added hastily. "But now I'll leave straightaway."

Kym waited an entire minute before leaving her room. She sprinted through the halls, unable to contain her excitement, bouncing off the walls before bursting into the entrance hall. She raced out the front door, which was left ajar, and ran the long way around the palace until she was directly below her bedroom balcony. She quickly gathered the coils of rope and stashed it in a patch of the tall, thick grass that peppered the sandy beach. Thinking there were worse hiding places, Kym ran straight into the sea.

She sped through the water, traveling away from her and Kat's meeting place since Stailin's realm, Silvaura, was on the opposite side of Princirum as Contellus. Since Nila said the demon was attacking the coast, Kym stayed as close to the coast as she could. The soft beaches she'd come to know slowly faded away, replaced by vast, white cliffs. Confident she was headed in the right direction, her mind quickly drifted to the coming battle, and more importantly, who'd be there.

Tomark lived at Alfonburg, so there was a chance he'd be there. Stailin had brought Tomark to the last Summit, after all, but did Stailin make him the Vanquisher of Air like Kai and Nila had for Kat and Kym? And if Tomark was there, Kym could ask him to join her and Kat if they got rid of the demon in time. There was little chance of Kat showing up, since Kai and Stailin didn't get along, but what if someone else came?

Kym swam on, fighting against the current as the waves grew steadily larger. Sand swirled up from the ocean floor, clouding the water so she could barely see a few feet in front of her. The water was so erratic and choppy that Kym's body started to tingle with discomfort. She couldn't wait to return to Wadita's calm waters. Suddenly, a massive tentacle, jet black and slimy-looking, darted out through the gloom, right in front of her.

Kym reacted at the last possible moment, making an oval-shaped shield just as tall as she was. However, she wasn't fast enough. The shield only partially formed when the massive tentacle made contact. It blocked the death energy emanating from the tentacle, but that was all. The shield shattered, and the force of the blow sent Kym flying high out of the water.

She flailed through the air, a newborn bird prematurely pushed from the nest. She felt her body slow as it rose higher into the air, then, for the slightest of moments, all time stopped. She neither rose nor fell as her heart pounded in her throat. Her stomach lurched, and instinctively she reached upward, but it was useless. She'd already started to fall back to earth.

The wind pressed harder and harder against her face, and Kym tried to think of something, anything, to get her out of this. She didn't care how magical she was; hitting the water from this height would be the exact opposite of painless. But then it came to her; she needed to hit the water as soon as possible. She directed her hands toward the water below, concentrating with all her might. A column of water rose into the air and would reach her in a matter of seconds.

A tentacle whipped out from the depths of the dark water, and Kym's heart sank. She took the water from the column, which was mere feet from her, and formed another shield. No longer concentrating on the column, it exploded into a million tiny water droplets. The tentacle swatted her, breaking Kym's shield and sending her even higher into the air.

She closed her eyes, bracing herself for the impact she knew would come. Then, something moving very fast slammed hard into her side. Kym's eyes snapped open as she crashed to the ground, the thing that hit her wrapped tightly around her middle. Winded, her mouth full of a mixture of dirt and her own hair, she looked around. Tomark lay on the ground a few feet away from Kym, his wavy hair coated in even more dirt than hers.

"Did you need to tackle me out of the sky?" she grimaced, clutching her side.

"Sorry," Tomark groaned, pushing his hair out of his face, "my flying skills are not the best."

"That wasn't flying."

"Hey!" a vaguely familiar voice called from several feet away. "I didn't come all this way to fight this thing on my own. Help me!"

Amber stood at the very edge of the cliff, illuminated by the massive tentacle she'd set on fire. Kym hurried to the cliff's edge, and from the light of the still-flaming tentacle, saw what they were fighting. The only thing she could think to call it was a squid. She'd read about them in school, but no squid should ever be that big. It was at least 200 feet long and attempting to pull itself up the cliff with a never-ending supply of tentacles.

A slimy, black tentacle shot up from the demon, slamming onto the ground, which blackened and cracked at its touch. Kym jumped back, not wanting to get hit by a tentacle for a third time, and looked for a source of water; but there was nothing. No river. No stream. Not even a pond. The closest thing was the seawater, but that would never make it up the cliff in one piece.

Kym backed away from the cliff, fear bubbling up inside her. Her foot caught on something hard, and she fell to the ground. Desperate, she looked at the sky, almost asking it to provide some water for her. And miraculously, virtually out of nowhere, it started to rain.

Kym stood, forming two bolts from the water falling through the air. She joined Tomark and Amber at the cliff's edge, where they were attempting to blast away the tentacle clinging there. Kym threw her bolts while Tomark sent a silvery blast at the ground beneath the tentacle. It recoiled, rearing up like a snake preparing to strike. Two bright-red bolts flew past Kym's head and hit the tentacle right in its massive suckers. Turning around, Kym stepped out of the way just in time to avoid Amber's blast. Kym shot one of her own at the tentacle, and together she, Tomark, and Amber forced the tentacle off the cliff.

But their victory was short-lived. Mere moments after the first tentacle returned to the squid, another rose up to take its place. Kym, Tomark, and Amber attacked, but before they could force the tentacle to retreat, another one appeared several yards away. Before Kym knew it, she, Tomark, and Amber were repelling five different tentacles at once.

"This isn't working!" Kym shouted through the rain as she threw bolts at tentacles in no particular order.

"We need a new plan," Tomark agreed, a tentacle shattering his shield.

"I got it," Amber yelled, looking over the cliff's edge. "It's just hanging onto the cliff now. We need to blast the body and stop attacking its fingers."

Amber stopped what she was doing and directed her hand at the rain-soaked earth. A jet of fire shot from her fingers and onto the ground, flickering feebly. Amber flicked her wrist, and the flame exploded into a sizable fire.

"If we use compact bolts," Amber said in a strained voice, pulling all the fire she'd made toward her, "it should dislodge it from the cliff."

"Um…" Kym sent a blast at a tentacle that was getting way too close for comfort. "I can't make a compact bolt."

"What?" Amber shrieked, her eyes popping as her compact bolt pulsed in her hands.

"I can't either," Tomark admitted. "They always just blow up."

"You two are worthless! How are you imbeciles the Vanquishers of Air and Water if you can't make a simple compact bolt?"

Amber ran forward, dodging between the wriggling tentacles, and threw her compact bolt straight down the cliff. The explosion made the cliff, which was already in bad shape after being touched by the tentacles, rumble and shake under Kym's feet. All the tentacles fell motionless. Amber had done it. But then, the tentacles sprang back to life and continued their assault with more vigor than they had before.

"This is pointless," Amber shouted over the renewed crashes. "How the Thed are we supposed to beat this thing if you two can't do anything at all?"

Amber was so busy yelling at Tomark and Kym that she did not see the tentacle coming. Her quickly formed shield broke instantly, and she flew through the air, landing hard on the ground. Kym ran after Amber, blasting the tentacle away as she did so. When she reached her, Amber was already on her feet.

"I know we aren't that experienced," said Kym, trying not to feel too insulted. "But you are. You're Amber, the Fire Princess. You've been doing this for sixteen years. There has to be something you can do. Some super-powerful magic, you know?"

At these words, a light seemed to go off in Amber's eyes. Slowly, much slower than Kym thought their present situation warranted, Amber walked to the edge of the cliff. Kym followed her, Tomark right on her heels until all three of them were standing together, looking over the demon and out to the sea.

"You want power?" Amber whispered, raising her hand, her red

Marks glowing. Her voice was different, like how she spoke when she was around a lot of people. "I'll show you power."

A jet of flame shot out from Amber's hand. It soared over the still-thrashing demon and out to open sea, where it finally stopped. Amber traced a large circle with her hand, and out over the water, the fire did the same, forming a ring that must be twice as tall as Kym. Mesmerized, Kym watched Amber close her hands into fists, and the ring floating offshore filled with fire. Amber opened her hands and extended one to the circle, like she was offering it to the fire.

"Amber," Tomark said quietly. Kym turned and saw a look of terror on his face. "Stop."

Ignoring Tomark, Amber gestured to the fire, as though beckoning it to join her. The sound of an explosion and the rushing of wind filled the air, and the circle of fire began hurtling towards the cliffs. But it wasn't ordinary fire. To Kym, it looked like a giant comet.

"Amber," Kym said, unable to keep the panic from her voice. Her eyes locked on the countless cracks in the still-shaking cliff. "Stop."

"Amber!" Tomark yelled, but she did nothing.

Tomark shoved Kym to the side, stepped in front of Amber, and formed a silvery shield dome around them. The comet hit the cliffs with an almighty crash, the ground trembled, and odd shrieks filled the air as the tentacles slithered over the side of the cliff. The force of the comet blasted the dome apart, sending the unhurt Kym, Tomark, and Amber into the air. They thudded to the ground, and the air filled with crashes as large pieces of cliff fell into the sea.

Dazed, her ears ringing, Kym staggered upright. Amber lay a little ways away, and she was slowly getting to her feet. White-hot anger boiled up inside Kym. She ran at Amber and shoved her back to the ground.

"What the Thed is wrong with you!"

"Kym," Tomark said, shocked.

"I-I did what you wanted," Amber spluttered, gesturing toward the cliff. "I blasted the demon off the cliff."

"You nearly blasted *us* off the cliff!" Kym was beginning to sound hysterical. "And the cliff off the cliff! Look around." She gestured to the giant cracks and pieces of missing stone. "What were you thinking?"

"Kym," Tomark said reproachfully. "It's not her fault."

"The Nothingness it is!"

Kym couldn't see straight. She was so mad she thought her arms might pop off. Had Amber thought about their safety before sending a comet at them? Amber's horrified look made it perfectly clear that she hadn't. How could she not think of that? If Amber could show such disregard for her friends' safety, maybe Kym didn't know Amber at all.

"Ah!"

The ground gave way beneath Amber, and she disappeared down the side of the cliff. Kym dove forward, her anger toward Amber evaporated, and she closed her hand around Amber's fingertips. But she was already too far down and ended up pulling Kym with her. They plummeted toward the ground, and Kym knew there was nothing either of them could do.

Something grabbed Kym's foot, and they stopped falling. The chunks of cliff continued to fall, landing on the demon with a squelch. Craning her neck, holding onto Amber like she was a lifeline, Kym saw Tomark, his silvery Marks glowing, floating in the air, her foot held tight in his hands. They slowly rose up the cliff, bumping roughly into the sides. Once at the top, Tomark dropped them in a heap before falling on top of them.

For a while they just lay there, not making a sound.

"I'm sorry. I-I wasn't..."

"It's fine," Kym sighed, and she meant it. "You just did what I asked. Sorry for freaking."

"But seriously," Tomark panted. "Don't ever do anything that stupid again."

"I won't," Amber promised. "Trust me. When I go into 'fire princess' mode, I kinda block everything out."

After several more minutes' silence, Kym slowly pushed herself into a sitting position. "Who wants to get out of here? Kat and I are hanging out tonight. We did it last week, and it's a great break from everything. You wanna come?"

"You can't be serious," Amber panted.

"I am. We planned it all out. She won't mind if you come."

"Why not?" Tomark shrugged. "A break could be nice."

"Amber?" Kym asked. She didn't answer. "C'mon. I want you to come."

"Fine," Amber said slowly. "Where are going?"

"A valley in Contellus. But I have no idea how to get there from here."

"I can get us there in seconds," Amber said, "if you two trust me."

Warily, Tomark and Kym agreed. They stood on either side of Amber, each holding one of her hands. Amber invoked her Marks and instructed Kym to do the same. Since Kym knew where they were going, Amber would use Kym's energy to guide her. So, Kym closed her eyes and focused her energy on a mental image of the meadow. There was a flash of light, a rush of flame, and Kym's body felt like it was pulled into a million tiny pieces.

The pieces of Kym flew through space, both filling it while feeling smaller than a grain of sand. But even though she felt pulled apart, she still felt Amber's hand held firmly in her own. She was both every-where and nowhere. Kym just wanted it to end. And an instant later, it did. Her body came crashing back together with more rushing of flame and flashes of red light. Her feet hit solid ground, and Kym gingerly opened her eyes. They were standing in the middle of the meadow.

"How'd you do that?" Tomark asked, his eyes wide as he looked around.

"It's a newer skill," Amber said. She sounded almost embarrassed. "Fire Favored have only really perfected it in the past year or so."

"Cool. Where's Kat?"

"She's…" Kym squinted through the darkness, but she see couldn't anything.

"What's that?" Amber pointed to a speck of light off in the distance.

"A firefly?" Tomark suggested.

Kym squinted at the little bobbing speck. There was something looming in the shadows around it. She marched over to it, Amber and Tomark trailing a little behind her. As they drew nearer, what they thought was a firefly grew larger and larger, and the shapes around it came more into focus.

"Finally," Kat shouted, getting up off the ground and punching Kym in the arm. "I thought you got lost. I see you brought friends," she added, noticing Tomark and Amber over Kym's shoulder.

"So did you," Kym smiled. She, Tomark, and Amber joined Kat, Pupil, and Ashlyn around a floating ball of light Ashlyn must have conjured. "So, we're all here."

"You did invite us," Tomark said slowly.

"I mean," Kym said slowly, "you all wanted to come."

"What?" Ashlyn asked gently. "Why wouldn't we come?"

"You all missed the introductory meeting," Kat said in a mock business tone. "We must bring you up to speed. The sneaking out on Saturday nights is for those who need a break from the crap that is our daily lives. We have our reasons, and we don't need to share them. But if you didn't have one, why would you come?"

"So what's the point of this?" Pupil asked.

"The point is to be free," Kym said, glancing at Pupil.

"Free?" Amber asked.

"Free," Kym repeated. "Free to be ourselves and speak our minds and do what we want without being judged. Everyone at Wadita has gone from hating me, to loving me, to now just putting up with me, and I'm sick of it."

Kym stared at the ball of light as it bobbed up and down every few seconds. The words slipped from her lips before she even knew what she was saying, but they were all true. Life at Wadita had become too much for her to handle, and there was no use denying it.

"My entire life I've always felt like part of the crowd." When no one responded, Ashlyn pressed on. "I'm the fifth kid out of seven, and all girls too. I was so excited when I found my magic. Finally, I was special. When Lady Evanna took me, I decided to make this experience a positive one.

"But when I got to Solaris, I was just part of another set, and everyone thought my positive attitude was too on the nose for a Light Favored. And among so many people, I was alone again. But lately," Ashlyn added, looking at the group around her, "I've finally felt like I belong. Like I have friends."

Kym stared at Ashlyn, taking her hand as tears slid silently down her cheeks. She looked around, taking in the odd selection of people around her. Kat, always speaking her mind. Ashlyn, just wanting to be seen. Tomark, who hated fighting. Amber, despising her legendary persona. Pupil, afraid of failing. How'd they all find each other? Her father's words seemed to bloom from someplace deep inside her. The gods must have a plan for her after all.

"C'mon," Kat said, standing and offering her hand to Ashlyn. "Let's go have fun."

C H A P T E R   F I F T E E N

P R E P A R A T I O N S

Sneaking out on Saturdays became the highlight of Kym's week. She perfected her escape plans and wasted no time racing off to the meadow, where at least one other person always waited. They spent their nights exploring the countryside, swimming in the river, and showing off the newest moves they'd learned. But mostly, they'd vent about things they couldn't talk about at the palaces.

As the weeks bled into months, the number of attendants at their "secret Summits" dwindled, as they were all called upon more and more to fulfill their Vanquisher duties. Pupil hadn't made an appearance since the very first night, and the rest of their track records were spotty at best. Even Kym had to miss a couple nights out. She'd been out of the palace so often lately she'd started falling behind in training again, but she promised herself she wouldn't miss the next Saturday.

Kym had a harder time than usual getting out of the palace that night. Nila cornered her in the dining hall, insisting she demonstrate all the moves Kenna and Aidan taught her. And Kym wasn't alone. Nila demanded the same of three other Favored before Kym escaped to the stairs. Once safely in her room, Kym bolted the door, retrieved the rope from under her bed, and swung off the balcony. She arrived in the meadow after sunset, the stars twinkling weakly in the darkening sky.

"'Sup, stranger."

"I could say the same to you," Kym smiled. "You weren't here the last time I was."

"I know," Kat huffed. "Kai's been acting loonier than usual, and that's impressive."

"Really?"

Kym was going to ask more when Tomark came soaring through the sky, his silvery Marks giving his body a ghostly glow. He circled over them several times before skidding to the ground, spraying Kym and Kat with dirt. Personally, she thought this was his best landing yet. At least he wasn't crashing anymore. A flash of fire appeared from out of nowhere, and Amber stood before them, looking very out of place in an elaborate red dress.

"You can't drop the princess act for even a second?" Kym smiled.

"Not when I only wear gowns," she groaned, trying to unfasten the buttons to the dress. "I even train in them most days. Don't worry. I've got regular clothes on underneath."

"You're crazy," Kat said, stepping forward to help Amber with the buttons.

"So, are we it?" Tomark asked as he sat on the small earth stumps Kat made for them.

"I think so," Amber flicked her wrist, and the pile of logs before them burst into flame. "Ash can't make it."

"When'd you see her?" Kym asked.

"Earlier this week. We fought a demon in Igmontis. Lord James' realm," she added when Kym looked confused. "She said Lady Evanna's been drilling the Light Favored day and night, so she wouldn't have the opportunity to slip away."

"You fought another one?" Kat asked. "How many does that make in the past few weeks? Like a million?"

"It's more like twenty, I think," Amber corrected her coolly.

"They just keep on coming. They're like weeds," Tomark sighed.

"Seriously. If more of them keep appearing the Rulers will need to appoint new Vanquishers just to keep up," Kym said.

"I doubt it," Kat said. "And Evanna isn't the only Ruler who's lost it. Kai's acting crazy, too."

"So is Nila. She cornered me tonight and made me show all these moves before she let me go to bed."

"What are they so worried about?" Tomark asked.

"Well, the Festival of Creation is in a few weeks," Amber said promptly.

"They're getting worried over a holiday?" droned Kat. "Lame."

"It must be this performance thing Nila talked about last week," Kym said, racking her brain as she tried to remember. "All of the Favored have to perform or something on their element's day of the festival."

"We do it every year." Amber nodded. "But, now that you mention it, I've never seen Lord James act like this before the festival. He's never seemed this nervous."

"It's like the Rulers think something is going to happen," Tomark said.

"Of course something is going to happen, stupid," Kat said abrasively. "We've all seen it, or am I the only person around here paying attention? There's been so much tension during the last couple of Summits I'm surprised the Rulers could see each other through it. They're up to something, and I bet it's gonna go down at the festival."

"C'mon Kat," Kym groaned. "They're not up to anything. Melana hasn't spoken to any of them in weeks as far as we know. And even if something were going on, the Rulers wouldn't be stupid enough to start it at the festival. That's insane."

"I'm not so sure," said Tomark. "Like Amber said, this festival stuff happens every year, so it can't be the reason the Rulers are acting strange. I agree with Kat. Something's going to happen, and we'll know it when it does."

"The Festival of Creation," Nila began one week later after everyone finished their dinner, "is nearly upon us. The eight-day celebration commemorates the gods' creation of Princirum and everything on it. Each day represents one of the elements: Life, Death, Light, Darkness,

Fire, Water, Air, and Earth. On all of the days except for the second, we give thanks to a particular god for everything they have done. On the second day, the Day of Death, we pay homage to those who have passed from this life.

"The Favored will give a performance demonstrating their power on their respective days. Since Lady Zara has no Favored, she will demonstrate life magic on the first evening of the festival. And of course, there will be no performance on the Day of Death. You will learn your parts of the water performance this week. I expect you will do your best to showcase the talent I know you possess."

Excited chatter filled the dining hall as everyone got to their feet. Kym stood silently, not really in the mood to talk. It seemed those at her table shared her feelings, since Kenna, Ryland, and Aidan left the hall without saying a word. Back in her bedchamber, all she wanted was to relax. After talking with Amber, Kat, and Tomark, Kym had expected Nila to announce the festival, as well as her high expectations for everyone. But to her, it just sounded like Nila wanted her Favored to give a good performance. Kat was probably just being paranoid.

Kym dismissed her maids after they removed the tight, new dress they made her wear. Pulling on her favorite training clothes, she walked over to her bed, crouched on the floor, and had begun pulling out the rope when there was a knock on her door. She quickly shoved the rope back under her bed. Nila must have sensed the appearance of another death demon. However, it wasn't Nila standing on the other side of the door.

"You'll never believe what just happened," Kenna said happily, pushing past Kym into the room, Aidan right behind her.

"What?" said Kym, taken aback by Kenna and Aidan's abrupt appearance in her bedchamber. They hadn't hung out during their free time in months.

"Lady Nila just put us in charge of the Water Favored's performance for the Festival of Creation," Aidan said excitedly, bouncing up and down on the balls of his feet.

"Oh," Kym said. She didn't know what she expected, but this wasn't it. Kenna and Aidan's faces fell at her lack of excitement. "I mean," she added quickly, "it's really cool; Nila letting you run the performance. But I thought she always put it together."

"She did," Aidan said seriously. "But she said she has too much on her plate this year. So we're doing it for her."

It was like the past couple of months hadn't even happened. They wanted to include Kym in their big moment. What changed? Why were they now suddenly ready to include her again? The change was so abrupt Kym actually felt dizzy. She sat down, clutching the edge of her bed.

"Please be happy for us. Planning the performance is a huge responsibility. We've never done anything like this before. This is our chance to shine and show everyone what we can do. And we want your help, of course," Kenna added, like she thought Kym's less-than-enthusiastic reaction was because Kenna hadn't included her.

"Great," Kym said, forcing a smile and trying her best to sound enthusiastic. "Sounds like a blast."

The next morning, Kenna and Aidan stopped everyone before they left the dining hall. They made everyone stand on the steps to the training rooms while they stood in the entrance hall, claiming everyone could hear them better from the high vantage point. Silence fell over the chattering crowd in waves, and Kym shuffled uncomfortably next to Kenna. She and Aidan refused to let Kym stand with the others, claiming she deserved to be there since she helped plan the performance they were about to describe.

Personally, she wasn't sure if she'd use the word "plan." Then, after thinking about it for another half second, she was positive she wouldn't use "plan," since she didn't help plan the performance whatsoever. Kenna and Aidan stayed in Kym's room for most of the night. She tried suggesting several ideas for the performance, but Aidan and Kenna always preferred one of their own. After being shot down for the tenth time, Kym stopped trying and only spoke to tell Kenna and Aidan how great their ideas were. So, she helped them plan the performance about as much as they helped her fight death demons.

"Lady Nila left Aidan and me in charge of our performance for the Festival of Creation. Overall, it will involve jets and orbs of water flying through the air in a choreographed sequence as the background. Several water constructs and Favored swimming from one water source to another will be the centerpiece of the performance. You all have a part to play, so everyone needs to pull their weight."

"We have one week to get this performance ready. We've postponed all regular training so you can focus on perfecting your parts of the performance. We'll now divide you into your groups and explain your individual parts in more detail."

Kenna and Aidan walked into the crowd, calling loudly as they divided everyone into their respective groups. They left Kym in the entrance hall, but it wasn't a real shock to her at this point. Why would they take her along to make the groups if they didn't even let her help plan? They weren't going to include Kym in anything since, as Kenna said the night before, this was their "time to shine." Kym just shook her head.

When nearly all the Favored were divided into groups, Aidan came to collect Kym. Her group was the smallest and consisted of Favored who'd been at Wadita far longer than Kym. She knew most of them as Favored Kenna and Aidan trained with from time to time, but couldn't remember any of their names. Kenna explained their role in the performance, and Kym could tell she was really trying to make the most boring job sound exciting. They needed to stand around the edge and make sure nothing went wrong. In short, they'd babysit everyone while Ryland, Jean, Kenna, Aidan, and Jax all received what Aidan called "performance" roles, placing them front and center.

Kym had never seen so many things go so wrong so fast. The performance was so intricate and precise that the smallest mistake sent the whole thing literally crashing down around them. The first deluge was pretty funny, since it happened thirty seconds into the performance, as four pool-sized orbs of water crashed to the ground.

However, by the sixth mistake, Kym was fed up and, apparently, so was Kenna. She marched over to Kym and her group, who watched the whole thing crumble, and started screaming at them, her voice echoing around the domed chamber they were in.

Apparently, Kym's job in the performance was harder than she thought. She and the rest of her group had to memorize every part of the performance and go through the motions so they could stop anything from going wrong. By the end of the day, Kym's entire body shook, as did the rest of her group. They'd finally made it through a performance without stopping, but only because Kym and her group of four assisted the work of fifty others.

The next several days weren't much better. The others relied heavily on Kym's group to save them when they made mistakes. This was most difficult during the performance's climax, where hundreds of bathtub-sized orbs, all continuously changing shape, danced around each other in the air. The performers leapt from orbs, throwing attacks that didn't actually hit anyone, before landing in the next orb. The performers made the most mistakes, like not being in the right positions at the right time. However, Kenna and Aidan insisted everyone else's mistakes were why the performers had messed up, and slowly, the performance did improve. Kym thought they were actually in good shape when Aidan announced Nila would watch the performance the next day.

The following morning saw a level of stress Kym didn't even know existed. Kenna and Aidan prowled around the room, critiquing everyone on everything, magical or not. One girl burst into tears after Kenna told her she would fail at everything in her life since she didn't walk the way Kenna liked. When Nila arrived to watch, Kenna and Aidan were white as ghosts, and everyone else looked like they'd rather be anywhere else.

Overall, everyone did pretty well compared to where they started. They all seemed to have gotten the hang of their parts, so Kym only needed to fix water runoff during the performance. She didn't even feel too tired by the time it was over. Nila stayed silent throughout the whole thing. When the performance was over, she gave Kenna and Aidan a significant look, then left the room.

"That was pathetic," Kenna spat at the group after the door closed behind Nila. "You'll need to do a lot better than that if we want to beat the other elements at the festival. Practice your parts so tomorrow won't be as big of a disaster."

"Aren't you being a little harsh?" Kym asked, staying behind while the others left the hall. Most looked ready to burst.

"No I don't," Kenna snapped, placing her hands firmly on her hips. "You could do so much better if you'd just listen to us."

"We've only been practicing for four days. It's not going to be perfect yet. Give us time."

"We don't have time," Aidan barked. "The festival's in three days, and this thing needs to be perfect by then."

"And if it's not perfect, all of you will have messed up our big chance."

"Don't worry. It'll be fine. You'll see."

Everyone improved over the next three days. Convinced the vast improvement was all thanks to their insane instructions and yelling, Kenna and Aidan softened, but only slightly. But Kym knew better. The improvements were thanks to Aidan and Kenna, but not for the reasons they thought. Everyone was sick of Kenna and Aidan screaming at them, so they did whatever they could to prevent it.

The day before the festival, after running through the performance one final time, Kym arrived in her bedchamber to find her lady's maids in a state of sheer panic. Her first instinct was to run for cover, but she fought against the impulse. It was as though her closet had exploded; shoes littered the floor, large trunks lay haphazardly all over the room, and clothes, both complete and half finished, hung off every available surface. Veronica and Isabel ran around the room at top speed, nothing more than high-pitched, brightly colored blurs.

Mustering her courage, Kym stepped into the fray. She grabbed each of her maids' arms as they passed and sat them together on one of the smaller couches. She tried asking what was going on, but they didn't take in a word as they sprang back into action. Their brains seemed to be on overload. All Kym got out of them was that she was going to an eight-day party, which meant morning gowns, evening gowns, outfits for leisure, and undergarments. And that was just for one day.

Currently, their chief concern, as they'd already moved on from others, was how they were going to transport all of Kym's clothes to Crystal Palace. Veronica, red-faced and sweaty, looked on the verge of passing out as she tried to fit nearly all of Kym's clothes into a single trunk. Kym was about to tell her to stop when Isabel burst back into the room.

"The housekeeper has upped the number of carriages for the Favored's clothes from three to ten."

"Thank Pheil," sighed Veronica. "There's no way Miss Kym's clothes would fit into two trunks. I'm glad the housekeeper finally saw sense."

Deciding it was best for her safety to be as far away from her maids as possible, Kym spent the rest of the evening in the back garden. She sat on the ground, back pressed against the smooth garden wall, her eyes closed as she held her knees close to her body. The air was cool and crisp with a hint of winter on the breeze, and she tried to relax as the waves crashed gently behind her. It didn't work. Despite their many, many faults, Kenna and Aidan seemed to have gotten one thing right. Kym felt the pressure of the performance.

Kym woke the next morning and found her room in another state of siege. Much to her surprise and slight annoyance, since nearly all her clothes were going to the festival, so were her lady's maids. In fact, all of the Favored were to be accompanied by their personal staff. Apparently, no one seemed to think they could, or even should, dress themselves. On the bright side, she'd only see her maids when she was changing clothes, which she hoped would only be a few times a day.

Kym began undressing when her carriage started up the black mountain to Crystal Palace. Her maids expected her to be ready when they arrived, and she was in no mood to contradict them. She placed her shirt and pants on the rack over her head and waited in her underwear for the carriage to stop. The door flew open the moment the carriage stopped, and her maids pulled Kym onto Crystal Palace's front drive, which looked unrecognizable.

Several large tents sat around the drive and the front lawn, each the color of a different element. Veronica and Isabel steered Kym into the closest blue tent and immediately set to work. They dressed her in a tightly fitted blue gown with shortened sleeves that reached her forearm. The hem and cuffs were bright gold, but the neckline swooped a little lower than Kym would've liked. They applied small amounts of makeup, put Kym in a pair of strappy blue heels, and, to top it all off, placed a delicate gold chain with a single pearl around her neck.

Veronica barely placed the chain around Kym's neck when another set of maids entered the tent and promptly kicked them out. Unsure what to do, Kym decided to wander around. This, she soon discovered, was easier said than done; she kept losing her footing on the gravel-covered drive. Several minutes later, she spotted Tomark emerge from a silvery-gray tent. Kym was surprised to see him wearing billowing gray pants, a puffy white shirt, a gray vest with silver and gold stitching, and tall, black boots. It was so different from the way he usually looked.

"You look amazing," he said slowly.

"Thanks," Kym said sheepishly. "You too."

Kym, still unsteady in her heels, stumbled as she hurried the last few steps over to Tomark. Luckily, he caught Kym around the shoulders just as her feet slipped out from under her. For some reason, she couldn't stop herself from staring into his bright green eyes, which looked so calm and peaceful. His wavy brown hair, which usually fell loosely around his face, was pulled neatly behind his head. His soft smile seemed to invite Kym's lips to do the same. She opened her mouth to speak, but a sarcastic voice rang through the air.

"Look at you two, dressed fancy and lookin' all bright and shiny," Kat said, walking toward them. Kym hastily stood back up. "Personally, I don't understand why we don't train dressed like this. I mean, look at us—so practical and not uncomfortable in the slightest. C'mon —everyone's waiting on the other side of the drive."

Kym and Tomark followed Kat over to the others, who were all wearing extravagant outfits, to wait for the festival to begin. Ashlyn's pale-yellow dress floated gently through the air, while Amber's dress was red and tightly fitted. They were both bedecked in jewels, and Amber even wore a thin, red tiara. Pupil's clothes were similar to Tomark's, though his, of course, were violet.

Everyone looked so different from the way she knew them. Oddly, it reminded Kym of her first school dance back home. No one really looked like themselves as they twirled around the dance floor. But this? This was on a whole different level.

"When is this thing supposed to start?" Kat complained. "My feet feel like they're gonna fall off."

"At sunset," Amber said with a superior air, looking down her nose at Kat.

"How long does it go every night?" Kym asked, directing her question to anyone but Amber. She didn't think she could handle the Fire Princess tonight.

"It depends on the night," said Pupil. "Nothing exciting happens the first night, so it might go by pretty quickly."

Kym craned her neck, looking over the excitedly talking crowd as she tried to see around the palace. She could just make out the top of the sun sinking lower and lower over the horizon. The sun would set any moment, and the festival would begin. She wondered what it would be like. She'd never thought to ask anyone until now. Back home, the whole celebration part of the festival lasted one night. They'd gather on the first night, and then everyone would return to their normal lives for the rest of the festival. Kym had a feeling she would be experiencing something far grander.

Ashlyn poked Kym softly on her side and nodded silently toward the sky. Kym watched the last rays of deep crimson fade as the sky turned indigo. Expectantly, Kym looked at the palace doors, ready for the festival to begin. But nothing happened. A whole minute passed while the crowd waited in silence for something to happen. What was taking so long?

The whole palace burst into brilliant white light, but it wasn't like lights were shining on it. The actual, physical palace seemed to be turned on like one massive light bulb. It was so bright that Kym, along with most of the crowd, turned away to shield their eyes. Kym squinted back at the palace, tears streaming down her face, not wanting to miss a thing. The massive front doors slowly swung forward to reveal nothing inside but pure, white nothingness.

CHAPTER SIXTEEN

THE FESTIVAL OF CREATION

THE LIGHT EMITTING FROM INSIDE THE PALACE WAS EVEN MORE beautiful than the light radiating from the outside. While the exterior glow was jarring and magnificent, the inner light was brighter but somehow softer. It enhanced all it touched, making everything appear more lively and vibrant. It engulfed the crowd, which seemed to hold its breath, like a single sound would disrupt its gentle work and break its spell. Slowly, a dark figure bloomed from the depths of the light.

"Ladies and gentlemen, it is my honor to welcome you to Crystal Palace for the Festival of Creation," Zara said, stepping onto the vast front steps and smiling down at the crowd. Her magnificent white dress radiated the same pure light as the palace.

"In the beginning, there was only Chaos. Then Pheil, Goddess of Life, Thilg, Goddess of Light, and Kensrad, Goddess of Darkness, defeated Thed, God of Death. They banished him to Nothingness, freeing the world from his grasp, and claimed this land for their creation. With the help of their children, Heirraph, Rai, Reta, and Thray, they created Princirum and her people. They watch over us, and grant us their wisdom to maintain balance."

Kym barely suppressed a snort. Everyone's version of the Creation of Princirum was different, but no matter who told it, they'd always make the gods' defeat of Thed the most fantastical and wonderful thing that ever happened. Even Kym's father, a much more devout man then Kym, had to admit that the version of creation told during the festival was a little over the top. But Zara's version made things seem so perfect it was laughable.

Needing to look at anything else to calm herself down, Kym turned sideways. But the look on Kat's face had the opposite result. It was bright red and her shoulders shook with silent laughter as she tried to keep her lips firmly pressed together. Turning away from this hilarious sight, Kym faced Zara, who was still addressing her guests.

"So we, humble servants of the gods, honor them with this celebration of their achievements and greatness. For the gods, who are always just and kind, allow magic to exist in the world and therefore allow us, their Favored among humankind, to exist."

Applause broke out at these words. It didn't last very long, as silence fell over the crowd only a few seconds later. Everyone gazed expectantly at Zara, who still stood on the top of the front steps, smiling down at the crowd before her. Zara raised her hands and clapped twice. Once the ringing of her claps had faded away, she spoke again.

"If the Rulers would join me on the steps, the Conduit shall be brought forth to open the festival."

The Rulers, who stood near the back of the crowd, stepped forward. They didn't make eye contact with anyone as they walked, their gazes fixed firmly above everyone else. They joined Zara atop the massive front steps, each bowing respectfully to her as they took their place in line, their faces blank. Kym stared at Melana, who stood on Zara's left side. Her eyes looked colder than ever, if that were possible, as she stared down her nose at the excited crowd.

Kym was so focused on watching the Rulers assemble she didn't notice the servant emerge from the still-shining entrance hall. Dressed in the signature white toga of Crystal Palace, he carried a small white box in his outstretched hands. It was no bigger than a breadbox, but the look on the servant's face made it seem much heavier. He presented it to Zara, who accepted it with a smile. The servant bowed low to the Rulers, then quickly backed down the steps.

"When the Rulers," Zara began, "first discovered we were not the only ones in Princirum to possess magic, the gods granted us this: the Conduit."

Zara tapped the lid of the box with her slender fingers, her Marks glowing pure white, and it opened. She set the open box at her feet, and the Rulers slowly stepped back as one. Kym's mouth fell open. An enormous diamond rose gracefully out of the box and floated unsupported in front of the Rulers. The whole crowd gasped as they watched the glittering stone revolve slowly on the spot.

"The Conduit," Zara continued, "is the source of all magic and the heart of Princirum. When the gods discovered the unintended magic of Princirum, they realized there was nothing they could do to stop it. So, instead of letting this unexpected magic roam free, they contained it within a vessel. It is our duty as Rulers, as proxies for the gods, to rejuvenate the Conduit at the start of the Festival of Creation each year."

The Rulers moved as one, like they'd done this hundreds of times, which Kym realized they probably had. They formed a semicircle around the Conduit, each raising an arm toward the stone. The Rulers invoked their Marks, and a dim rainbow of light appeared against the still-bright palace walls. Clouds of colored mist, which matched the Rulers' Marks, formed around their arms, obscuring them from Kym's view. The glowing mist shot forward, engulfing the Conduit as the Rulers stepped back.

The multicolored storm swirled around the Conduit. Then, it was like someone hit the pause button, and the mist froze. Kym squinted up through the gloom and could barely see the Conduit's faint outline through the frozen, multicolored haze. The cloud of mist contracted, growing smaller and smaller as it concentrated around the Conduit. For a moment, everything was still, then a pulse of energy surged from the Conduit. It rushed through the crowd, and the hem of Kym's dress flapped around as her hair blew backward.

The Conduit, still floating before the Rulers, was no longer a clear diamond. The white, yellow, violet, red, green, gray and blue mist the Rulers conjured swirled around inside it. It reminded Kym of a kaleidoscope; the colors spiraled around, forming many strange shapes and images. The crowd broke into applause, and this time it lasted. Zara stepped forward, lifted the white box from the ground, and brought it up to the Conduit, which sank silently back inside. The togaed servant returned, taking the box from Zara as she addressed the crowd.

"With the Lighting of the Conduit, the Festival of Creation has officially begun. We will gather inside the palace for the opening banquet and the presentation of life magic. Tonight, as with all nights for the duration of the festival, you shall sit according to palace. Follow your Ruler into the dining hall. They will show you where to sit."

Kym quickly waved good-bye to the others and ran to join the Water Favored, who'd already gathered near the front of the crowd. Ignoring Kenna's clear look of disapproval, Kym stood on the opposite side of the group. Kym knew Kenna was upset she didn't stand with the Water Favored for the opening of the festival, but, honestly, she didn't care. Once everyone had assembled, Aidan and Kenna led them up the steps, where Nila stood waiting for them.

If she hadn't spent so much time in the dining hall during her previous visits, she wouldn't have known they'd entered the same room. The white walls, which had been bare, were now draped in the various, shimmering banners the colors of the elements. White hangings covered the front wall, while two different colors covered the sides and the back was divided into thirds. Long tables surrounded by benches replaced the round ones from the evaluation, and lined the room's perimeter, leaving the middle bare. Nila led her Favored to the section draped in blue on the left side of the back wall.

"Our position will change based on the element and god we are honoring. The front will be black tomorrow, and the white will move to the front of the left wall. We will be on the back wall for the first three days. Those who have not attended the festival as Favored will sit near the front."

Six Water Favored hadn't been to the festival before. Kym tried to sit by people she really hadn't spoken to before, but much to her dismay, Chloe and Matt sat on either side of her. She hadn't spoken to them in months, and she could tell they weren't too happy with the seating arrangement. So much happened over the past few months that her first weeks as a Favored felt like a bad dream. But with two living reminders of her torment sitting beside her, it was hard to block it all out.

"The Great Mother," Zara said, and the whole hall fell silent, "who watches over all that is living, smiles upon us on this, her greatest day. Pheil," Zara looked at the ceiling, and everyone followed her lead, "Queen of the Gods, bringer of life and family, bless us this day, for we honor you with this bounty before us. Take us into your loving embrace, and let us share our love for you as we feast in your honor."

White-togaed servants appeared in the still-silent hall, their arms laden with trays. Her stomach growling loudly, Kym dove into the first of many courses. They ate their way through salads, soups, roast beef, fish, steamed vegetables, potatoes, chicken, turkey, and finally, an array of finely iced cakes. When the clink of cutlery started to die, the torches set in brackets along the walls began to dim.

Everyone turned to Zara, who sat in front of the white wall, along with a large group of her assorted guests. She rose from her seat and glided to the vast open space in the center of the hall. Five servants carried large, brightly colored plants into the hall and placed them in a circle around Zara. She pointed her hands at the pot directly in front of her, taking a deep breath.

A faint white mist, similar to what Zara conjured to light the Conduit, shimmered around the plant as her Marks glowed. It grew larger and denser, drifting lazily around the plant. Then, Zara pulled her outstretched arms into her chest, and the white mist flew toward her, where it hovered between her hands. Zara repeated this on each of the plants, drawing out what Kym guessed was the plants' life energy. The plants, though still alive, looked weak and feeble as their yellowing leaves fell from delicate branches, settling in heaps on the floor.

Once Zara drew the life energy from all the plants, she stood in what looked like a thin, white cloud. From within the cloud, Zara slowly extended her arms, and the cloud of life expanded outward, reaching those sitting nearest the center of the hall. The second the energy touched Kym, she felt so light, like she'd never be tired again. It was like air filled every little space inside her. Zara quickly brought her hands together, and with a whoosh the cloud of life compacted between her hands, forming a glowing white orb. This orb, whose light was much brighter than the mist's, floated peacefully in Zara's hand as she ambled around the hall.

"Life is fragile," Zara said softly, staring at the orb as the entire room gazed at her. "It can so easily be snuffed out if a person does not handle it with care. But life is also mighty. Life can cause the most horrific destruction in the world."

Zara turned to the white-draped wall behind her. A stone pillar Kym hadn't seen before stood in the middle of the wall. A servant must have placed it there while Zara demonstrated her magic. Zara threw the orb of life at the pillar with unexpected speed and precision, striking it directly in the center. The place where the bolt hit the pillar seemed to disintegrate, reduced to a fine powder rather than breaking like they did when Kym's water bolts hit them.

"The hand of life is always present," Zara continued as the remaining pieces of the pillar crashed to the floor. "It is the bringer of death and the cause of darkness and light, which created fire, water, air, and earth."

Zara turned to the plant nearest to her and pulled the life energy from the plant more aggressively than she had before. As the energy soared away from the plant, the yellowing limbs and leaves shriveled and darkened, crumbling in a black heap in the pot.

"But life can also undo the horrors and destruction of death," Zara said, looking almost longingly at the cloud of energy in her hands.

Zara approached the blackened heap and released the energy from her hands. It floated gently, resting around the black flakes of the plant, which began to swirl within the cloud of energy. The flakes seemed to absorb the cloud of life around them as they turned from black, to yellow, to green. And under Zara's careful supervision, the plant reformed. But it didn't look the same as it had before. The once-large bush was no taller than five inches, with only three leaves on its fragile-looking stem.

"Life is precious. Life holds us all together." Zara turned to face to the white hanging behind her, gesturing to the symbol embroidered upon it. It was a simple circle with a black bottom and white top, with the white and black halves seeping into each other in the middle. "The Bleed. For without death, there is no life, and without life, there cannot be death. They are forever one. Embrace and enjoy life. Use yours to its fullest extent. For you never know when death might be near."

Cheers and applause erupted as Zara returned to her seat at the front table. Excited chatter filled the hall as the lights slowly returned to their original state. Everyone was discussing Zara's life magic, and Kym had to admit she was impressed. The way she pulled the life from the last plant was incredible, but how she brought it back filled Kym's mind with unanswered questions. She knew Zara could heal people; her maids told her so after her first sparring match. But was there a limit to what Zara could bring back? She now understood why Kenna and Aidan pushed them so hard when training for their performance. Because what Lady Zara just did was completely extraordinary.

Nila led her Favored out of the dining hall as soon as the banquet was over. However, they didn't go to the palace's many guest rooms as Kym predicted, but back out onto the front drive. Since so many people, including returning, powerful Favored and prominent members from the Temples, had accepted Zara's invitation to the festival, all the training Favored couldn't stay in the palace along with Zara's other guests. So they and their servants would stay in tents on the grounds.

The tents were grouped according to palace, so Kym followed the Water Favored to where the blue tents stood waiting. Servants flanked each entrance flap, all marked with the symbol of water, the Wave. Kym wandered aimlessly, knowing her lady's maids would spot her before she saw them. Sure enough, their squeals led Kym straight to her tent.

The tent was much larger on the inside than it looked on the outside, containing a bed, several puffy cushions, and two thin sleeping pads, presumably for Veronica and Isabel. They undressed Kym, chattering endlessly about Zara's presentation since they'd never seen life magic either. They quickly shepherded Kym into bed, insisting she needed beauty rest to look her best. Kym's protests were completely ignored.

When Veronica and Isabel's heavy breathing filled the tent, Kym slipped out of bed and through the entrance flap. The night was quiet and dark, with the palace no longer emitting its bright light. She wandered through the city of tents, wanting to find Kat, Ashlyn, or somebody to talk to, but she had no idea where their tents were. And unless she poked her head into every single one, there was no hope of finding them. Kym decided to turn back when two white togaed servants, each carrying lanterns, stopped her.

"What are you doing, Miss?" one of them asked.

"Just wanted some air," Kym said innocently. "Is something wrong?"

"Oh dear," the other attendant said. "I'm afraid you've strayed too far in the dark, Miss. A Water Favored has no business here among the Fire Favored. Follow us, and we'll get you back where you belong."

Confused, Kym walked slowly between the two servants. Hadn't Zara and her servants encouraged the Favored to mix and mingle when they were all here for their evaluations? She even let them pick their own roommates. But now it was like Zara didn't want the Favored communicating with each other at all. Kym stayed silent as she followed the servants back to her tent. Once there, she got into her bed, trying her best not to wake her maids, and stared at the canvas until she finally fell asleep.

Hours later, though it felt like mere moments to Kym, her maids shook her awake. Still dressed in her bedclothes, they led Kym to one of the washing tents. They reserved it early in the morning, ensuring they'd have plenty of time. It was early all right; the sun wasn't even up. Kym grumbled all through her bath, eating the assorted fruits set beside the tub, though Veronica and Isabel didn't acknowledge her grumbling. They were back in her tent before she knew it, Veronica and Isabel dressing Kym in the first of two dresses she'd wear that day.

"Such a somber affair doesn't warrant many wardrobe changes," Veronica said wisely.

Looking in the full-length mirror, Kym saw she wore a dark-blue dress with black trim. Assuming this was just the beginning, she stepped back to let them continue their work, but Isabel only offered Kym a pair of black heels.

"This is a little subdued," Kym said, putting on the shoes.

"Today is a day for the dead," Isabel said. "It's not a day for happy colors."

Kym joined the rest of the Favored, all dressed in darker versions of their usual bright colors. Kym followed the crowd up the steps, through the entrance hall, and walked through corridors she'd never explored until they finally reached their destination: the palace Temple. The Favored and guests sat on benches around the room while the Rulers stood in the middle, where the high priest usually stood in the city Temples. Unlike the Temple at Wadita, this one looked just like Kym's Temple back home, though much nicer.

"On this day," Zara said quietly through the sheer black veil draped over her crowned head, "we honor those who have left this world for the next. We honor Thed, the King of Nothingness and Watcher of the Dead, and pay tribute to him."

Zara turned to the altar at the center of the room. Usually, this is an altar to Pheil, but it's changed once a year to honor Thed. So a statue of a man replaced the one of a smiling woman, her arms open wide. The man's arms were also open, but his face was impassive and blank. Zara knelt before the statue, and everyone else followed suit.

"Oh ever watchful King of Nothingness, we beseech you. Here on this day, we honor you as you watch over those we have lost. As they wander through the vastness of Nothingness, we present these offerings to sustain and nourish you."

At these words, several servants approached the altar, their arms laden with food, flowers, wine, and gifts of jewels, gold, and cloth. They placed them silently around the statue's feet, then backed away as Zara continued.

"As you shepherd those who pass from this life to Nothingness, take special care to watch over those who have fallen in the service of the gods."

Zara, along with the other Rulers, recited the names of every Favored who'd died that year. The list was short, but each Ruler spent about ten minutes honoring the fallen. They spoke of their deeds and accomplishments, recounting the stories of their deaths. Most, it seemed, died of old age, though there were some who died of other causes. A Fire Favored in his thirties died when his magic backfired, killing him and all the servants in his estate. These were the only non-Favored deaths the Rulers mentioned.

When the Rulers finished they stepped aside, granting the others the opportunity to ask Thed to watch over those who they'd lost. The line was slow-moving and long, giving Kym plenty of time to make her decision. Her aunt and uncle died years before, and Kym's mother always prayed for Thed to watch over her brother and his wife, but aside from them, there was no one else Kym could think to pray for. In front of her, she heard more and more people ask Thed to watch over the same dead Favored. Then it dawned on her. She knew who to pray for.

"Thed, watcher of the dead," Kym whispered, bowing her head to the statue, "watch over the unwatched. Give the souls no one speaks for a chance as they wander through Nothingness."

They exited the Temple in silence. Kym returned to her tent, where Veronica and Isabel stood waiting, each wearing dark blue. They dressed Kym in a simple blue dress and a shawl for the evening festivities. And much to her surprise, Isabel presented Kym with a pair of blue flats instead of high heels.

"You've been standing all day. Let's give your feet a break."

The dining hall was transformed yet again. Black hangings covered the front wall, and a shrine to the dead stood in the middle of the room. Embroidered upon the black drapes was the Bleed, but this time, the black half of the circle was on top, while the white was on the bottom. The usual chatter that filled the hall was absent, and the food was more understated than the night before. When everyone finished eating, Zara stood at her table on the left side of the hall, tapping her glass with a knife.

"Make you way to the center of the hall as we honor those who are no longer with us."

With a scraping of benches, everyone stood and walked into the middle of the hall. Seeing an opportunity, Kym fell back through the crowd of Water Favored until she was at the very back of it. She scanned the crowd and saw her friends gathering near the back of the room. Kym joined them, happy they'd had the same idea, while Zara called for silence.

Zara's moment of silence lasted a lifetime, and no one seemed to want to move. It was like they thought their movement would somehow ruin the silence pressing against Kym's eardrums. Unsure how much longer she could keep this up, Kym craned her neck, trying to get a look at Zara. Her head was bowed, and she was clearly not stopping the moment any time soon.

A ray of sunlight shone through a gap in the black drapes, hitting Kym squarely in the face. Kym turned away, squinting at the floor, which was crisscrossed with the shadows of the crowd. Her eyes no longer stinging, she started turning back to the altar when something caught her eye. A dark shape glided quickly across the floor, darting between the dark shadows painted across it. This black mass slipped under the door, and vanished from sight.

H I D D E N   I N
S H A D O W

"THANK YOU," ZARA SAID, "FOR PAYING YOUR RESPECTS. ENJOY THE rest of your evening."

The crowd began to disperse, but Kym didn't move. She stared at the door, her mouth slightly open. Had she imagined it? It had been a long day, so her mind could be playing tricks on her. But if it was her imagination, why would she see that?

A pair of hands clapped sharply in front of Kym's face. She jumped and blinked for what felt like the first time in months. Ashlyn stood in front of her, her hands prepared to clap again, a concerned look on her face. Looking around, Kym saw that look mirrored on the others' faces. She ignored them and once again looked back at the door.

"Did you see that?"

"See what?" Ashlyn asked cautiously.

"That black thing. It slid under the door during the moment of silence," Kym said, pointing to the door. "Didn't you see it?"

They looked at the door like they expected to see the dark shape sitting there. At least Tomark and Ashlyn seemed mildly interested. Amber and Kat clearly thought Kym had lost her mind.

"Um, no. I didn't," Kat said, laughing slightly.

"What? None of you saw it?" Had she really imagined it?

Tomark timidly grasped one of Kym's shoulders. "Are you feeling okay? You seem out of it."

"You do look strange. Do you want to lie down?" Amber asked. "I'll summon a servant."

"I'm fine," Kym said, her temper starting to rise as she jerked her shoulder out of Tomark's grip. "And I don't want to lie down." Was seeing a dark shape so impossible?

"Well, you saw something no one else did, and that's not good," Ashlyn said softly. "Did you get enough sleep last night? Are you tired?"

"What do you think you saw?" Amber asked.

"I *saw* a black thing slide under the door while everyone was looking at the altar."

They all exchanged skeptical looks. Why did they find it so hard to believe her? She didn't go around saying crazy things all the time for no reason. The more she thought about it, the more she knew it must be true, but that didn't help her figure out what it was, or convince the others. She looked around, searching for some evidence to prove her story, and noticed something she hadn't registered before.

"Where's Pupil?" she asked, momentarily caught off guard.

Kat, Amber, Tomark, and Ashlyn looked around like they thought Pupil was right behind them, but he was nowhere in sight. There were only four people in the entire room wearing purple clothes, so he shouldn't be too hard to pick out in a crowd. Amber and Ashlyn pushed through the jostling mass of people, hoping to find him. But after several minutes passed without their return, Tomark invoked his Marks. A slight gust of air issued around him as he rose slightly into the air.

"I can only see two Darkness Favored," Tomark said, looking over the heads of the crowd, "and they're on the other side of the room."

Tomark landed gently next to Kat. Amber and Ashlyn pushed their way out of the sea of people a few moments later. They'd found the Darkness Favored Tomark saw, but neither of them would speak to Ashlyn or Amber. That's when Melana showed up.

"So we tried asking Lady Melana, but she told us to stay out of Darkness business," Amber said bitterly.

"Where'd he go?" Ashlyn asked no one in particular. "I saw him over here when Zara asked us all to stand. I thought he got here before me and was standing where I couldn't see him."

"No," Amber said. "He would have passed me, and I never saw him."

"Maybe you just lost him in the crowd?" Tomark suggested.

"Because it's easy to misplace a big guy wearing bright purple," Kat said.

"Wait a moment," It was like a switch went off in Kym's brain. "A shadow. The sun was in my face, and when I turned away, I saw all of the shadows on the floor. Then one broke free from the others and slid under the door."

"Really?" Kat asked, clearly thinking Kym was grasping at straws. "Why would Pupil sneak out on his own? I mean I get it, this party is really boring, but still."

"Why not?" Kym retorted. "He's sneaked around before."

"To listen in to the Rulers. But they're all here, Kym," Amber said, exasperated. "Why would he leave?"

"It's not the only time he's done it," Kym breathed.

She'd never told the others about the night Pupil came to Wadita to frighten her. She'd forgiven Pupil for it and saw no reason to bring it up when she wanted to let it go. But she knew Pupil could do something like this, and she was more than ready to tell them what had happened.

"Why'd he do that?" Ashlyn asked. "Going to Wadita to frighten you doesn't sound like him at all."

"It wasn't his idea," Kym said firmly. "He only did it because Melana…" She trailed off. Another thought just occurred to her. She looked into the crowd, where she knew Melana was. Why didn't she think of it sooner?

"Snap out of it," Kat said, punching her hard in the arm. "So Melana had him frighten you? Big deal. What does that have to do with him sneaking out of here now?"

"Because he told me he'd do anything to stay in Melana's good books," Kym said. "I bet he's doing something for her. That's why he sneaked out."

"We don't even know—"

"Yes, we do," Tomark cut across Amber. "I trust Kym. We all trust her. So, now that we *all*," he put a lot of emphasis on the word, "agree Pupil's not here, we need to find him. Whatever Melana's asked him to do can't be good. Maybe we can talk him out of it."

Kym's insides swelled at Tomark's words. Whether he believed she saw the shadow or not, he was on her side. The anger that bubbled up inside her melted away, but nerves soon took its place. What was Pupil up to?

"All right," Ashlyn said slowly. "Let's look for him. But how are we going to leave? The Rulers will notice if all five of us walk out. The banquet won't be over for at least another hour."

"Leave it to us," Kat said, nodding toward Amber and giving her a sinister smile. "Wait by the door until you hear us yelling, then you can slip out."

"And how will you two get out?" Tomark asked.

"Don't worry about us," Amber said, comprehension dawning on her face, her eyes alight with thought. "Just get out and hide in the hall. We won't be far behind."

Amber and Kat pushed their way into the crowd, while Kym, Ashlyn, and Tomark slowly backed toward the doors. Kym tried to be discreet, but she reached the door sooner than she expected, and ran right into it. She stumbled awkwardly, but luckily no one seemed to notice. Amber's shouts rang through the hall, and Kym knew every eye was locked on her. Between the two of them, Kat and Amber knew how to draw people's attention.

"You idiot!" Amber's shouted, in top Fire Princess form. "You bumbling little piece of filth! How dare you touch me!"

They didn't wait to hear Kat's response. With every eye glued on Amber and Kat, Kym pushed the door open as quietly as she could. She, Tomark, and Ashlyn slipped into the corridor and hid behind the massive pillars supporting the ceiling. They didn't even wait one whole minute before the door to the dining hall burst open. Amber stormed out, her face white with fury as she turned to face the mass of people staring at her from inside.

"You all will burn, and I'll enjoy watching it!"

The doors closed and Amber walked down the corridor. She joined Kym and the others behind their pillar while they waited for Kat to show up. Kym stared at Amber, her shock mirrored on Tomark and Ashlyn's faces. Tomark even looked like he might fall over.

"A little over the top, Fire Princess?" Kym asked breathlessly.

"It had to look good. Everyone's heard the rumor that Kat and I despise each other, so Kat just bumped into me and I made a giant scene. It was actually kinda fun."

"I meant that bit at the end."

"Oh that," Amber said absentmindedly. "They needed to be frightened. At least now no one will come looking for me for a while."

Kym smiled. It really was a good plan. But where was Kat? How was she going to get out? Suddenly, a door on the other side of the hall opened, and Kat's head poked out of it. She looked around, saw the others standing behind their pillar, and hurried to join them. Her shoulders shook, and she looked like she was on the verge of falling over.

"Everyone in that room is a complete and utter moron. After you stormed out, everyone rushed over to see if I was okay. Kai summoned a servant to take me to one of those small rooms off the hall so I could 'recover.' Ha!"

"Well, now that we're out, what are we gonna do?" Tomark asked.

Now that they were out of the dining hall, no one seemed to know what to do next. Kym didn't have the faintest idea what Pupil could be up to. Crystal Palace was enormous, and none of them knew it that well. It would probably take them days to search the entire thing, and by then Pupil would definitely be gone.

"What the Thed could Melana want Pupil to do that he'd need to sneak out while everyone was looking the other way?" Kat asked.

"Who knows," Ashlyn said. "I just hope we can stop him before he does whatever he's supposed to do."

A terrible, drawn-out scream echoed and reverberated around the corridor. It was faint, but sounded like it was coming from the direction of the entrance hall. Without even speaking they sprinted in that direction, sliding around corners until they finally reached the entrance hall overlook. But the hall was deserted. Another scream filled the air; it was closer, but sounded like it came from far below them.

They descended the steps, searching frantically for the source of the screaming. After several minutes of hectic searching, Tomark called out to the others. He stood before a small, white door, which led to who knew where. Kym took one last glance around the empty entrance hall, then pushed through the door and down into the lower levels of Crystal Palace.

They'd only run down the first few steps when a third, louder scream reached Kym's ears, piercing her heart. They were definitely heading in the right direction. She ran on and reached the bottom step sooner than she expected. The vast stone tunnel was far different from the glittering white palace above, with torches set in brackets at regular intervals. But the most peculiar thing about the tunnel was the scene about ten feet in front of Kym.

A boy no older than ten, a palace servant based on his white toga, lay in a heap on the floor. Gashes and bite marks covered his arms and legs, and there were rips along the bottom of his toga, like something tried to pull it off. More scratches and bites appeared out of nowhere along his arms, and Kym couldn't understand what was hurting him. Ashlyn gasped, pointing at the wall behind the boy.

His shadow stretched along the tunnel wall, cowering as he was. But the boy's shadow wasn't the only one on the wall. Crouching next to his shadow, ready to pounce, was the shadow of a large dog. Kym looked around the boy, expecting to see the dog, but there was nothing there. The shadow dog bit the boy's shadow, and new bite marks appeared on his flesh.

A blast of brilliant yellow light shot so close to Kym's arm she felt the heat radiating from it. But it didn't strike the shadow of the dog on the wall, but where the dog would be if it had a physical body. The beam vanished, and a gaping hole appeared in the shadow where the blast struck it, like the attack burned it away. Next to Kym, Ashlyn's arms were outstretched, her yellow Marks glowing.

"It's a darkness construct," she panted. "Pupil's doing, no doubt. He probably set it here to stop anyone from following him."

"Why can't we see its body?" Tomark asked.

"Darkness magic exists in the plane of darkness. We're in the plane of light, so we can only see darkness magic if Darkness Favored bring it into this plane."

"I've seen Pupil make bolts and stuff," Kat said, staring at the now-motionless dog.

"Bolts and blasts and other attacks require a lot of energy and focus, which brings them into the plane of light."

Personally, Kym was more concerned with the bleeding boy than the planes of darkness and light. She took a step toward him, but Amber threw her arm out in front of her. She was staring at the darkness construct, and a moment later Kym realized why. The hole Ashlyn blasted into it was slowly filling in. In a few seconds, the construct would be ready to attack again.

But it never got the chance. Both Amber and Ashlyn threw bolts where the dog would be standing, not even giving it the opportunity to bare its fangs. Ashlyn's light bolt hit it in the middle once again, while Amber's fire bolt hit it directly in the head. The construct writhed around before fading away, leaving no trace of itself behind.

Kym ran to the boy, wrapping the worst of his wounds with her shawl, her fingers trembling the entire time. Tomark carried the boy, who seemed ready to pass out, back up the stairs while the girls moved deeper into the tunnel. About a hundred feet down, the tunnel turned, revealing a new, unlit passage. They looked at each other, none of them wanting to step into this new tunnel. Finally, when

Tomark returned, Kym took a deep breath and peered cautiously around the corner.

The darkness was too dark. After taking a few tentative steps in, Kym couldn't see the others behind her, even though she could still hear them breathing. But when she stepped into the tunnel, Kym saw something she hadn't seen outside of it. A purple man glowed faintly at the end of the tunnel, right in front of a giant, circular door. Something grabbed tightly around Kym's wrist, making her jump.

"Shh," Tomark's voice hissed.

But Tomark's whisper carried eerily through the dark. The purple man faced Kym and rushed toward her with incredible speed. There was a flash of light, and suddenly the tunnel was full of brilliant sunlight, which glinted off the shining walls. Ashlyn's Marks glowed, and a miniature sun floated over their heads. The purple man vanished, replaced by a long shadow cast along the floor. The shadow bulged and rose off the ground, where it transformed into a young man.

"What are you doing here?" Pupil demanded, and Kym heard the fear in his voice.

"We could ask you the same question," Ashlyn answered, apparently shocked that they actually found him.

"Go back to the party."

"Not without you," Kym said, stepping toward him.

"No," Pupil said, invoking his purple Marks. "I have to do this."

"You don't—" Amber began.

Pupil sent a darkness swipe at them, and they dove to the ground to avoid it. Kym looked wildly around for a source of water, but there was nothing. Another darkness swipe soared through the air, and again they scrambled away from it. Kym struggled to her feet, pulling herself up on the glistening wall. Pupil was about to send a third swipe when Kat hit him with an earth bolt, knocking him back.

Desperate, not knowing what to do, Kym ran her hands over her face, leaving it damp. The crashes of battle filled the tunnel as Kym examined the wall. It wasn't made of shiny stone as she originally thought. The walls were wet. A darkness bolt soared toward her, and she focused all her energy on the wet wall.

Kym's small shield formed just in time, deflecting Pupil's bolt while remaining intact. She reformed the shield into a bolt and threw it at Pupil, who seemed to be crumbling under the weight of their five-pronged attack. His back pressed against the round door, he looked frantically around, but Kym and the others had him cornered.

"No!" Pupil called. His Marks flashed momentarily, but nothing happened.

"Give up," Tomark shouted, inching closer to Pupil. "You're outnum- Ah!"

Tomark was hoisted into the air by his ankle, though nothing was holding onto him. Kym spun around. At least ten shadows covered the tunnel walls behind them. There were several dogs, a snake, a couple of large birds, and one that was so giant Kym couldn't think of a word for it. One of the birds held the shadow of Tomark's ankle in its shadowy beak, suspending him high in the air. Blood trickled down Tomark's leg as he fought to free himself from the bird's clutches.

Before Kym, Kat, Amber, or Ashlyn could move to save Tomark, the rest of the darkness constructs charged. Kym pulled water from the walls, formed another shield, and watched the wall. The shadow of a large dog lunged at her shadow, and Kym ducked behind her shield. The dog shadow hit her own, and Kym felt something very hard and solid collide with her shield. On the wall, Kym saw the shadow dog lying on its back, and she seized her chance. She deformed her shield and shot a blast down the middle of the hall where she thought the construct landed. She guessed right, and the shadow on the wall vanished.

Panting, Kym looked around. Kat and Amber each fought a different construct, while Tomark blindly threw bolts at the bird still holding him in the air. Ashlyn was also in the middle of battle, ensnaring several constructs in a large ring of light. At the other end of the tunnel, Pupil was trying to force open the massive round door.

Kym ran at Pupil, but something hard hit her in the stomach, knocking her back. The massive construct was standing in the middle of the tunnel, blocking her path. Kym saw the large shadow raise its arms, and quickly formed a shield. It blocked the attack, but shattered under the immense force. Unable to defend herself, Kym stumbled backward. An arch of yellow light soared over her head. On the wall, the large shadow was cut cleanly in two.

In front of her, the large round door finally swung open. Without even looking back at his fighting friends, Pupil ran through it. Ashlyn, her bright yellow dress ripped in several places, raced past Kym, still sitting on the floor.

"I'll handle Pupil!" she shouted as she ran through the door. "Help them!"

At the other end of the tunnel, Tomark, Kat, and Amber were in trouble. Kat was fighting three constructs at once, Amber seemed to be pinned down, and Tomark still hadn't freed himself. Kym pulled all the remaining water from the walls, and threw a bolt over Amber's pinned body. On the wall, the shadow of a snake wriggled and writhed before it vanished. Together, Amber and Kym defeated the bird and two dogs attacking Kat, Kym using the last of her water in the process.

Turning their attention to Tomark, Amber and Kat both threw bolts into the air. Kat's missed, but Amber's was a direct hit, and the bird dropped Tomark. Kym raced forward to catch him, but she was late by seconds. Tomark fell to the ground, and there was a loud crack as his bleeding leg hit the stone. Amber shot a blast into the air, and the bird construct finally vanished.

"Are you okay?" Kym asked, kneeling beside Tomark. His face was green, and his foot stuck out at an odd angle.

"I'm fine," he grimaced.

"Where's Ash?" Kat panted, looking around.

"She chased after Pupil," Kym said.

"Can you walk?" Amber asked, bending down to help Tomark to his feet.

"No," he winced, lifting his injured foot quickly off the ground. "But I got it."

He invoked his Marks and rose several inches into the air. Thinking this was the best they could do, Kym followed Kat through the circular door and into the chamber beyond. They stood at the top of a small flight of stairs that led down to a stone walkway, lined on either side by long pools of clear blue water. Torches covered the walls, but they didn't seem to give off much light. A raised altar sat at the end of the walkway, topped with a little white box and illuminated by a spotlight from overhead. The chamber would have looked peaceful if there wasn't a battle raging within it.

Ashlyn and Pupil were locked in combat, and it was unlike anything Kym had ever seen. Ashlyn moved so fast it seemed impossible. She would stand in one place, then after a yellow flash, Ashlyn would be on the other side of the room, attacking the entire time. Multiple light bolts exploded from the giant orb in her hands, soaring through the air and following Pupil around the walkway. Most of the time he stayed a shadow, sliding around the walkway, and only became human long enough to send several bolts and blasts at Ashlyn.

Kym, Tomark, Kat, and Amber sprang into action. Tomark flew over Ashlyn, staying off his injured leg, and hovered over Pupil as his shadow slid across the ground. Kat dove into the walkway and Amber sent a jet of flame flying over Ashlyn's head, hitting where Pupil had been seconds before. Kat rose out of the ground, but Pupil grabbed her shadow and threw it, sending Kat flying through the air. Tomark flew to catch Kat, and Kym charged forward. She formed two bolts from the pools and threw them at the slithering shadow on the ground. At the same time Ashlyn, Tomark, Kat, and Amber all sent attacks to the same place.

Their combined attacks blasted Pupil's shadow off the ground. He flew through the air, oddly distorted as he turned back into his human form. He landed in a heap and rolled into the base of the altar. He immediately tried to stand, but Kym was thinking ahead of him.

"We need to bind him." There had to be some rope somewhere in the room.

Ashlyn had a better solution. She waved her hand, and a ring of yellow light appeared around Pupil's ankles. He toppled over, landing flat on his stomach as the others surrounded him, Tomark still floating several inches off the ground. Pupil tried to crawl forward, but Ashlyn waved her hand again, and several more rings of light appeared around his body, as well as his hands.

"I didn't know you could do that," Amber panted, sounding impressed.

"Nor did I," Ashlyn breathed. "I just kinda went for it. And it worked!"

They closed in around Pupil. A powerful pulse of darkness, stronger than any Pupil had produced, rippled through the chamber. It knocked Kym off her feet, sending her flying through the air while Pupil stayed where he was. She slammed into the ground, and heard multiple voices cry out in pain around her. Her head throbbing, Kym saw the yellow bands around Pupil's body begin to fade. Then the bands glowed bright purple and vanished in a flash.

Pupil stood and stumbled up to the altar. He opened the small white box, and a rainbow of multicolored light filled the chamber. Pupil thrust his hand inside and pulled the glowing, multicolored gem from within. He paused, looking back at Kym and the others, all lying motionless on the ground. Then, he transformed back into a shadow and slithered from the room, taking the Conduit with him.

C R Y S T A L
C L E A R

KYM TRIED TO STAND, BUT HER LEGS AND ARMS TREMBLED AS SHE tried to push herself from the ground. She collapsed, falling face first to the floor. Lifting her head the few inches she could, Kym saw she was better off than the others. She'd been the farthest from the strange darkness pulse, leaving the others to get the worst of it.

Ashlyn, who looked like she was having trouble lying on her back, was closest to Pupil when the pulse went off. She held her head in her hands, moaning quietly. Amber and Kat tried to help each other stand, but with very little success. Tomark looked like he was willing himself not to throw up while he clutched his broken ankle.

Kym forced herself up. She crawled over to Ashlyn, and the room spun wildly around her. She sat behind her, lifted Ashlyn's head into her lap, and brushed her long, red hair from her face.

"Are we ignoring the fact that Pupil stole the Conduit?" Kat asked thickly.

"We have bigger problems right now," Kym said.

"Like what?"

"Them," Kym hissed, her eyes darting between Tomark and Ashlyn. "Ashlyn? Ash? Can you hear me?" Ashlyn merely groaned in response. "This isn't good. She needs help."

"Tomark's no better," Amber said. "I think he landed on his bad foot, but I'm not sure."

"Get him up," Kym ordered, looking back down at Ashlyn. "Can you stand?"

"Uh-huh," Ashlyn moaned.

Slowly, Kym pulled Ashlyn into a sitting position. She draped one of Ashlyn's arms over her aching shoulders, and hoisted Ashlyn to her feet. She swayed ominously for a moment, but luckily, Ashlyn didn't pass out. Amber supported Tomark similarly across her shoulders, while Kat just stood there, her arms folded tightly across her chest, staring at the altar. Kym and Amber hobbled their way down the stone walkway toward the round door, but with Tomark's one good foot and Ashlyn's swaying, they stopped every few feet to rest. Kat finally joined them when they reached the stairs.

"We need to talk."

"About what?" Kym demanded. "Tomark and Ash are hurt. We need to get them out of here."

"Don't you get it? We've been waiting for this."

"What are you blathering about?" Amber snapped.

"Me-lan-a," Kat said through gritted teeth. "This is what she's been planning."

"What?" Ashlyn asked groggily.

"How'd you work that out?" Tomark asked.

"Look," Kat snarled, clearly frustrated. "Melana needs power to overthrow the gods, and the Rulers won't help her. So she needed to find some. How about the giant, magical"—she paused, searching for the right word—"battery, the Rulers just recharged."

"And you thought I'd lost it when I said I saw a shadow sneak out of the dining hall," Kym said, stopping dead in her tracks.

"It makes sense," Kat said defensively.

Kym was about to retort but stopped mid-word. Something wasn't right. The sounds of flickering flames and bubbling water that filled the chamber moments before were gone. Even her voice faded into silence faster than it should have. It was like something was sucking the sound from the room. Kym looked around, Ashlyn still supported on her shoulder, but the chamber was empty except for them.

Could the Conduit's absence be causing the silence? Kym looked at the altar, which looked exactly like it did before. Then, one of the shadows broke free from the vast, curved wall behind the altar. Kym and the others stumbled away from the shadow, which drifted through the air like smoke. It landed silently and solidified in the form of a tall, elegant woman.

Melana towered over them, a vicious smile playing around her lips, but Kym wasn't scared of her smile. There was something strange happening to Melana's face. Her light skin seemed to be drained of color, and dark veins covered her smooth features. And Kym distinctly remembered Melana's eyes as brown, but now they were black. The blackness overtook the whites of her eyes, and when she spoke, something mingled with her cold voice—something ancient and powerful.

"I must say I am impressed." It was like two voices were coming from her mouth. "I did not expect children would discover my plans, especially you," she added, staring at Kym. "Had I not intervened, you would have captured my Pupil, and my plans for this world would fall to ruin."

"You blasted us back!" Kat shouted.

"Of course I did. You should have died, but you seem to be more resilient than I anticipated."

"It's five against one," Amber said. "Even with all your power, you're outnumbered. Now let us go."

"With all of you hurt? No. You may outnumber me, but I have you out-magicked."

Melana raised her hands, her Marks shining, and the walls of the chamber glowed purple. She waved her hand through the air, and with a sound like a cannon, a tear opened in the space above her. Wind howled through the rip like a hurricane. Melana smiled, her face still oddly distorted, as she turned back into shadow. She spun on the spot, and with a faint pop, vanished just like Amber had so many times.

An unearthly roar filled the chamber. Long, skeletal hands forced their way through the tear. Kym's insides turned to ice as the creature fell into the chamber. Nearly as tall as the vast room, it looked like a black skeleton. Giant, leathery wings flapped on its shoulders, spraying water and dirt in all directions while it stared at them with eye sockets full of bright black flame. It was a death demon.

Fear rooted Kym to the floor. Maybe, if they didn't move, the demon would leave them alone? Amber, Ashlyn, Tomark, and Kat all seemed to be thinking along those same lines, as none of them made a sound. The eerie stillness lasted five seconds before the demon spread its wings.

They scattered. Letting go of Ashlyn's arm, Kym ran to the closest pool while Kat dove into the stone walkway and Tomark zoomed over her head. Over her shoulder, Kym saw both Amber and Ashlyn running for the door, reaching the stairs as she dove into the water. She sank to the bottom, took a second to collect herself, and then pushed back to the surface.

Tomark threw bolt after bolt of spiraling air down at the demon while Amber and Ashlyn attacked from the ground, blasting its legs. Their attacks had no effect on the demon, which looked almost bored. It swatted lazily at Tomark, Amber, and Ashlyn, who dived sideways to avoid its touch. Kym saw Kat rise out of the walkway right in front of the altar. The two girls looked at each other, nodded, and ran into the fight.

Kat broke two giant boulders off the walls while Kym made two columns of water rise out of the pools. The columns looped around and spiraled together, forming one large jet that shot straight toward the demon's back. Realizing what was happening just in time, Amber, Ashlyn, and Tomark ran for cover. Kat's boulders smashed into the demon's sides as Kym's jet of water hit it in the back, knocking it over.

After twenty seconds of relief, the demon was back on its feet, and it looked angry. The black flames in its eyes grew larger and brighter, and it let out a roar that shook the ceiling. Chunks of stone fell to the ground, but Kat redirected them toward the walls, away from Kym and the others.

Kat pulled hundreds of tiny, glowing green rocks from the walls, and sent them flying at the demon. Roaring, the demon smashed its skeletal fist right where Kat had stood moments before. Amber and Tomark fired alternating blasts of air and fire at the demon's middle, slowly forcing it into the center of the room. Ashlyn and Kym threw what felt like hundreds of bolts at the demon from either side of the chamber, preventing it from moving.

The demon went berserk, spinning around and attempting to knock each of them back as it swung its long, skeletal arms. Kym rolled across the water, narrowly avoiding the deadly touch of its hand. It switched targets to Amber, who wasn't as fast. The demon touched the hem of her dress, which turned black and crumbled into dust.

Amber shrieked. She conjured a giant wall of fire, separating herself from the demon. It spun around, flapping its leathery wings as it tried to avoid the flame, and rammed into the ceiling. Kym seemed to watch in slow motion as Kat, standing on the other side of the room, sent the stone falling over Ashlyn flying in another direction, unaware of the piece right above her. The stone landed with a sickening crash, and Kat fell to the floor. Her mind wiped blank, Kym ran to Kat and saw her arm pinned beneath the rubble.

"Are you okay?" Kym asked.

Kat sat up, phasing her arm through the solid stone. Momentarily relieved, Kym's horror returned when she saw Kat's arm. It was bright red and puffy, and Kat was having trouble moving her fingers.

"I didn't see it," Kat groaned. "I couldn't phase through."

Kym ripped a piece from her already-destroyed dress and wrapped Kat's arm in a sling. Kat grimaced, and Kym hoped the bone was only broken.

"That's your dominant arm," Kym said.

"I'll manage. Move!"

Kym didn't ask why. She dove to the side while Kat sank into the walkway. Looking back, her hair flying around her, she saw the demon's foot right where she and Kat had been, the ground blackened and cracked. It must have retreated from the other end of the chamber, trying to avoid the walkway Amber set on fire.

"Are you crazy?" Kym was back on the edge of a cliff, squid tentacles flying around her.

"It was trying to leave the chamber!" Amber yelled over the roar of the flames, bringing Kym back to the present. "I couldn't let it pass."

Screams filled the chamber as Ashlyn flew through the air, knocked back by the demon. She smashed into the wall and fell with a splash into the pool below her. Panic coursing through her like ice, Kym dove in after her. She pulled Ashlyn, her eyes unfocused, to the surface. She dragged her onto the walkway, trying to be as gentle as she could in her haste.

"Ashlyn?"

Before Ashlyn could answer, the demon's skeletal fist appeared. Kym formed a small shield dome around her and Ashlyn, stopping the demon's hand. Cracks spread through the dome like spider webs, but miraculously, it didn't shatter. The demon moved on, and destruction continued to rain down around them.

Kat continued attacking one-handed while Amber attempted to hold the demon at bay. It flapped its wings angrily, hitting Tomark, who fell and landed with a thud next to Kym and Ashlyn. Bolts and blasts weren't going to stop this thing, even if they were at full strength. They needed something stronger.

"Tomark," Kym said, grabbing his wrist and pulling him into a sitting position. "We need to end this before anyone else gets hurt."

"How?" Tomark grunted, clutching his side. "Nothing we do works."

"Then we need to try something stronger."

Kym looked into his eyes, and comprehension dawned on his face. He rose back into the air, and Kym helped Ashlyn to her feet, explaining what she had in mind. After blinking several times, there was a flash of light, and Ashlyn swayed in front of the altar. Hoping Kat would catch on, Kym shouted at Amber.

"Hey! Princess!" Amber looked at Kym, still trying to keep the demon back with her wall of fire. "Time for me to not be worthless."

Amber smiled, and Kym dove into the nearest pool. She energized as much of the water as she could, and forced it all into the size of a small bolt, using more than half the water in the pool. The compact bolt shook violently in her hands, and arcs of energized water flew in every direction. Kym concentrated as hard as she could, willing the compact bolt to not blow up in her face.

Kym saw tongues of flame and chunks of earth fly through the air, and she redoubled her efforts. The others were counting on her. They needed to end this. She rose slowly out of the water, and saw the others with their compact bolts in their hands; Amber blocked the door, Kat and Ashlyn stood in front of the altar, and Tomark hovered above the other pool. Kym looked down at her bolt. It pulsated smoothly above her hands, but she wasn't surprised. It was time. They were ready.

They threw their compact bolts, and the attacks, willed by their throwers, hit the demon at the same time. A massive, multicolored shock wave reverberated through the room, sending them flying back for what felt like the millionth time as the demon roared. Kym landed in the water, stars popping in her eyes. She swam to the surface, and peered cautiously over the edge of the pool. The death demon lay motionless on the floor, the fires in its eye's extinguished. It was over. They'd done it.

Kym dragged herself onto the walkway, lying flat on her back. She covered her face with her hands, closed her eyes, and breathed a sigh of relief. Her hands slid slowly down her face, and when she looked at them, they were covered in blood. She crawled to the center of the walkway, unable to think of a better place to go. She just lay there, her face pressed against the cold stone.

She didn't know how much time passed, but when she finally looked up, Tomark, Kat, Amber, and Ashlyn were lying around her. Using what felt like all the strength she had left, Kym pushed herself to her knees, and began to rouse the others.

"We need to get them out of here," Kym said to Amber. She, like Kym, only seemed to be cut and bruised.

"Agreed," Amber breathed. "I'll take Ash if you get Tomark."

Together, they hoisted Tomark to his feet, and once Amber pulled Ashlyn up, the four of them and Kat began hobbling up the walkway. It took them much longer to find their way back through the tunnels. They only ever walked for a few minutes before one of them needed to rest. Ashlyn was in the worst shape. She vomited halfway up the steps to the entrance hall, but they still kept going. When the five of them finally reached the glittering white room, they collapsed in a heap on the floor.

Soon, the sound of footsteps reached Kym's ears. Several white togaed servants were running toward them, the little boy they saved in the tunnels leading the way. They whispered frantically to one another, though Kym didn't take in a word they said. A servant knelt beside Kym and lifted her into his arms. He carried her into a room filled with small beds and many potted plants and flowers. He placed Kym on one of the beds, and she watched groggily while the others were carried in. A few moments later, the doors to the room burst open, and Zara swept into the room, closely followed by Evanna, James, Kai, Stailin, and Nila.

"What happened?" James demanded.

"Who did this?" hissed Evanna.

Kym tried to sit up and speak, but the Rulers were yelling and arguing so much her head hurt. A sound like a gunshot rang through the room and silence fell. Zara held her hand over her head, a dark look on her usually calm face.

"This is a place of healing," she said menacingly, "not the location for your most recent screaming match."

She shepherded the other Rulers out of the door, closing it swiftly behind them. She waved her hand over the door, which glowed momentarily white before returning to normal. Zara approached Kym's bed, and the little boy pulled several large flowers to her bedside. Zara removed the life energy from the plants, which crumbled to dust, and let the energy drift over Kym, who felt substantially better. Zara pressed her hands to the cuts on Kym's cheek and forehead. Immediately, they felt like Zara had filled them with white-hot fire. Kym groaned and jerked her head, but Zara didn't remove her hands. When the pain finally faded, Zara let go, and Kym felt perfectly normal.

"That is all I can do," Zara said, her voice gentle once again.

Kym watched Zara heal Amber. The burning sensation she'd felt was Zara forcing life energy into her wounds. Amber struggled as Zara sent the life energy from four plants into the long gash down her left arm. Tomark and Kat's injuries took much more life energy to heal, each using at least ten plants carefully selected by the little boy. Zara, hardly speaking to any of them, moved to Ashlyn, where both she and the servant boy stopped. Ashlyn lay motionless on her bed, not even reacting as Zara and the servant examined her body.

"She hit her head." It wasn't a question, and Zara didn't look up from her work as she continued. "How many times?"

"Um…" So much had happened during the battle. "Maybe twice?" Kym finally said.

Zara and the servant looked at Ashlyn. It was odd watching her debate with the little boy. How long had they known each other? Nila never let her servants speak with her like that. Kym didn't even know if Nila knew her servants' names. But they finally reached a consensus, and the boy dragged nearly twenty plants and flowers around Ashlyn's bed.

Zara summoned the life energy, and after letting it float around Ashlyn's body for a few moments, she placed her hands on Ashlyn's temples. The energy forced its way into her head, but Ashlyn didn't cry out as the others had. Instead, she just lay there, motionless, not making a sound. When all of the energy finally vanished, Ashlyn slowly opened her eyes.

Kym, Kat, Tomark, and Amber surrounded Ashlyn, embracing her and each other in one massive hug. A sigh of relief escaped Kym as she felt each of the bodies pressed against her own. It was all right. They'd made it out alive. It took them a long time to finally pull away from each other. When they did, they saw Zara staring at them, perched on the bed opposite Ashlyn's.

"Would you five like to tell me why you were discovered in such a state?"

"It," Kym began. "It all started when I saw a dark shape slip under the dining hall door during the moment of silence. I thought it must be Pupil since we could only see two other Darkness Favored and I thought the dark shape I saw might be a shadow."

"So we wondered," Ashlyn continued, "why Pupil left since he clearly wanted to slip away unnoticed. We tried asking Lady Melana, but she shooed both Amber and me away. We know Pupil would do whatever she asked, so we figured he must be doing something for her."

"We needed to get out of the feast without being noticed. Amber and I made a big scene to distract the rest of the idiots in the hall—no offense, sorry—so the others could sneak out, and we'd follow," Kat said.

"After we got out," Tomark continued, "we were wondering where Pupil went when we heard a scream. We found that boy cowering on the floor. He was being attacked by a shadow construct."

"We got rid of the construct, and Tomark brought the boy up here. We found Pupil at the end of the tunnel, where he set about a dozen darkness constructs on us. He got through the door at the end of the tunnel, and Ashlyn raced after him while Kym, Tomark, Kat, and I fought off the constructs," Amber said.

"The four of us went to help Ashlyn," Tomark continued, "and we quickly overpowered Pupil."

"But before we could bring him up here," Kym said, "something knocked us back. Pupil took the Conduit from its box and ran from the room."

Zara's eyes flashed at Kym's words. Her eyebrows contracted, and she looked at each one of them in turn. Kym felt like she was being examined.

"Was that all?" Zara asked coldly.

"No," Kym shook her head.

"We were trying to come back up here when Melana appeared," Ashlyn said. "But there was something wrong with her. Her eyes were all black, and her face looked different, and when she spoke her voice sounded all echoey and strange."

"She said she couldn't let us live," spat Kat. "So she summoned this giant death demon to kill us and disappeared. We were barely able to fight it off."

Kat's words were followed by one of the loudest silences Kym ever heard. They just stood there, waiting for Zara to do something. Her usually impassive face had become lined, and she held her hands together so tightly her knuckles turned white. Finally, she spoke, and Kym could tell Zara was fighting to keep her voice steady.

"That is a very serious accusation."

She stood so abruptly Kym and Tomark fell back onto Ashlyn's bed. Zara swept over to the door, which glowed once again before she opened it. Kym and the others hurried after her, unsure of what they were supposed to do. Out in the hall, Zara spoke very quickly with the other Rulers, and their mouths fell open one by one.

"Where is Melana?" Nila demanded. "We must find her."

The Rulers sprinted down the hall and Kym, Tomark, Kat, Ashlyn, and Amber hurried after them. They found Melana in the entrance hall, walking toward the open front doors. She froze when she heard them approach, and turned slowly to face them, looking at the floor.

"Lady Melana," Zara said from the front of their little party. "These Favored accuse you of stealing the Conduit of Princirum, as well as attempted murder. What do you have to say about these accusations?"

"Well," Melana said in the same strange two-in-one voice, "there is no use denying it. It is all true."

"Melana?" Zara breathed, approaching her cautiously. "What have you done?"

"No, not Melana." Melana's voice was gone, and only the deep one issued from her lips. She looked up and revealed her pale, black-veined face. "I am Thed, God of Death."

CHAPTER NINETEEN

HOW THE MIGHTY HAVE FALLEN

Ashlyn screamed. Several of the Rulers gasped, backing away from Melana. Kym's brain felt like it had been unplugged. It was impossible. How could Thed, the god of death, be in the land of the living? And how could Melana be Thed? Only Zara stood her ground, seemingly unsurprised by the god of Death announcing his presence.

"How are you here, Thed?" Zara said coldly. "The gods banished you to Nothingness when you failed to destroy their vision for humankind."

"Oh, little Zara," Thed said through Melana. "You already know how I came to be here. This young woman came to me as a friend when you denied her what she rightfully deserved. Naturally, I assisted her, as I do for all those who feel the changing tides. You, little life-giver, know better than any; death always finds you when you least expect it."

Thick, black mist appeared around Melana, seeping from her body until Kym couldn't see her. It rose into the air, swirling like storm-clouds and carrying Melana with it. The black cloud spun faster and faster, dissipating into the surrounding air. Melana fell to the floor in a heap of various purple fabrics, her face and eyes returned to normal. Zara pulled Melana up by her dress, her eyes alight with anger, and waved her free hand at Melana, her white Marks glowing. Melana gasped with pain, clutching at her forearms. It was like Zara set her on fire.

"Prepare the throne room for an emergency Summit of the Rulers," Zara ordered the boy, who seemed reluctant to leave her side.

The little boy ran up the entrance hall stairs. Melana wrenched herself from Zara's grip, who didn't try to maintain it, causing Melana to stumble back. She pointed her hand menacingly at Zara, and though Kym knew what Melana intended, her Marks didn't appear.

"Do not even try, Melana," Zara snapped. "Your energy flow is blocked. You will not use magic until I decide otherwise. Restrain her."

Evanna and Stailin stepped forward at Zara's command. Melana tried to brush them off, but they each took one of her arms in their hands. They pulled her away from the rest of the group and formed bolts, which they held menacingly close to her back. Melana stopped struggling. The servant boy returned a minute later, announcing the throne room was ready. The Rulers walked toward the stairs, Evanna and Stailin dragging Melana between them. Kym, Tomark, Kat, Amber, and Ashlyn stayed where they were, unsure what to do. Then, Evanna's voice rang out from the top of the stairs.

"Well," she said impatiently. "What are you waiting for?"

When Kym and the others only exchanged confused looks, Zara stepped forward.

"You are needed at the Summit. You must present your story officially before we can proceed."

Kym silently led the way up the stairs, keeping a healthy distance between her and the Rulers, and in the quiet, the events of the night came more into focus. She wanted to go after Pupil. Melana tried to kill them. Tomark and Kat broke bones and Ashlyn barely made it out of that chamber alive. And now they were attending an official Summit, covered in blood and wearing the rags that were once their clothes. And it was all her fault.

"I'm sorry," Kym whispered. "I caused all of this."

"No, you didn't," Tomark said flatly. "All of this. It's on Melana."

"I said we should go find Pupil. I'm the reason you got hurt."

"But we're fine now," Ashlyn smiled. "And thanks to you…"

"Melana's getting exactly what she deserves," Kat finished.

Even though it was almost midnight, it looked like the middle of the day in the throne room as a soft, warm glow issued from the walls and ceiling. All of the Rulers sat on their thrones, and Zara ordered her servant to bring in extra chairs for the Favored. Zara smiled down at Kym, Tomark, Kat, Amber, and Ashlyn from her raised throne as they sat behind their Rulers.

"I call this Summit to order," Zara began. "Our first and only order of business is to discover the truth of this evening's events and, if they are indeed true, how they came to be. We will discuss punishments for the guilty when necessary. If the Favored would please give their account of what happened this evening, we can begin."

Kym didn't want to relive the whole night a second time since, no matter what the others said, she was responsible for at least some of what happened. If she'd just kept her mouth shut about seeing Pupil leave, none of this would be happening. She'd be out on the grounds, fast asleep in her tent like all the other Favored who knew to not stick their heads where they didn't belong.

But that wasn't Kym. She'd go after a friend she thought was doing something wrong. She'd speak out against a Ruler's cruelty. She'd do her best, no matter what anyone else said. She'd pull garbage out of the river just to glimpse the world beyond.

Slowly, Kym stood, stepped into the middle of the throne room, and began, officially, telling what happened. She went through it all— second by second, blow-by-blow, broken bone by broken bone. She took her time, not leaving out a single detail, and it was like every- thing happened all over again. She felt the blows, heard the bones crack, and felt the death demon's chill.

When she finally finished, explaining how they collapsed on the floor before the servants found them, the room was silent. The Rulers took in her words, staring at her with such intensity Kym was surprised it didn't knock her over. But Kym stayed where she was, not wanting to disrupt them. Finally, Evanna leaned forward in her throne, her forehead covered in lines.

"Why, when you thought something was happening, did you not inform a Ruler of your suspicions? Why try and go after the Darkness Pupil yourself? It would have been simpler to alert someone with the authority to—"

"Because," Ashlyn said, stepping forward and cutting across Evanna, "Pupil is...was...is our friend. We thought he was doing something that he might not want to do. We thought we could stop him."

"I understand, Ashlyn," Evanna said, her tone frigid. "But you have not answered my question. Why did you not inform someone capable of handling the situation?"

"I mean no disrespect, Lady Evanna," Amber said, ruining the effect by refusing to drop her superior tone, "but would you, or any of the Rulers, have believed us if we'd told you what we suspected?"

"Of course we would believe you," Evanna said simply.

"Do not kid yourself, Evanna," James laughed dryly. "We all know if anyone came up to us and said what these five thought was happening, we would have waved them off."

James stared at the other Rulers as if trying to see each of their reactions to his statement. Most avoided eye contact, shifting uncomfortably on their thrones as they stared in random directions. Kym tried to imagine herself in the Rulers' shoes. If a Favored had come up to her and said they thought another Favored sneaked out of a feast to do something for another Ruler, Kym would have thought they'd gone crazy.

"It doesn't matter whether or not we would have believed their suspicions," Zara said. "The time when we could have intervened has passed. What matters is the events of this night did happen. I tended to their wounds myself, which were consistent with both the girl's story and known injuries by such beasts.

"And now we must discover why these events occurred. There is a power at work here I have not seen for centuries. Melana appears to have been possessed by Thed. Lady Melana, do you deny this claim?"

Everyone in the hall turned to face Melana, who sat on her throne, her cold smile in place. Her eyes moved slowly over every single person in the throne room, like she wasn't the one being accused of being possessed by the god of death. Finally, she looked directly at Zara, whose throne turned to face her.

"I do not deny these claims."

"Melana," Zara said, looking stunned for the first time. "By saying this, do you realize what you confess?"

Melana fixed Zara with her emotionless gaze. "Enlighten me?"

"Godly possession is no easy feat," Zara began. "It is a complex and volatile relationship. Most believe possession is a god forcing entry into one's body and mind, taking complete control over the person while the host cannot resist. This is not true. Possession is a relationship; a partnership; an agreement. The host is always conscious of the god's presence in their body and mind, and the god must always want to be present within the body. The two must be in constant harmony. One cannot work without the other while they share a body.

"By confessing to possession by Thed, Lady Melana admits to willingly aiding the sworn enemy of the gods by helping him carry out his plans on Princirum. You have knowingly plotted the destruction of all we protect. Do you have anything to say for yourself, Lady Melana?"

"Am I supposed to get on my knees, brimming with remorse, and beg for your mercy?" Melana asked silkily. "I will not, for I regret nothing. None of you would act and help me seize that which is rightfully ours. Princirum is our birthright. But none of you, for all your talk, could see the future I envisioned for us. So, I looked for allies elsewhere, and Thed presented himself to me.

"He agreed that our parents have not done what is best for Princirum. He offered to assist me in destroying our parents, and I, his devoted niece, accepted. He showed me how to get more power; enough power to stand victorious against our parents. The Conduit, newly charged at the Festival of Creation, would grant me enough power to accomplish my goal.

"I instructed my most powerful student to steal the Conduit for me, for I could not be seen stealing it myself. He was to slip away unseen during the moment of silence on the Day of Death and return before any in the crowd noticed his absence. Everything went just as I planned; I sensed him leave the room and make his way to the Conduit chamber. But then, something went wrong."

Melana glared at Amber and Ashlyn, and her tone seemed to become icier if that were even possible. "These two girls came up to me mere minutes after my Pupil left, asking if I knew where he was, for they could not find him. It seemed odd that Favored from different palaces were looking for my Pupil, and I told them to mind their own business. Then, a short while later, I sensed something else had gone wrong. I teleported to the Conduit Chamber and saw my student subdued by these five, who'd magically bound him in a way I have never seen Favored do before.

"I acted quickly, knocking them back and releasing my Pupil from his bonds, who completed his task. I thought I had dealt with the children, but they soon awoke. They deduced that my Pupil stole the Conduit for me, but they did not know why. Naturally, I could not let them leave the chamber alive. I showed myself and, with Thed's power, summoned a death demon to killed them."

Melana looked down at Kym and the others, and the loathing in her eyes was unmistakable; like it was their fault they didn't want to get killed. Kym's insides turn to fire. Did she really care so little about everything else in the world that she was willing to kill anyone to get what she wanted?

"Your Pupil—is the Conduit still in his possession?" Nila asked.

"Of course."

"Summon your student, Melana, and have him return what is rightfully ours," Zara demanded.

"There will be no need for that, Lady Zara. He is already here."

Melana snapped her fingers, and the shadow of her throne swelled upward. Pupil stepped out from behind the throne and stood beside Melana. He seemed intent with examining his shoes and didn't look up from the floor.

"Bring the Conduit forward," Zara ordered.

Slowly, his eyes still trained on the floor, Pupil walked toward Zara's throne. He unbuttoned his purple vest and pulled the Conduit, large and multicolored, from inside it. He handed the glittering stone to Zara, who sent her young servant to return it to its chamber. Pupil walked sheepishly back to Melana's side, refusing to look at anyone. But even though he tried to hide it, Kym could still see the disgust on his face.

"Pupil," Stailin barked. "Did you know Thed had possessed Melana?"

Slowly, Pupil shook his head.

"She told me stealing the Conduit was a test," he whispered, "like going to Wadita to scare Kym. She said doing it would prove I'm the most powerful Favored she's ever trained. I wanted to prove myself and show her I'm the best, because she only ever keeps the best."

Kym could almost picture Pupil walking into a dark room where Melana waited for him. She could hear her cold words, telling Pupil this was the only way to stay her student forever. Part of her felt sorry for Pupil; she knew how hard it would be for him to resist such an offer. But she still couldn't believe he actually went through with it, and hurt his friends in the process.

"How could you do this, Melana," Kai demanded, getting to his feet. "How could you turn against your own family? What did we do to deserve such a fate?"

"You did nothing," Melana said coldly. Kai sat back down, almost recoiling in fear. "And that is the point. I used to be able to count on all of you. But now, you are too scared to do anything that might disrupt your precious lives. You were too worried about what would happen if we failed. Thed acted as family should."

"If Melana fell under Thed's influence," Nila said, apparently following her own train of thought, "are any of us truly safe? Can we trust anyone?"

"Don't be paranoid, Nila," James said dully.

"She has a right to be paranoid, as do we all," Evanna said. "When was the last time any of us truly confided in one another? Years? Centuries? I do not know who any of you are anymore."

Kym couldn't believe her ears. The Rulers were supposed to be discussing how Melana betrayed them by joining forces with Thed. Wasn't that the whole point of this Summit? They weren't here to argue about whom they did and didn't trust anymore. She'd always imagined the Rulers as a single unit; sure, they didn't always agree, but in the end, they'd always stand as one. But as the Rulers pointed and jeered at one another, Kym was sure she'd lost her mind. To her left, she saw her shock reflected on Kat's face.

"Are you sure it is wise to make enemies out of your closest allies, Evanna?" Stailin asked.

"When my closest allies are all of you? You know what they say: 'Keep your friends close and your enemies closer.'"

"I would have never thought it possible," Nila said. "Being in a room with so many idiotic people."

"And what do you mean by that, Nila?" Kai asked hotly.

"It means you cannot see what is plainly right in front of you."

Kai looked as though he was about to retaliate when a deafening boom sounded through the hall. It echoed around the round room, bouncing off the smooth walls until it finally died out. The Rulers looked at Zara, who alone remained silent, her eyes flashing dangerously.

"This is getting us nowhere," Zara said. "We are here to discuss Melana's actions and pass judgment on them. Your little squabble has no relevance to our goals tonight. I believe we can all agree Melana is guilty. Now, we must determine the punishment for her crimes."

It was clear from the looks on their faces that the Rulers weren't ready to let the subject drop. Evanna's nostrils flared, Kai's face was blotchy and red, and James panted like he'd just run a marathon. All these feelings seemed to have been lurking below the surface, and Melana's actions were just enough to blast them over. They stared at the floor, refusing to look at one another, their large crowns all in danger of tipping off.

Kym glanced across the room at Tomark. He was staring at Pupil, still standing beside Melana's throne, his entire body deflated. Tomark's gaze was so intense Kym was surprised Pupil didn't wince. Apparently sensing her eyes on him, Pupil lifted his head slightly in her direction. For a moment, she did nothing, then, seeing the look on his face, she smiled. Pupil looked back at the floor, but she thought she saw the corners of his mouth twitch.

"I feel there should be no punishment for Melana's crime."

"Of course you think that, Kai," James snorted. "You have always been scared of Melana."

"I am not—" Kai began.

"Enough!" Zara roared. She rose to her feet, glaring down at everyone in the room. Power seemed to radiate from her, and everyone fell silent. "Obviously, you are not going to let this go. So I will reach a decision on my own. You will all leave this throne room immediately. I will summon you when I have reached my decision."

Eager to escape the throne room as fast as possible, Kym walked over to the door without a second thought. When she reached the door, she saw the other Favored also making a beeline for the exit; however, all of the Rulers remained seated on their thrones. They stared at Zara, and each one looked like she'd slapped them across the face. Zara cleared her throat loudly, but still, the Rulers didn't move.

Seconds turned into minutes as the Rulers still refused to leave, and Zara didn't do a thing about it. She sat on her throne; her hands pressed together, her throne rotating slowly on the spot. She gazed down at the Rulers, an odd smile playing around the corners of her mouth. Finally, James seemed to have had enough.

"This is pointless!"

He stood up, throwing his arms in the air as he stormed out of the throne room. Soon after, Evanna followed suit, then Kai, then Stailin, then Nila. Melana was the last to leave her seat. Finally, she stood, her lips pursed together as she sauntered from the throne room. Once in the hall, the Rulers went off in different directions, skulking around the shadowy columns supporting the ceiling. Kym gazed into the now-nearly-empty throne room, and the massive doors swung shut with an ominous thunk.

C H A P T E R   T W E N T Y

B A C K   T O   N O R M A L ,
M A Y B E

EXHAUSTED, BARELY ABLE TO KEEP HER EYES OPEN, KYM SANK TO her knees in the middle of the hall. Kat plopped down next to her, and Tomark and Ashlyn practically fell to the floor, while Amber sat with a bit more grace. Pupil stayed standing, a little apart from the rest of the group. Everyone but Kym refused to look at him. She was over all the fighting they'd witnessed that night. She offered Pupil her hand. He took it, and she pulled him to the floor.

The silence seemed to last forever. Personally, Kym thought she'd done enough talking that day to last her about three lifetimes. The silence was nice, almost peaceful. But she knew it couldn't last. So much had happened, and if they didn't talk about it, they'd end up down a very dark road. Just look at how the Rulers responded when their true feelings finally came out. Eventually Kat, with about as much sensitivity as a hammer, broke the silence.

"All right, let's get this over with. And for the sake of time," Kat yawned, "can we not beat around the bush?"

They looked expectantly at Pupil, who seemed even more fascinated by the floor than he had been with his shoes in the throne room. He had dark circles under his eyes, and his large, muscular body seemed deflated. It was strange, seeing such a large person look so small. And even though they were all looking at him, Pupil didn't make a sound.

"Fine," Kat burst out, apparently unable to take it anymore. "I'll start. Pupil, why did you do it?"

Pupil seemed to be going through some intense internal struggle.

He kept opening and closing his mouth like he was trying to speak, but no sound came out.

"I…" he finally said. "I did it…my family has no money."

Of all the answers he could have given, this wasn't what Kym expected. She thought he'd talk about respecting his Ruler and showing blind loyalty wherever possible. But being poor? How was that supposed to justify his actions?

"Look," Pupil continued. "My parents never had much. I was always the kid wearing second-hand clothes and buying all used books and things for school. But when Melana found me, I wasn't poor anymore. I was rich. I lived in a palace full of servants and jewels. Everything there was brand new, and it was all mine.

"But there's a price for being Melana's student. She's not like the other Rulers. The Great Fortress isn't full of Darkness Favored; there's only ever three of us there, and if she thinks she's found someone better, she'll throw you out without any warning. She only cares about power, and if you're not powerful, you're of no value to her.

"So we're constantly trying to prove ourselves, and show her how powerful we are. All we do is train until we literally can't go on. Then, Melana gives us each a task; if we complete it, no questions asked, we're in the clear. But if we fail, she'll kick us out that night, and have our replacement already waiting."

"So," Amber asked skeptically, "you stole the Conduit to save your place at the Fortress? You do know that the Rulers give all their Favored land and estates within their realms when we leave the palaces?"

"It's not the same as being a Darkness Pupil," Pupil said. "Nothing is like living in the palace."

Amber snorted. "Take it from someone who's been doing this a lot longer than you; living in a palace for your entire life isn't all it's cracked up to be. And don't worry about what will happen when you get chucked out like every other Darkness Favored. The houses they give us are really nice. My dad's is enormous."

"Sorry, I don't buy it," Tomark said. "There had to be something in it for you. What did she offer you to get you to do her dirty work? You had to know it was wrong."

Pupil looked to the side, and Kym could see his body tense. He was staring at Melana, who was watching the Favored as they talked in their little huddle.

"All right. Melana said she'd use the Conduit to give me more power if I got it for her."

"Oh, Thed," Ashlyn said, rolling her eyes.

"What?" Pupil asked, a note of resentment in his voice.

"You're telling me you believed her when she said she'd give you more power?"

"She said she would. She gave me her word."

"Yeah, and we all know Melana's the most trustworthy person in the whole wide world," Kat said sarcastically.

"We trusted *you*!" Ashlyn shouted. "You were our friend, and you turned on us. Did you think we wouldn't find out what you did? I thought we knew you. Guess I was wrong."

"Didn't you think it was odd that we were trying to stop you?" Amber asked.

"I-I didn't…" Pupil stammered.

"Is power really so important to you that you're willing to hurt your friends to get it?" Tomark asked.

Kym looked at the ceiling, rubbing her eyes as she felt an odd tremor run through her body. Did it really matter why Pupil did what he did? She was sick and tired of everyone picking apart everyone's motivations. Zara said it was in the past, so what was the point of arguing about it now? It wasn't like they could go back and change it if they talked about it enough. All they were doing was making each other angrier than they were before.

The others continued to argue about Pupil's unbelievable reasoning. Kym, her skin still crawling, tore her gaze from the ceiling. It was like someone was watching her. Sure enough, the Rulers were staring at the circle of Favored from their shadowy corners. They wore expressions of displeasure on their faces, but Melana looked particularly vengeful. Her hands were balled into fists, and her eyes were mere slits. Kym turned back to the others, where Kat was telling Pupil how much of a moron he was.

"Hey, wait," Kym interrupted.

"What? You don't think he's an idiot for doing everything he's told?" Kat asked hotly.

"What? No, it's not that. Look. The Rulers are staring at us, and they don't look too happy, do they?"

The Rulers quickly looked away, but not before Kym and the others saw them watching their conversation.

"They really don't look happy," Kat said, smiling at the thought. "Dang."

"It's like they don't want us talking to each other. You don't think it's because they all don't trust each other now?" Amber said.

"That's ridiculous," Tomark said. "They don't need to be frightened of each other, or us talking on the floor. What do they have to be scared of anyway? They're all powerful and immortal. The only things more powerful than them are the gods."

"I know," Kym shook her head. "I don't get it either."

"If I were them," Ashlyn said, "I'd want to help the other Rulers. Melana only went to Thed in the first place because the other Rulers wouldn't help her. And now they're only going to make things worse by isolating themselves."

"This has been building since their little talk after our evals," Pupil said quietly. "Couldn't you feel it when they all started screaming at each other? They want more power than the others, but they're scared someone else might become more powerful than they are."

"Why are you talking?" Kat snapped. "Who said you could—"

"Kat," Kym said, actually throwing up her hands in frustration. "Look, Pupil did what he thought he needed to do in the moment. Was he completely wrong and out of his mind? Yes. But we've all made mistakes. None of us are guilt-free here. So, can we agree to just let this go? If we don't, we're going to end up just like them."

They turned to look at the Rulers, all separated around the hall, then, one by one, they nodded. A flash of multicolored light burst from the gap between the floor and the bottom of the throne room doors. All of the Rulers perked up at the sight of the light, apparently mesmerized by the multicolored display. Seconds later, the doors swung open, and Zara stood on the threshold, her face lined with concentration.

"You may reenter at this time," she announced to the hallway at large.

The Rulers practically ran through the doors, overjoyed that they were allowed back in the throne room, before Kym even realized what had happened. Kym and the others, on the other hand, took much more time to enter the throne room. Sitting on the floor was a lot easier than standing. Once on their feet, they all ambled back into the throne room and sat in their seats, already exhausted from that small amount of exertion. Kym hoped the rest of the Summit wouldn't take long, her mind drifting to her tent and bed on the grounds.

"I have reached a decision regarding the behavior of the Ruler of Darkness, Lady Melana," Zara said officially once everyone had settled. "Since no one in this room could offer me any assistance, I was forced to seek help elsewhere. I prayed, and the gods graced this hall with their presence tonight. But by calling upon their wisdom, I revoked my right to make the final decision. Melana's fate now rested in the gods' hands. They listened to the events of this evening, and together the gods reached a decision.

"This ruling comes straight from the lips of the Great Mother, Pheil, herself. There will be no further discussion on this matter once I deliver her verdict. Rai, god of Air and Judgment, declared the Great Mother's ruling fair and just. After much debate and deliberation, the gods decree that Lady Melana, Ruler of Darkness, for the crimes of treason and attempted deicide, shall be stripped of her authority within this throne room for the next eight months.

"The gods knew all along of Melana's plans against them, and are therefore most generous and forgiving in their punishment, They also knew of her treacherous alliance, and assured me that they have already taken steps to rectify the situation."

For not going to Temple and criticizing the gods and Rulers in public, the priests killed Kym's aunt and uncle. But after making a deal with Thed and planning to destroy the gods, Melana didn't get to vote at Summits for eight months. She must have misunderstood Zara. Melana tried to steal the source of magic, she tried to kill Kym and her friends, and the gods, who knew all this was happening, decided to put her in a timeout? How was this justice?

"This plan the gods spoke of," Stailin said, pulling Kym momentarily from her fury, "what is it?"

"They did not tell me. All Pheil said was that greed and power could tempt even the best of us and once one has a taste, they can only crave more. But, the gods did say we should not expect this level of leniency from them again. The next time they feel threatened, the gods will deal with the culprit personally."

Zara stepped down and walked over to Melana's throne. She waved her hand, and Melana breathed a sigh of relief as she rubbed her forearms. With Melana's magic unblocked, Zara returned to her throne, but she didn't take her seat. Instead, she stared at the ground before turning away from the rotating chair.

"The events of tonight have shaken me. I feel a kind of fear I have never experienced, and not just for ourselves, but for all of Princirum. Death is a parasitic entity. Even the tiniest speck will begin to fester and grow if left unchecked. It will consume everything until there is nothing left but death itself. Melana's actions opened Princirum to death's clutches. I can feel them, even now, those tendrils of death, already working their way into our paradise. We must prepare ourselves against Thed's forces. For now, they will surely come.

"Now," Zara continued, sitting at last, "I know the Favored in this room are extremely tired and deserve to rest. In light of this evening's events, I believe we should cancel the rest of the festival. All of those in favor?"

Every Ruler raised their hand without hesitation.

"It is unanimous. We will celebrate the remaining elements tomorrow, allotting each god an hour of praise. Then the festivities at Crystal Palace will end. Good night to you all."

Kym stood, swaying slightly as she tried to maintain her balance. Nila walked up to her, and without even speaking, grabbed tightly around her upper arm. She steered Kym out of the throne room and through the maze of halls. But instead of taking Kym to her tent, Nila pulled her into a shadowy corner when they reached the entrance hall and began to speak in a whisper.

"You look exhausted, Kymbralyn. Are you feeling all right?"

"Tired," she said, taken aback by this sudden show of affection.

"I could not be more proud of you," Nila said, stroking Kym's shoulder with her free hand while refusing to release her hold on her arm.

"Thanks," Kym said gingerly, feeling very uncomfortable.

"When I plucked you from that awful city, I knew I had found something special. You are truly one of a kind, Kymbralyn Collins."

Nila had never shown her this much affection since she arrived at Wadita. Nila was cold, and mean, and uncaring, and never tried to make others feel better. So why was she petting Kym's arm like she was some kind of dog? If Kym weren't so exhausted, she'd have run as far from Nila as she could.

"I will have Kenna and Aidan accompany you to the remainder of the festival tomorrow."

"What? Why?"

"Because your Ruler commands it," Nila said, her soft tone quickly regaining its usual sharpness.

"Okay. But can you tell me why I have to go with them?"

"Those Favored you were with this evening, if you had the choice, you would see them again tomorrow."

"Yes," Kym said automatically. Were they seriously talking about this?

"They are a bad influence on you," Nila said, all pretense of niceness gone. "You will not see them again."

"Why?" Kym asked, finally succeeding in jerking her arm out of Nila's grip.

"I am your Ruler," Nila said, stepping forward and towering over Kym, "and you are my Favored. You will do as I command. Kenna and Aidan will remain by your side until we return to Wadita. Maybe then you will stay out of trouble."

"This isn't fair!" Kym yelled, unable to handle the injustice of the past five minutes.

Nila practically dragged Kym back to her tent. Once inside, she ordered Veronica and Isabel to get Kym to bed and let her sleep through breakfast. They were to wake Kym just before the remaining festivities started. Nila swept from the tent with a huff, and Kym was happy to see her leave. Veronica and Isabel silently undressed Kym, which mainly meant pulling the remaining pieces of destroyed fabric from her body. She collapsed on top of the bed covers before they could even put her in her nightdress.

Kym woke the next morning, her eyes heavy and her body aching, to find Kenna smiling down at her. Kym groaned. She grabbed her pillow and placed it over her head. Maybe, if she went back to sleep, Kenna would go away. No such luck. Veronica pulled Kym from her bed and hurried her over to the bathing tent. It took Veronica twenty minutes to scrub all the dried blood and dust of the previous night off her body. Isabel dressed her at top speed, and before she could even protest, Kenna led Kym out of her tent.

They spent the entire morning in the Temple as the Rulers tried to cram six days' worth of rituals and offerings into half a day. Kym sat in the middle of a bench, wedged between Aidan and Kenna. Both acted way too excited as they encouraged Kym to follow along as they paid tribute to the gods. But she wasn't in the mood. Every time someone said the word god or mentioned one of the gods, her mind flashed to the previous night and filled with more unanswered questions.

She couldn't get this plan of the gods out of her head. From what Zara said, the gods' plan wasn't just about Melana's crimes, but for something bigger. But what was the plan? What steps had they taken to make things better? Nothing in Princirum had changed. When was this plan of theirs going to start working?

Kym tried to get away and see her friends whenever she thought she could, but Kenna and Aidan were excellent jailers. Every time she tried to make a break for it, Kenna and Aidan were there, literally dragging her back to the other Water Favored. However, when Kenna and Aidan were praying to Reta, Kym thought she saw Kat among the Earth Favored. But when she looked back, Kat wasn't there.

The festival ended in the afternoon. When the last prayers to Rai were said, Zara announced the festival's completion, and Nila led her Favored out of the Temple and straight for the carriages. Apparently, the sooner they left Crystal Palace, the better. Their servants packed their tents and trunks during the day's ceremonies, so the grounds looked oddly bare as they walked onto the graveled drive. Kym heard Nila screaming at the stable master, insisting that all her carriages needed to be ready to leave in three minutes. She must have scared the stable master out of his mind. The blue carriages were packed and ready to leave two minutes later.

Kym rode in a carriage with Aidan, Kenna, and Ryland, who kept shooting her odd looks, like she was some strange animal on display at the zoo. Kym ignored them. Nila must have told Kenna and Aidan everything that happened the night before, and Aidan probably wasted no time filling Ryland in. They must be itching to hear the details firsthand, but Kym didn't want to give them. She didn't know why, but she wanted to keep it to herself, especially everything that happened at the Summit.

Realizing Kym wasn't going to tell them what happened, Aidan and Kenna sighed as they relaxed in their seats. Aidan leaned back against Ryland, who stared out the window with his eyes half shut. Kenna stretched out along her side of the seat, her feet propped on top of Aidan's on the opposite bench.

"I can't wait to get home and for things to get back to normal," Kenna sighed to the ceiling.

Ryland and Aidan agreed while Kym gave a noncommittal grunt. She gazed out the window, Kenna's words floating through her head like gas. Home. It was strange for her to admit, but after all this time, Wadita was starting to feel like home. But normal? There was a lot Kym didn't understand, but there was one thing she was certain of. Kym's life hadn't been normal since the day Nila found her, and it would never be normal again.

ABOUT THE AUTHOR

Logan Young is a Colorado-based young adult author. He graduated from the University of Colorado, Boulder in 2017 with a Bachelor of Arts in English, Creative Writing. As a child, his overactive mind never seemed to shut off, filling his head with all kinds of stories and worlds. Now as an adult, he's decided to put those stories on paper. When not writing, Logan enjoys getting out and exploring in nature whenever he can.

Connect with Logan Young for more books and updates:

www.imloganyoung.com

 twitter.com/imloganyoung

 instagram.com/imloganyoung

facebook.com/imloganyoung